THE SANCTUARY KEEPERS

ALEXANDRA BARBER

Storm

Ebook ISBN: 978-1-83700-220-7
Paperback ISBN: 978-1-83700-221-4

Cover design: Rose Cooper
Cover images: Shutterstock

Published by Storm Publishing.
For further information, visit:
www.stormpublishing.co

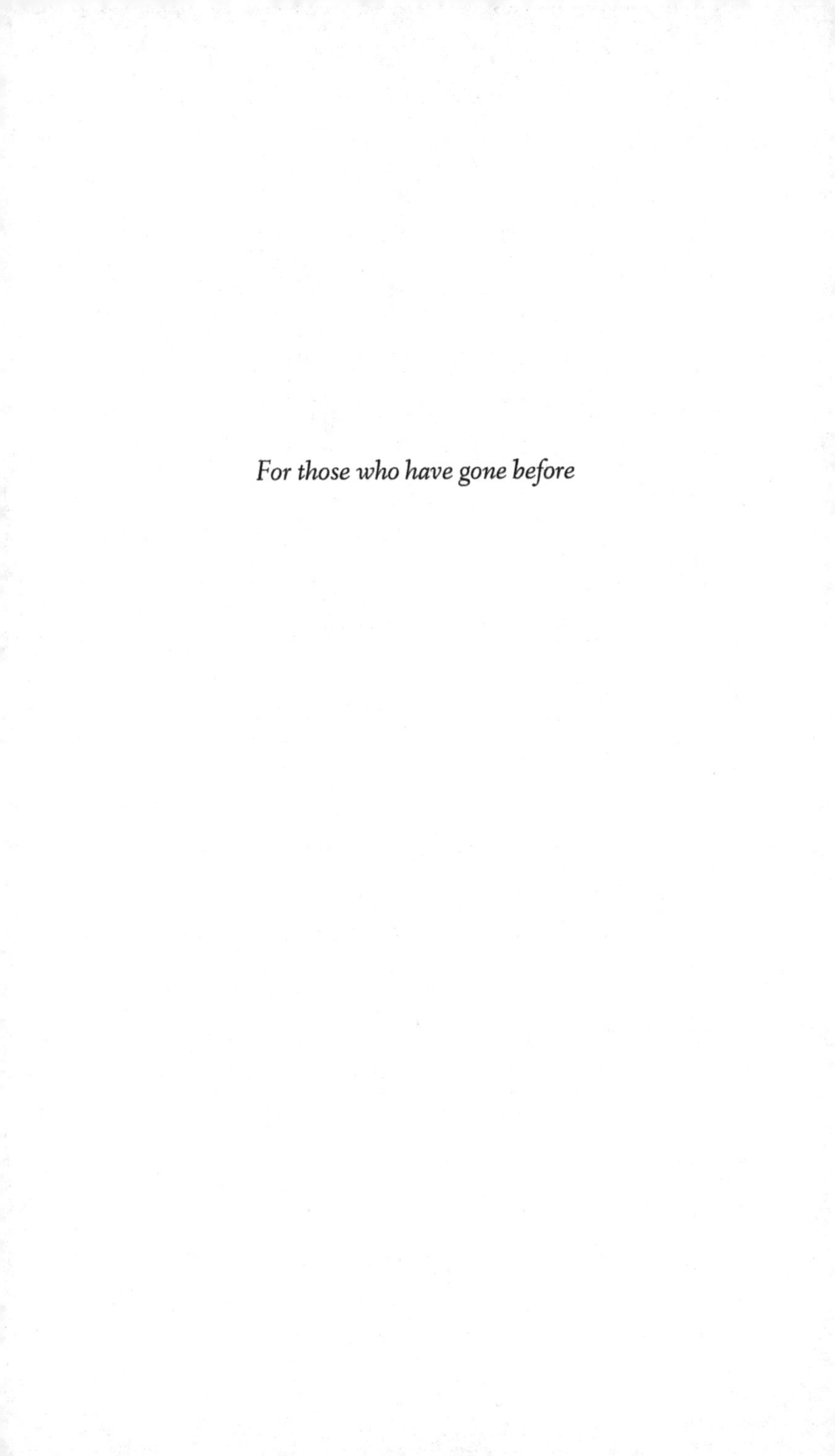

For those who have gone before

'Be kind, for everyone you meet is fighting a hard battle.'

Philo of Alexandria (c 20BC–AD50)

PROLOGUE
PROMISES

'Are you ready, my love?'

Eliza turned from the view of the sea and looked back towards her beloved home. Hideaway Cottage had been her sanctuary for so long.

'I'll never be ready,' she whispered.

'But we agreed,' Isaac said, placing a strong arm around her shoulders. 'Once the house was restored, we would move on. Guy hasn't let us down – it's looking fine, isn't it?'

Eliza sighed and nodded. On this sunny, spring morning the house was looking prettier than she had ever seen it. The window frames were freshly painted in a pale turquoise blue – her favourite colour – the thatch had been totally replaced, and the window boxes were planted up with miniature daffodils and purple pansies. On the ridge of the roof the thatcher had created a small border terrier, tail outstretched and ears pricked. This house had always offered a home to a dog and Eliza loved the way this extra touch brought a smile to everyone who passed by.

'Guy's done well,' she agreed, leaning into her husband.

'Oh, Isaac, I love it here so much. I'm not sure that I can bear to leave.'

He pulled her closer.

'It's hard for me, too.'

'Then why do we have to go?'

Gently, slowly, he turned her to face him, tucking a stray tendril of her thick hair, once a rich shade of chestnut, back behind her ear.

'Because it's time.'

Eliza stared back at the face she had loved for so long. He would do anything to make her happy. And she for him. It was how they had survived everything that life had thrown at them – not that she could remember everything, especially those early days. They were so long ago now. She tilted her chin, lifted her face to the refreshing breeze blowing off the sea. The one thing she was sure of, apart from Isaac's devotion, was that she belonged here. Somewhere deep inside herself she knew that a great deal had been taken away, but Hideaway Cottage had given her so much. It had helped to heal her, as much as any place could. She and Isaac had always welcomed people here, friends and the members of their families who hadn't shunned them. Now it was time to gift her refuge to strangers, people who needed its tranquillity, its restorative powers. There were people who would be helped by coming here. She was sure of it.

Eliza smiled up at Isaac. Where on earth would she have ended up without him? Not here, for sure. Her parents had other plans for their youngest daughter, and they certainly didn't involve a ramshackle cottage, as it was then, on the Isle of Wight. She stood on tiptoes and kissed his lips, closing her eyes to allow the bliss to spread through her.

'Perhaps we could remain for a little longer,' she pleaded, 'to ensure that there aren't any mishaps?'

Beside her Isaac stiffened a little. Eliza wrapped her arms around his waist to prevent him moving away. Always she marvelled at how they blended together, as if they were one.

'We made a promise to each other, didn't we?' she said. 'That we wouldn't depart while we're still needed here. With the world in such turmoil, with so many people struggling, I feel that's the case now more than ever.'

Isaac took the long tapering fingers of her right hand in his left.

'You have a great capacity for love, Eliza. I know that shouldn't be wasted but I worry that you'll succumb to exhaustion. I worry that you'll give too much of yourself.'

'And that there won't be enough left for you,' she replied, with a teasing smile.

Eliza drew his hand to her cheek and inclined her head. He had always given her strength, always shown her the right thing to do.

'So long as you're with me, Isaac, I can find the resources needed.'

He shook his head and smiled.

'How can I say no to you? From our very first meeting on the beach, I've been unable to deny you anything.'

Eliza did a little jump on the spot.

'Then we shall stay?'

'Just until our first guest arrives.'

'And is settled in.'

Isaac laughed.

'Yes, until our first guest is settled in. Except I don't believe there is a first guest quite yet?'

'Oh, there will be very soon. I'm sure of it.'

A tingle of excitement rippled through her. She grasped Isaac's hands and danced him around the magnolia tree until they both collapsed on the dew-bejewelled grass. She knew that somewhere out there was someone who needed to discover Hideaway Cottage, even if they themselves weren't aware of it yet.

ONE

Carrie nibbled at a corner of the sourdough toast which Jules had put in front of her, before pulling a face and pushing it away.

'You need to eat.'

Carrie shook her head.

'I can't. I feel sick. I know it sounds ridiculous, but this does feel as if it's one of the most important days of my life.'

'Which is why you need to eat,' Jules said.

'You sound like my mother.'

Carrie took a sip of her strong black coffee and stood up. Her stomach was churning, her heart already hammering as she imagined the scene to come. After seven and a half years at Winterson's PR Company she was going to be offered a partnership. All of those late nights and early mornings, all of her incredibly hard work, was about to be rewarded. The rumours had been flying around the office for weeks and everyone knew it would be her. There just wasn't anyone else in the running and this morning the partners had asked her in for a meeting. It couldn't be about anything else.

'How do I look?' Carrie asked.

Jules leaned back against the work surface and twisted her lips.

'You scrub up well, when you make an effort.'

'Thanks! It *was* an effort, too. I've no idea how Paloma manages to look so put-together all the time. It's such hard work.'

She ran a palm over her hair, which had taken ages to pin up. Paloma had straight, dark, impossibly glossy hair. Every time Carrie seemed to have the upper hand with her unruly mouse-brown mop, a recalcitrant curl would spring out in a scarecrow-like way.

'It shouldn't matter what you look like,' Jules said.

'But it does,' Carrie whispered, 'especially in PR.'

And especially since Paloma. Carrie blinked, unexpected tears pricking at her eyes. Wow, she was emotional today. *Take a deep breath,* she instructed herself. *You need to be calm, composed, concentrate on the matter at hand, not think about other stuff.* But it was impossible. Paloma haunted her thoughts, day and night. If she was being honest with herself, she wanted to look good for Mark, too. Every day for the past few months she'd made an extra-special effort. She'd even managed to stop biting her nails. There was no way she was going to see her ex five days a week and let him think that she was a broken woman. Jules, her parents, all her friends had said that she really should move jobs.

'I don't know how you do it,' her mother said, 'not just seeing him, but having to work with him, too.'

'It's fine, Mum. Really. We're still friends.'

'If you say so, darling,' Deborah said, 'but if it was your father, I would find it torture.'

Actually, it was torture, but there was no way she was going to let anyone else know that. Besides, working with him was better than no contact at all, even if, for now, he did belong to someone else. She'd vowed to show him how much he was missing by looking amazing and doing her best to be wittier and wiser and more supportive. Not that he seemed to notice. But now she was going to be made a partner. Surely that would get his attention and make her irresistible once more?

'Maybe he wouldn't have strayed if I hadn't looked like such a scruff, a jeans and t-shirt sort of girl,' she murmured.

Jules opened her arms wide and gathered Carrie up into a big hug.

'Sweetheart, you're not and never have been a scruff. And you're better off without that rat. Everyone thinks so.'

'You didn't know him when we first met,' she protested, not for the first time. 'When he was kind and funny and—'

Jules rolled her eyes and Carrie stopped mid-flow. She was wasting her time. Jules had never liked Mark.

'Besides, we both know that wasn't the real reason, don't we?' Carrie added. 'We both know that it was because I can't—'

Jules pushed her away a little but still held on tightly.

'No! No! No! Now isn't the time to be thinking about that.'

'Except I think about it nearly all of the time,' Carrie whispered. She shook her head and gave herself a little shake, dabbing at the outer corners of her eyes with her ring fingers. 'But there's no point feeling sorry for myself. The challenge of being a partner will be really good for me, take my mind off things. Anyway, I better go.'

Jules yawned.

'I'm off to bed – it was a long night. Who'd be a midwife, heh?' She grabbed a towel and headed towards the bathroom. 'Send me a message as soon as it's confirmed, and a picture of manky Mark's face, too. I'd pay a month of my meagre salary to see his reaction.'

Carrie's answering laugh was lost in the sudden whoosh of the shower.

'Don't forget to take an umbrella,' Jules bellowed. 'April

showers are a given in the north. And make sure you have something to eat before you hit the champagne bar at lunchtime,'

'You're actually worse than my mother!' Carrie shouted back. She made one final check in the mirror, glanced out of the window at the pale blue sky, dismissed the need for an umbrella and headed out towards her bright and shining future.

Waiting at the bus stop, Carrie took a deep breath and checked her phone. It was dead. Damn! She'd attached the charger last night but obviously not switched it on at the plug. She rolled her eyes but wasn't overly worried – she'd left plenty of time. When Ian, the senior partner, had asked for this meeting, she'd felt her heart skip a beat. In fact, it had barely stopped skipping for the last couple of days and Thursday had always been her lucky day. She'd been born on a Thursday, she'd been offered this job on a Thursday and way, way back, she'd met Mark on a Thursday.

Everything would have been perfect if Paloma hadn't sashayed into their lives and ruined it all. Now, that had been a Tuesday. Not a day she'd forget in a hurry. With hindsight, she should have checked out Paloma's appearance before vaguely suggesting her for the office interior design job. A client had said how good she was so Carrie had just dropped Paloma's name into conversation with the partners. If she'd taken the time to check out the quite seductive website photo first, she might have thought twice; all that infuriatingly glossy hair and gleaming skin. On the other hand, it might not have made any difference. After all, she'd trusted Mark. Implicitly.

Carrie felt the familiar lump in her throat and gave herself a shake. *Don't go there. Breathe. Keep calm.* She looked down the road and tapped her foot on the pavement. Where *was* the bus? She'd better start walking and hope she could catch it at the next stop. Ten minutes later, the sky was darkening. *Please,*

please don't rain, she silently begged, glancing up just as the largest raindrop ever to have formed into existence landed splat in her eye.

Carrie was turning her head to assess whether she'd make it to the next bus stop in time when she was drenched with water from a 4x4 ploughing through a blocked drain. This was closely followed by the bus she needed to catch whizzing down the bus lane and giving her a second soaking. Carrie stood for a moment and let the dirty water drip from what felt like head to toe. She didn't have time to dab at her face, the bus was about to make its next stop. She broke into a run, hair breaking free from its myriad of grips and sweat gathering at the nape of her neck.

'Wait, wait!' she shouted, waving frantically, but it was useless.

She stopped and bent double as the bus pulled away.

'Everything's going to be fine, Carrie,' she puffed. 'Remember, Thursday is your lucky day.'

Carrie almost threw herself into the lift. She was already twenty minutes late for the meeting. She glanced at her reflection in the glossy silver interior and groaned. An Irish Water Spaniel would be proud of her hair and her eyes looked like one of those old black and white horror films her brother loved. She ran her fingers through her frizz and dabbed around her eyes with a tissue before applying some concealer which only made her look as if she'd been punched in the face and was trying to hide it.

'It doesn't matter, it doesn't matter,' she repeated, as the lift pinged for each floor. 'It's about who you are, not how you look. This is going to be your moment. The fact you don't look perfect isn't going to make any difference.'

As the doors slid open there was a burst of applause. Carrie's heart lifted, her already flushed face turning even more pink with pride. Several bottles of champagne stood open on the reception desk and everyone was holding glasses aloft. She put a hand to her chest. This was wonderful. Like a surprise party. She'd always said that she wouldn't want one of those, but actually, it was incredible. So why had the room fallen strangely silent and why was Beth, her assistant, scuttling towards her, eyes wide with alarm? It must be because Beth knew she hated a fuss, but it was okay. It really was okay.

'I've been trying to get hold of you,' Beth muttered. 'Where have you been? Why weren't you answering your phone?'

Carrie beamed at Beth. 'I know, sorry, I forgot to charge it. Too busy thinking about other things.'

Chuckling, she looked down at the puddle forming on the floor around her and then towards a roomful of taut faces. She obviously looked more dishevelled than she realised.

'Bus issues,' she said, 'and then the rain. But it doesn't matter.' She touched her head. 'Anyway, I'm here now and this is amazing. I can't believe it.'

Beth tugged at her arm.

'Carrie, I need to talk to you.'

Carrie half turned. Out of the corner of her eye she saw Paloma skulking in a corner. What was she doing here? She didn't even work here. Then Mark was bearing down on her, face wreathed in smiles, a glass of champagne in his hand.

'See?' she murmured to Beth. 'Jules was wrong. He's taken it well, after all. I knew he'd be pleased for me.'

'You don't understand,' Beth hissed. 'He's not pleased for you. He's pleased for himself.'

Carrie stared at her, trying to absorb this information. She shook her head slightly and raindrops scattered around her in a circle. Just like tears, she thought.

Beth placed a hand against her shoulder.

'I'm so sorry, Carrie. It's just been announced. Mark's been made a partner.'

Carrie wobbled on her heels. A blister was forming on the ball of her foot. She could feel it filling up with fluid. There *must* be some mistake. But Beth didn't make mistakes and Carrie suddenly saw the embarrassment that was coating everything and everyone, apart from Paloma, who looked nauseatingly triumphant. Carrie could barely breathe. Only the truth could be that suffocating. Her dream lay at her feet in a thousand pieces like that favourite Christmas decoration of her mother's, which she had broken when she was seven years old.

And now Mark was in front of her, looking taller and more handsome than ever. Had Paloma bought him lifts? Or perhaps she was stretching him on some form of torturous rack which they'd had fitted in the home that used to be *her* home not so long ago. Paloma was five foot eleven and Carrie remembered her complaining that heels were out of the question when she and Mark went out together. Was she wearing flats now? She couldn't see. Anyway, why did that matter? Except it did because she'd been the perfect height. The top of *her* head used to nestle comfortably under Mark's chin. *Don't even think about nestling, or even nesting for that matter*, she told herself. Somehow, she took a deep breath into her bone-crushingly constricted chest and arranged her mouth into what she hoped looked like a smile. To her horror Mark was leaning forward to kiss her on the cheek. Instinctively, she ducked her head to the side and he missed, getting a mouthful of rain-soaked curls instead.

'Carrie,' he said softly, his eyes darting nervously across her face. 'Will you celebrate with us?'

She swallowed and pressed her lips together as he held out a glass of champagne. *How brave of him*, she thought. Surely he must realise the overwhelming temptation would be to throw it back in his face? Instead, she curled her fingers tightly around the air-blown, spiral twist stem. Not usual office fare. Someone had brought them in especially.

'A present from Paloma,' he said, as if reading her thoughts. 'Very expensive. I've only got six, but I saved one especially for you.'

Carrie raised her eyebrows, acutely aware of the whole office watching, almost holding their breath. Humiliated she may be, but blatantly bitter and twisted was not how she wanted to come over. She could vent later, back in the house with Jules or on the phone long-distance to her brother. Shame her parents were visiting him in New Zealand – she'd have to pick a time when they weren't around. Didn't want them to know yet. That would really ruin their visit. They'd had such high hopes for both of their children and now she'd let them down, too.

'You got me this job, Carrie,' he continued, 'and I'm so, so grateful. Who would have thought...'

Yes, who would have thought that Mark, who was always coming to her for help and advice, always offering adulation for her creativity, would be The Chosen One? She tilted her head, stood up straighter. It was amazing how that slightest change in posture eased her breathing and gave her a much-needed boost.

Carefully, she set the champagne down beside her and perched on the desk, rubbing the velvety leaves of the scented geranium which she had bought for Beth's birthday. Jules was always extolling the benefits of geranium and how good it was for anxiety. Secretly she'd bought it for herself as well as for Beth. Carrie placed her fingers briefly in front of her nose and breathed in the uplifting scent. But it wasn't enough. She needed a greenhouse full of plants to calm her.

'I can see that you're upset,' he continued.

'Can you blame me?'

He did actually look slightly contrite. Carrie felt the bubbling anger inside her chest subside slightly. *Wait! Perhaps the beautiful geranium was working its magic, after all. But hang on, he was still talking...*

'Paloma said you'd take it badly.'

He reached out but didn't quite touch her.

'I want you to be pleased for me, Carrie.'

Hah! Fat chance of that, she thought, but was pretty sure she had managed to maintain her aroma-zoned face because Mark's shoulders drooped a little, small wrinkles furrowing his brow. Now he leaned really close.

'I appreciate that's particularly difficult to do when you're still in denial about us,' he whispered.

She might as well have been slapped by Paloma herself.

'What?'

'Well, obviously it's not just the job you're upset about.'

He'd lowered his voice, but the office was so quiet everyone would be able to get the gist of what he was saying. 'You've never been able to accept that it's over between us. I know it, you know it, everyone knows it.'

Was that really what everyone thought? Scanning the assembled faces she saw only a study of pity.

'That's absolutely not true!'

She'd started to shake. Why did her body always give her away when she was angry? Why couldn't she stay cool and collected, at least on the surface? *Don't blow it, Carrie. Don't make a complete and utter fool of yourself in front of everyone, especially not* her. How dare she be here? It wasn't *her* office. Why wasn't she off interior designing someone else's space? Mark leaned forwards and took her arm. Carrie shook him away, almost toppling off the end of the desk. Righting herself, she stood up and faced down the people she spent time with almost every day of the week; people who obviously knew her better than she realised. There was no way she was going to admit the truth, not here, not now.

'Is it? Is that what you all think? That I'd have gone and got another job months ago if it wasn't for...' Her voice cracked.

Beth gave a short, horrified shake of her head and Carrie felt a small curl of gratitude in her chest, but she suspected that even her trusted assistant thought the same deep down. Somehow, from somewhere, she found her strength again.

'Well, you're wrong. I did *not* stay for that reason. I did *not* stay because of you, Mark, much as your over-inflated, puffed-up, pretentious arsehole of an ego would have you believe. I stayed because I love my job, because I'm good at it, because I'm loyal and because I hoped that one day I might be rewarded for those qualities.'

She swivelled towards Ian and the other partners. She knew she was signing her death warrant here, but she was past caring.

'Apparently those qualities don't count for anything.'

Suddenly spent, she reached behind to pick up the champagne. She really was intending to drink it, not to celebrate but for a much-needed sugar boost. But the urge to throw something was huge. She knew it would make her feel so much better, even if only temporarily. It was only meant to be a flinging of liquid, but her hands were shaky. Try as she might, her fingers couldn't grip the glass properly and she watched in horror as it flew from her grasp, twirling balletically through the air.

'Edinburgh crystal!' Paloma shrieked, as Mark looked on aghast.

As if in slow motion they leapt together, each with an arm outstretched as the other hand still gripped their own precious glasses. There was a mid-air tangle of limbs and then a sickening thud, both landing heavily on the expensive, and Carrie thought pretty tasteless, new carpet that Paloma had chosen. Mark lay underneath with Paloma spread-eagled on top, brandishing the airborne glass like a major sporting trophy.

'Ow! Ow! Ow!' Mark groaned. 'I think I've broken my back.'

Carrie had the urge to laugh. Mark had always been a drama queen. Except... an arc of light emanated from Paloma's direction. At first Carrie thought it was the reflection from the beautifully cut glass. But no, it was…

'You need to go,' Beth whispered, but she was rooted to the spot as the entire office clustered around Mark.

'Oh my God!' Carrie gasped.

'He'll be fine,' Beth said, virtually dragging her away from the scene.

'No, it's not that,' Carrie gasped, as if in a trance.

She couldn't take her eyes off the rock of a diamond on the third finger of Paloma's left hand.

'He didn't tell you about that either, did he?' Beth murmured.

Carrie shook her head.

'Disgusting,' her assistant said. 'But it doesn't change things, Carrie. In fact, it means that you *definitely* need to go home. Now!'

She hustled Carrie over to the lift and jabbed at the button for the doors. Putting an arm around Carrie's shoulders, she whispered, 'Remember to charge your phone up when you get home. I'll call later.'

And with a gentle shove she pushed Carrie into the lift where, as soon as the doors closed, she sank to the floor. It was probably filthy, but who cared? How could this have happened? How could potentially the best day of her life have suddenly turned into the worst?

TWO

She walked until her blister felt on the point of bursting. Had she really just done and said that, or was this some horrible nightmare and any minute now she would wake up? In the distance the sound of an ambulance mirrored the alarm in her chest. No, this was real and perhaps Mark wasn't being a drama queen this time. That ambulance was probably speeding him towards the hospital for emergency surgery on his back. What if he had a bad reaction to the anaesthetic or the operation went wrong? What if he was left crippled or worse? It would be all her fault. Then the loss of her job would be nothing compared to the guilt that she would have to live with for the rest of her life. Paloma would probably sue her, and she'd end up destitute or living back with her parents. No, not with her parents. They'd be so horrified by what she had done, so disappointed that she had let them down, that they'd probably disown her. New Zealand – that's where she'd have to go, if she could afford the airfare, to live with her drop-out brother, as their mother always secretly thought of him; all of them squashed together in his camper van: Charlie, Lucy, their two little girls, Carrie and the rescue collie. How the future of a life could change in a matter of moments.

The flat was hushed as she let herself in. On the kitchen table was a huge bunch of flowers, zinging pink roses, huge white snapdragons and those purple bell-like flowers which she could never remember the name of. Beneath was a card which said *Congratulations!!* in Jules' exuberant flowing script. Carrie buried her face in one of the blooms, inhaled the scent, sank onto the rickety chair and wept.

'I need to get away,' Carrie whispered. But could she even afford to? And what if the partners needed her? They might be trying to get hold of her even now...

She reached for the iPad on the side table, scrolled down the messages. Suddenly, one from Jules caught her eye:

My mum sent me this – it's from her friend, Claudia. The owner of this newly renovated holiday cottage on the Isle of Wight is looking for someone to try it out before it's available to the general public. Mum wanted me to go, but not sure we've reached that stage yet so I've told her there's no way I can get away – too many babies born in the spring. It's gorgeous, though. You should go! You've been working so hard recently. You need a break, and this looks like the perfect place to celebrate and recuperate.

Carrie barely knew where the Isle of Wight was – some small island off England's south coast. If she was going to take a break, she would definitely need to go further away than that – probably thousands of miles. In fact, as far away from Mark and Paloma and Winterson's as she could get. But Jules was bound to ask if she had even looked at the details, so with a sigh she clicked the link... and the picture completely stopped her thoughts in their tracks. The little thatched cottage reminded her of a jigsaw she'd had when she was a child, except the windows were painted the prettiest shade of turquoise blue and there was a heart-shaped knocker on the front door.

Need to get away from it all?
Unwind and immerse yourself in tranquillity.

Despite herself, Carrie stared at the picture of the cottage. Already she felt as if it had drawn her in, wrapped itself around her, even helped her to feel a little bit calmer. *For goodness' sake, Carrie,* she told herself, *it's just a picture with an artfully written description. You of all people should be immune and yet... there is something about this place.* Maybe she ought to think about it. She did feel exhausted and was in no fit state to be contemplating her future, but first she really, really needed to know that Mark was okay.

Her heart was thudding as she waited for her phone to charge just enough. It wouldn't be a long call and he probably wouldn't even pick up when he saw it was her, but at least she'd have tried. And he'd ring her back because, whatever Jules said, he was a decent person underneath and he'd want to say that he knew how much he'd hurt her, wouldn't he?

'What do you want, Carrie?'

Mark sounded even more stressed than she was. She strained to hear hospital noises, but all was quiet in the background.

'I wanted to check that you're all right.'

She was proud of herself for doing this.

'Of course I'm not all right.'

'Is it your back?'

'What?'

'You thought you'd hurt your back?'

'It's not me,' he snapped, 'it's Paloma. I've had to bring her home. She's delicate at the moment.'

Carrie frowned. Delicate and Paloma were not words she would ever have put together.

'Oh dear! Too much champagne?'

'Don't be ridiculous, Carrie. She's not drinking champagne in her condition.'

Carrie had never felt words fail her as they did in this moment. She could barely remember how to speak or move. She should put the phone down, but she couldn't. Maybe she had misheard or misinterpreted. Please, please let that be the case.

'I was going to tell you,' he said at last. 'It's early days.'

'H-how early?'

'Ten weeks.' He lowered his voice. 'It was an accident.'

Carrie closed her eyes for a moment. Surely life could not be this cruel. All of that tracking her ovulation and waiting each month for yet another disappointment and Paloma had fallen pregnant in a flash. They'd barely been together for ten weeks, or had they? What else hadn't he told her? *Put the phone down, Carrie,* a voice in her head instructed. *Save your self-respect. Don't say another word. He does not even deserve another breath.*

'I'm sorry,' he said.

Do NOT cry. Do not let him hear so much as a sniffle.

'I suppose I should offer my congratulations.'

He didn't reply.

'Mark, who is it?' she heard Paloma call.

'No one, honeybun,' he replied.

No one. Carrie shook her head a little as if it contained batteries and they had slightly lost contact with their terminals.

'Carrie, are you still there?' he whispered.

No, Mark. No one is here.

With tears cascading down her face she turned off her phone and with shaking hands picked up the iPad.

THREE

Two days later, Carrie was on the ferry to the Isle of Wight. If she was going to be out of a job, there was no point blowing her savings on an exotic holiday. And she probably was going to be out of a job unless some miracle occurred. And that miracle obviously wasn't going to be Mark putting in a good word for her. He'd made that quite obvious. He must have known that she was going to receive *that* email the following day. The partners, and she almost choked thinking about it, must have discussed it. She'd tried to get through to Ian on the phone, but he was 'busy, busy, busy' according to Beth and 'in meetings' all day. Not too busy, it turned out, to authorise the pinging of an email which referred to the 'unfortunate incident' and advised upon a '*cooling off period... take some time to consider your options*'.

'Stop procrastinating and just book the cottage,' Jules had said. 'What's the worst that can happen? Normally you'd say it's a sign. I'll call if you like.'

Carrie didn't believe in signs anymore, but she was too shattered to protest, so she let Jules dial the number and put the phone on speaker. Hopefully the cottage would already be taken and she wouldn't have to make the effort to go anywhere. She could just vegetate and eat doughnuts, but the cheerful woman at the end of the line – Rita, she was called – sounded so thrilled to hear from her and Jules was adopting one of her sternest looks. Carrie didn't dare tell her that she really didn't want to go to the Isle of Wight, after all, even if the cottage in question was the stuff of fairy tales – she knew that fairy tales were the meanest of stories, leading you down an illusory path of happy ever after.

'You won't be disappointed,' Rita said. 'It's the prettiest of places and just perfect for a few quiet days away.'

So it was arranged, there and then. She'd committed and it was only for a couple of weeks, not a lifetime. And, as she put the phone down Carrie had the strangest sensation that Jules might be right; that the cottage being available and the letter telling her to take some time off were a sign. It almost felt as if the whole process had been out of her control. *Trust, Carrie*, she said to herself. *Go with the flow...* but it was easier said than done. She took her cup of tea on to the deck and sat on one of the front seats, watching small sailing boats scudding past on the stiff Solent wind. It was uncanny how travelling across such a small stretch of water could really make you feel as if you were getting away from it all. It seemed strange, too, to be going away entirely on her own but it was too short notice to ask anyone to join her. Besides, Jules had said that the space to think would be good and she was definitely right about that. Her mind was a complete jumble.

'You need to be by yourself,' she'd said, as Carrie fretted about what to take, 'and try to just be for a change. You're always doing. It's not healthy. It leads to burnout. Believe me, I know what I'm talking about. I've got new mums who are burnt out before they even have the baby because they work up until the very last minute or they take time off but won't give themselves permission to stop for a moment. Sometimes I think the whole world needs to unwind.'

Unwind, Carrie thought, throwing her head back and letting the breeze attempt to de-tangle her hair. How long had it been since she'd felt able to do that? Could she even remember what it felt like? She had a vague memory of lightness in her limbs, blazes of colour from foreign getaways with Mark, and simple pleasures from further back such as the intense taste of her grandmother's ginger cake tingling on her tongue. She had a sudden sense of loss, and it wasn't just for the job or even for Mark. It was more than that. It was for a whole part of herself.

Once off the ferry Carrie took her time, trying to take in the scenery. She passed signs to Osborne House, Carisbrooke Castle and Tennyson Down. Under a benevolent blue sky, she drove through pretty villages and along country roads where the hedges hugged the verge so closely they almost tickled the car. Occasionally she caught a tantalising glimpse of the sea in the distance, a slip of silver which gave her a disproportionate sense of excitement. She had been brought up not far from the sea in Norfolk and it would always have a claim on her. But approaching her destination Carrie's heart skipped a beat. What if the cottage didn't look like the pictures? What if it was awful? What if she couldn't bear her own company? Even worse, what if it was a scam and didn't exist at all? No, that wouldn't be true. After all, Jules' mum's friend had recommended it.

'You don't have to stay,' she murmured. 'Nobody made you come here. Not really. You chose it yourself. Or it chose you...'

She blinked in the sunlight. Where had that thought come from? Places didn't choose you, did they? They couldn't, especially not ones you had never been to before. She braked sharply as a couple of plump brown chickens scuttled across the road in front of her. She wound down the window.

'Silly birds,' she called, as the hens clucked frantically, squeezing themselves underneath a five-bar gate adjoining a converted stone barn. 'It was nearly roast chicken for dinner!'

Carefully following Rita's instructions, she passed the church, its graveyard speckled with primroses, and turned right opposite The Manor. Turning down a narrow lane luminous lime green angelica crowded the hedgerow. Carrie could almost taste it as she inhaled the gentle aniseed scent mingled with spring sunshine and salt air. And once again tears began to trickle down her cheeks. She had to stop crying. She would shrivel up at this rate.

Hideaway Cottage was right at the end of the little winding road and came into view through blurred vision. She stopped the car and wiped her eyes with the back of her hand. Contrary to her fears, the photograph of the outside hadn't done it justice and it was, without a doubt, the most enchanting place she had ever seen. Almost triangular in shape, the newly thatched roof swooped so low in places that Carrie was sure she would be able to reach up and touch its rough underside with her fingertips. A small window framed each side of the front door, and another looked out above the larch lap porch. The picket gate opened on to a gravel path edged by borders frothing with lady's mantle and forget-me-nots, threaded through with orangey red tulips that rocked slightly in the breeze. Carrie placed her palms together in a prayer position and took a deep breath. The relief she felt was indescribable.

'Thank you, Jules,' she murmured, and she felt a tiny portion of her spine, just at the base of her neck, begin to soften. 'Key under pot by front door,' Carrie reminded herself, as she deposited her suitcase on the gravel. But which pot? There were several, some with a greenish blue glaze, others formed of beautifully weathered terracotta. All were full of violas, pansies, tulips and miniature daffodils. Finally, locating the weathered key under the last pot she tried, Carrie placed it in the lock and marvelled at how easily it turned. She opened the door slowly, prolonging the unexpected sense of anticipation. It felt important, this moment. Not something to be hurried. She wasn't sure why, but had a feeling that she might want to look back and remember it exactly. With that thought uppermost in her mind she took her first step across the threshold into Hideaway Cottage.

The hall was almost square with a polished parquet floor, beamed ceiling and endearingly lop-sided staircase tucked against the back wall. The air was scented with a mixture of lavender furniture polish, warm wood and a large bunch of yellow chrysanthemums which occupied a pretty blue-speckled pottery vase on the central hexagonal table. Next to this was a hand-painted card of The Needles. Someone had written in a pleasing rounded hand:

Welcome to Hideaway Cottage. May it be everything you hoped for. If you have any queries or problems, please give me a ring or pop into Orchard Farm – back to the top of the lane, turn left and take the unadopted road. We're right at the end and the kettle's always on! Otherwise, all the numbers you might need are in the book in the kitchen dresser plus lots of other information, too. I'll pop in to check everything's all right before too long.

Yours,

Rita

Carrie slipped out of her shoes and placed her case at the bottom of the stairs. To her right was the sitting room, its pale green carpet soft beneath her bare feet, the grate already laid within the rough-hewn stone fireplace. More flowers decorated the coffee table alongside a pile of magazines and a hardback book about the island. Already she longed to sink into the sofa and snuggle amongst those plumped cushions but first she needed to see the rest of the house.

Through an old oak latch door was the light-filled kitchen. A range emitted a gentle warmth and above the butler's sink a large picture window gave views of the rear garden and once again, in the distance, the glimmering sea. On the pine table a tray was laid with delicate, vintage bone china in palest pink, a pair of silver sugar tongs balanced on top of a mountain of sugar cubes in a bowl. On a whim, Carrie reached for one and popped it in her mouth. She hadn't done that since she was little and the sudden sweet rush on her tongue made her want to laugh. There hadn't been much of that lately either, not free, impetuous laughter which made you feel about three years old again. Under a glass dome a homemade cake waited – carrot, her favourite. Had she mentioned that to Rita on the phone? She couldn't remember. In the fridge was a well-chilled bottle of rose wine, some butter, milk and eggs. Carrie filled the kettle, placed it on the range and meandered back through to the hall. Already the mainland felt like a different life.

There were only two bedrooms, one to the front of the house and the larger one at the rear. She tried out the king-sized bed, bouncing up and down a few times before moving to the window. From here, as well as the sea, she had a good view of the next-door field, studded with sheep and bleating lambs. Carrie pushed open the diamond paned window and perched on the little window seat with its jaunty, striped cushion. This would be the perfect place to sit and write the journal that Jules had placed in her hands as a parting gift.

'I find that writing things down can help to sort out your thoughts,' she'd said. Carrie used to write a diary, but she hadn't had time for ages. She wasn't quite sure how spilling everything out into a notebook, even a very beautiful one with gold foil decoration on the front, would save her job, but she did know that it could help her to decide where to go next. One thing was certain, she couldn't stay at Winterson's, whatever the partners decided. *Don't think about that now*, she instructed herself. *It's too soon. You're exhausted. You'll make a knee-jerk reaction and then regret it.*

Lifting her legs she leaned back, knees crooked, bare feet pressed against the opposite wall and studied the chipped nail varnish on her toes; the frosted pink was a favourite colour, but she always had to apply it in such a hurry and then she'd put her shoes, socks or tights on too soon and smudge it. Everything was done in a hurry these days. She sighed. Whatever she did, it just never felt good enough. She'd known she was stressed. There was no escaping the aching shoulders, the ever-threatening headaches, the inability to sleep deeply. She'd lie awake thinking about the things she wanted to do, friends she wanted to see, places she wanted to visit, books she wanted to read. And then the guilt would course through her, so much more acutely in the deep of the night. And she would resolve to change, to make more time for others, for herself, to be a better person, one she could feel happy to be. Sometimes her transformation would last a couple of days but never more than that before life took over again.

Suddenly, reading a book from beginning to end felt like a matter of life and death. *If not now, when?* Who said that? Padding to the bedside table she investigated the neatly piled selection: Charlotte Brontë, Barbara Kingsolver, David Nicholls, Daphne du Maurier and a book of poems by Tennyson. A bookmark decorated with a botanical drawing of lily of the valley lay at an angle right across to one side. It felt as if she was staying with someone who knew her inside and out, someone who would look after her no matter what. She picked up *Jane Eyre* and ran her fingers over the cover before turning to the first page. *There was no possibility of taking a walk that day.* Carrie closed her eyes and let the familiar words settle over her. How she used to love this story. The companionship of it felt like having a friend with her, after all. From downstairs the kettle's whistle demanded her attention and, clasping the book close, she headed towards tea, cake and a promise to reclaim a part of her long-lost self.

Walking up the track, Rita swung the basket and scanned the fields, her eyes flickering over every sheep and lamb, alert for anything untoward. Satisfied that all was well for now she looked up at the clouds.

'We've got our first guest, George,' she said.

Funny how she'd said that, as if the cottage belonged to her. Of course, it could have done. Some would say it *should* have done but she wasn't one to hold grudges. After all, she had the farm. As Rita rounded the corner and Hideaway Cottage came into view she felt her spirits lift. There was no doubt this was a very special place.

Carrie was sitting on a wooden seat at the back of the house feeding cake crumbs to a greedy blackbird when she heard footsteps on the gravel drive.

'Hellooo!' called a sing-songy voice.

She stood up quickly, almost knocking over the empty cup and saucer by her feet.

'Hello,' she replied, as a woman with glowing cheeks and a face wreathed in smiles came into view.

'There you are! I knocked at the front but there wasn't any answer, so I guessed this was where you'd be. It's a real sunspot, isn't it, and you've brought good weather with you. We've had quite a lot of rain up until now but it's marvellous for the plants. Oh, listen to me prattling on and I haven't even introduced myself. My husband always said that I talked too much. He was right, of course. God bless him.'

She held out a generous hand with short, square-cut nails.

'I'm Rita. We spoke on the phone.'

Carrie placed her small hand inside Rita's firm and surprisingly soft one.

'Of course you are,' she replied, smiling broadly as the older woman pumped her arm up and down. 'I'm Carrie.'

Rita beamed back at her.

'And you're very welcome, Carrie. I can't tell you how pleased we are to have you here. Did you have a good journey? You're from the north, I think you said, didn't you? My, my, that's a long way. I've never been there myself but I'm sure it's lovely.'

Carrie felt a little pucker between her eyebrows. That wasn't quite how she'd describe it.

'Well...' she began, wondering whether to puncture Rita's rosy view of where she lived.

'And vibrant, I expect,' Rita continued, barely pausing for breath. 'I do hope you won't find it too quiet here. It's a sleepy little place.'

'Actually, that's just what I'm looking for,' Carrie replied. 'Peace and quiet.'

Rita's gaze was casual, her features remained soft, but there was a knowing expression in her eyes.

'Well, I hope you'll find all that you need here. As it says in Matthew: "Come to me, all you who are weary and burdened and I will give you rest." I sometimes think he could have been talking about this place as well as the Good Lord!'

Instinctively Carrie's hands flew to her face as if to smooth out the wrinkles – she must look even more tired and defeated than she realised. Her mother always used to say that she wore her emotions on her face. *Another disappointment to add to the many which she'd inflicted on Deborah over the years...*

'Now, there are some bits and pieces in the fridge,' Rita continued, 'just to tide you over and there's an excellent shop in the next village with lots of delicious fresh produce. Much of it local. It's important to know your food hasn't travelled too far, isn't it? Talking of which, I figured you wouldn't want to go out shopping as soon as you got here so I've made you a shepherd's pie.'

Rita thrust the wicker basket, which had been dangling over one freckled arm, towards her.

'Couldn't get more local than that,' she chuckled, inclining her head towards the sheep in the field. 'But you can't be too sentimental about these things when you're a farmer and our lamb is the best on the island, even if I do say so myself.'

Suddenly, Rita placed a hand to her exuberant bosom, which was doing its best to escape from the disorderly buttoned, pink cardigan that covered a flowery dress.

'Heavens above!' she exclaimed, her vivid eyes widening. 'You're not a veggie, are you? It's no problem if you are. One of my granddaughters is a vegan, so I've got a nice leek and mushroom casserole in the freezer. I can pop back and get that for you?'

Carrie peeled the tea towel away from the top of the basket.

'No, I'm not a vegetarian or a vegan.' She laughed. 'And that looks delicious. It's so kind of you. Actually, I've got a grocery delivery arriving shortly but—'

'Oh, of course you have. You young things are so organised. My daughter-in-law said as much and not to bother you.'

For the first time Carrie detected a slight cloud pass across Rita's face.

'But she's a bit...' Rita stared over Carrie's shoulder and seemed to give herself a mental shake. 'My pa used to tell me that if you couldn't find anything good to say about someone you shouldn't say anything at all, and he was right, God rest his soul.'

She took a deep breath.

'Enough of that. We've all got our troubles, haven't we? And I am blessed, really I am. I don't want to become one of those old biddies who moans and groans all the time.'

'I'm sure you won't be,' Carrie said, with a sympathetic smile.

'Now, did you like the cake?' Rita asked, eyeing the clean plate.

'It was delicious. Did you make that, too? Carrot's my favourite.'

'Baked it this morning and I had an inkling that you'd be partial to it. If you don't want the pie, I can take it for the Major and pop it in his freezer.'

'Oh no,' Carrie replied, 'I'd love the pie. It'll be so much better than anything I've ordered.'

'Well, I'd better be off,' Rita said, 'and get back to my chores. There are always things to do and the devil makes work for idle hands. If there's anything you need to know, just give me a buzz. I go shopping on a Tuesday morning but apart from that I'm not usually far away. You'd be very welcome to pop in for a cup of tea if you'd like some company.'

'Thank you,' Carrie replied.

'I'm not pressuring you, though,' Rita said. 'Sometimes we all need to have time on our own, don't we? Even me.'

And with her laughter ringing in Carrie's ears, she turned and bustled away.

FOUR

'I don't believe this!' Carrie fumed, as she marched from one room to another, waving her phone above her head. She leaned out of the bedroom window. She walked to the bottom of the garden and balanced on a fallen log. It was hopeless. Even worse than no phone signal was the fact that the house didn't have any internet, so she couldn't check her emails or anything. If work, or anyone else for that matter, was trying to get in touch she wouldn't have a clue. 'I'd never have come if I'd known,' she said to Jules on the landline, aware that she sounded like a petulant child.

'It will be good for you,' she replied. 'It's hardly the end of the world, is it? You're only there for a fortnight.'

'You knew?'

'It was in the details. You obviously didn't read them properly. Anyway, aren't I always saying that you spend too much time on social media and stuff?'

'It's part of my job,' Carrie said defensively.

'Not all of it. It's addictive, you know. It gets in the way of real life.'

'So you keep telling me.'

Jules ignored the annoyance in Carrie's voice and focused on the panic.

'You'll be fine. Think of it like a detox.'

Carrie bit her lip and tried to ignore the swirl of adrenaline that was interrupting her breath.

'It's just that I'm here on my own and I don't know a soul and I'm aware that it's fewer than twenty miles from the south coast, but it feels really remote and not being able to keep in touch with everyone and everything going on in the world feels—'

'Carrie, get a grip! You're not in the Kalahari Desert without water or whatever. It's the south of England. There are newspapers. There's a television. There are people, neighbours even.'

Carrie gulped.

'Sorry, I sound pathetic, don't it? Actually, I met one of the neighbours earlier.'

'And did they try to eat you alive?'

'No, no, it was Rita who I spoke to on the phone. You remember? She's really nice. She brought me a shepherd's pie.'

'There you are then,' Jules said. 'Who'd have believed it? They eat shepherd's pie on the Isle of Wight. It must be civilised, after all!'

Carrie chuckled, despite herself.

'I wish you were here, Jules. What if I'm one of those people who just isn't good at being on their own? I probably should have gone to a hotel instead.'

'Just so you could have been surrounded by strangers and felt awkward if you didn't want to talk, or sitting at a table for one at dinner. I don't think so,' Jules replied.

Carrie scanned the corners of the room.

'What if a big hairy spider comes out to greet me? What do I do then? The thatch could be full of them. What if they're mutating up there?'

She shuddered and lifted her feet up off the carpet.

'There won't be any mutating spiders,' Jules said, with a chuckle. 'Forget about giant arachnids, that idiot of an ex-fiancé of yours, work and what your parents will say. Just shut it all out. Give yourself a nice, relaxing evening. Run a bath, heat up your shepherd's pie, read a book, watch something nice on television. The television does work, doesn't it?'

'I think so. It's got a remote so that's a good sign!'

'Get a good night's sleep,' Jules instructed. 'We'll speak tomorrow. Everything's going to turn out absolutely for the best. I'm sure of it.'

'Thank you,' she murmured, but she wasn't sure that it would. Not at all.

Carrie was convinced that she wouldn't sleep. The absolute darkness outside was unfamiliar; a morbid invitation to let her imagination run away with her, to conjure up visions of ghosts and ghouls, witches and werewolves. She had drawn the curtains tightly and early, lighting the house with all the lamps, even in the upstairs bedroom which she wasn't using. At bedtime she left one light on at the bottom of the stairs, hoping it would act as a form of protection for the night ahead.

The bath had released some of the tension in her shoulders and, as she slipped beneath the super soft duvet with its crisp white cover, the scent of lavender mixed with geranium invaded her nostrils. She leaned back against the plump pillows and opened her book. A floorboard creaked, and she sat up a little straighter, aware of her muscles tensing, ears straining. Was that whispering she could hear? *Don't be ridiculous*, she told herself. *It's just the house settling, which is what you need to do.* She listened for a while longer and when all was quiet, she returned to reading while telling herself every few minutes that there was nothing to worry about. She was perfectly safe.

· · ·

Amazingly, she slept on and off for most of the next day. At one point she woke with the distinct feeling that someone was stroking her hair. It was a wonderful, comforting feeling and reminded her of how her grandmother used to smooth her hair when she was little. The next time she woke, she was sure that the bedroom door was further open than she had left it, but perhaps there had been a breeze – and there was the slightest perfume trail, which she couldn't quite identify, definitely something from the garden.

'Do you know how long I've slept for?' she said to Jules, when she checked in that evening. 'Nearly twenty-four hours.'

'You obviously needed the rest,' Jules said.

'I don't want to spend my whole time here sleeping.' Carrie yawned. 'It seems such a waste.'

'To me it sounds like absolute bliss,' Jules replied. 'And you won't worry about being on your own if you're asleep.'

'I need to tell my parents where I am. It's really inconvenient not having a phone signal or any internet connection.'

'But not so inconvenient as to make you venture out and find one?' Jules retorted.

No, Carrie thought, after the conversation finished, *perhaps she wasn't as desperate for that constant feeling of connection as she thought she was.* But sooner or later she was going to have to talk to her parents. At least she could try to keep the call brief. Her poor brother would probably take the flak. Deborah was bound to go over and over 'what had gone wrong' and 'how they had done their best, the sacrifices they had made' etc. etc. *Payback time*, she thought with a wry smile. She'd spent plenty of time over the years defending Charlie's lifestyle choices and trying to make her parents see that a rejection of the conventional way they'd brought up their children wasn't a rejection of themselves. She'd wait a little longer before calling, for Charlie's sake and her own.

. . .

On the second morning, Carrie took her coffee, a cushion and Charlotte Brontë out into the garden. She hauled one of the teak chairs into a patch of sunshine beside the old magnolia, which was in full bloom, and shrugged off her old plimsolls. The tufty grass was cool and grounding beneath her outstretched toes. Jane Eyre was just meeting Mr. Rochester for the first time when a chocolate brown Labrador bounded across the lawn and dropped a slobbery tennis ball between Carrie's bare feet.

'Oh! Hello.'

She stroked the top of his head.

'You're very handsome. Where did you come from?'

The dog looked up at her expectantly, a startlingly pink tongue lolling out of the corner of his mouth.

'I'm so sorry!'

Carrie half-turned towards the slightly dishevelled looking man who was striding across the lawn towards her.

'I didn't mean for him to disturb you, but he just loves meeting new people. Obviously, he finds me very boring!'

Carrie stood up, shielding her eyes as she looked up into a lightly tanned face and blue eyes which were crinkling attractively at the corners. Gosh, he was tall! Even taller than Mark. The top of her head barely reached his shoulder. The man stooped, almost bending himself in half, to pick up the ball, and threw it overarm. From where they were standing it was quite possible to be uncertain about where the garden ended and the fields began, but the throw was perfectly judged.

'I'm Guy, and that,' he said, as they both watched the dog take a flying leap over one of the borders in hot pursuit of the ball, 'is Wilbur, named after one of the Wright brothers due to his ability to take flying leaps into the unknown.'

He held out the hand which hadn't picked up the ball and Carrie took it, his strong fingers briefly wrapping around hers.

'Carrie,' she replied. 'I'm staying here for a couple of weeks.'

'I know. I look after the garden and wondered if you'd mind me mowing the lawn? We've had so much rain recently I haven't been able to get on it for a fortnight. I reckon it might just be dry enough now.'

He paused, glancing at the book.

'But I don't want to disturb you. Good choice, by the way. Where have you got to?'

Carrie told him and he nodded.

'I'll definitely come back later then.'

Carrie placed the little lily of the valley bookmark between the pages, closed the book and rolled her shoulders a little.

'No, please don't. To be honest, I'm ready to be disturbed. I've dreamt of having the time to sit and read like this, purely for pleasure, without any distractions, but now I've actually got the chance...'

She shrugged and felt herself colouring as he gazed down at her. The tips of his eyelashes were fringed with gold. Mark's eyelashes were thick and dark, as were Paloma's. Their baby would have the most amazing framing to their eyes. She sucked in air as a stabbing pain sliced through her abdomen.

'You okay?'

Why could she not get Mark and his baby out of her head, even for a few seconds, even when trying to hold a normal conversation with someone else?

'Yes, fine. Sorry.'

He looked unconvinced but obviously decided to return to the safer topic of reading.

'It takes time to get back into anything if you've left it for a long time,' he said, 'including reading. It's like riding a bicycle. You never forget how to do it, but you do get a little rusty.'

'Well, I'm certainly that,' she said, desperate to be distracted from thoughts of Mark and Paloma having passionate sex to create the luscious-lashed baby. Talking of rusty, she would probably be totally rusted up in the sex department, too, by the time she met someone she actually wanted to leap into bed with. Guy looked as if he'd be good in bed. Athletic. *What are you thinking, Carrie? He's really not your type and you've only just met him. You're really not that kind of girl. At least, you never have been. But who are you now? Maybe someone quite different, maybe someone who jumps into bed with the first...* He was smiling down at her, looking quizzical.

'Are you sure you're okay?'

Now she was definitely blushing.

'Yes, yes. Sorry, I was miles away momentarily.'

'I tend to have that effect on people.'

He smiled ruefully. He had a nice smile, gentle but maybe tinged with sadness. *Most people had sadness to contend with,* she thought, *but some managed to hide it well.* She liked the fact that he wouldn't or couldn't. People were too good at pretending to be fine when they weren't. She needed to work on that, to open up more. But not yet. Now she needed to get back to the conversation. What was the conversation? She frowned up at him.

'Gosh, I'm a complete airhead at the moment. What were we talking about?'

'Reading.'

'Ah, yes! I used to be a fast reader and now I have to keep going back over bits. I'm so slow.'

'Is that a bad thing?' he asked.

'Well, no. I don't suppose it is. Not here, at least.'

And going forwards it looks as if I might have more time on my hands anyway, she thought. *But no need to tell him that.* Although there was something about the way he stood there, so comfortable in himself, with the most direct gaze that she had ever come across. He looked completely trustworthy. She could easily embarrass herself even more and offload all her life problems. Thankfully, Wilbur thudded to a stop in front of her, dropping the ball once more at her feet, and she bent down to fondle his ears.

'Wilbur warning,' Guy said, with a mischievous grin. 'If you pick up that ball and throw it, you won't get any more time for reading. You'll have a job for the entire time you're here.'

'Well, I could be looking for a new job,' Carrie blurted, her fingertips reaching for the slobbery ball, 'and maybe a complete career change would do me good – professional ball lobber for Labradors. Now that would be a good occupation, wouldn't it?' She addressed Wilbur. 'I bet that it really doesn't take very much to make you happy, unlike a lot of the people I normally have to deal with.'

She flung the ball as far as she could manage, which was about half as far as Guy had thrown it.

'Except maybe I need a bit of training,' she said.

Within seconds Wilbur was back.

'Told you,' Guy said. 'He'll attach himself to you like a limpet.'

'There are worse things to be attached to,' Carrie said, 'and he *is* gorgeous.'

'Doesn't he know it?' Guy sighed.

Wilbur looked up at Carrie with his melting brown eyes.

'He's also the most terrible flirt with the ladies. And if you happen to have food, he's yours for life!'

How wonderful, Carrie thought, *to have someone who was yours for life.* For an awful moment she thought that she might cry. As if sensing her struggle Guy looked away diplomatically. That giveaway face of hers again. She moved backwards, her knee knocking into the corner of the chair. She'd have a bruise there tomorrow.

'I might be able to rustle up a plain biscuit for Wilbur. It's a shame to mow up the daisies but if you want to press on with the lawn, that's fine. I'll go and put the kettle on, shall I? Tea, coffee? Oh, and Rita left me a very large carrot cake. Do you know Rita? She's a very good cook. Would you like a piece of that, too?'

The words came out in a rush. He must think she was barking mad, gabbling away like this but if she stopped talking now, if there was the slightest of pauses, who knew what would happen? Most probably all of those tears puddling inside would spout out like geysers and soak this poor man to the skin. What she really wanted to do was curl up like a dormouse, close her eyes and forget everything, stop feeling everything – although she was sure that dormice did feel. Why was she still talking? Goodness knows whether she was saying anything sensible. She barely recognised the words coming out of her mouth as her own.

'You'd be doing my waistline a service if nothing else. That carrot cake is irresistible.'

She was blushing even more now. She hugged herself. His eyes were going to drop to her waist now, she knew it. But his gaze returned steadfastly to her face.

'I do know Rita and she is indeed an excellent cook and a wonderful lady. Coffee and a slice of carrot cake would be good,' he said. 'And I've never known Wilbur to say no to a biscuit. I'll go and get the mower out of the shed.'

He had given her the opportunity to escape, and it didn't feel as if he was running away from an over-emotional stranger like a scared rabbit of a man. It felt as if he was giving her some space to compose herself because he knew that was what she herself wanted. She grabbed at the lifeline.

'Come on then, Wilbur,' she said. 'Follow me.'

Without any hesitation, as if he'd understood every word in addition to 'biscuit', Wilbur trotted closely by her side back towards the house.

Carrie placed the coffee and cake on the garden table and left the back door ajar so that Wilbur could wander in and out. She sat on the sofa and began to sift through the pile of brochures which had been left in a wicker basket underneath a side table. For a small island there was an enormous amount to see and do: Osborne House, Carisbrooke Castle, the Donkey Sanctuary, the Garlic Farm, the multi-coloured rock at Alum Bay – and that was before exploring any of the pretty villages or beaches. It was definitely time she got out and about. She'd been sitting there for well over an hour, trying to decide where to go first, when the comforting rumble of the mower stopped.

'All done for now,' Guy called.

Carrie stood up, smoothing her Breton top, and walked through to the kitchen. Suddenly, she really didn't want to be on her own. In fact, just having him standing there in the doorway, his hefty gardening boots careful not to cross the threshold and mess up the honey-coloured floor, was reassuring. He leaned forwards and placed his mug and plate on the work surface before running a hand through his unruly brown hair. The gesture didn't have the slightest effect.

'Thanks for the drink and the cake. Not everyone offers, especially if they're in a holiday cottage.'

'Why would that make a difference?'

He shrugged his shoulders.

'Too relaxed, maybe.'

'Or can't be bothered?'

'Or maybe it just doesn't occur to them. I don't take it personally.'

He shot her a lop-sided smile which reminded her of the dog. He had some grass cuttings stuck to the stubble on his jawline. Jules liked someone who was a bit rumpled and crumpled and she would definitely go weak-kneed at the sight of that smile. Maybe Guy would be the person to tempt her to try a relationship that lasted longer than six weeks. Perhaps she ought to try and get her over here, then she could introduce them and...

His eyes took in the couple of brochures she was still holding.

'If you're looking to explore,' he said, 'the walk up to the Longstone is one of my favourites and the gardens at the other end of the village are pretty special, if you like that sort of thing. Mind you, I'm a bit biased because I work there. My gran always says to me 'not everyone's into plants, Guy' when I'm in danger of boring someone silly about how to prune the different types of clematis or droning on about the joy of taking cuttings. She's always there to put me right. Good thing, too, or I'd probably be unbearable.'

Carrie smiled and automatically twisted the slim eternity ring on the ring finger of her right hand.

'You're lucky. My granny died recently. I wish she was still here to give me advice. She always used to say that it's good to be passionate about something.'

'True. It can come at a cost sometimes, though, can't it?'

Instinctively, Carrie knew that he didn't really expect an answer. Again, she thought of Mark. Had her dedication to the job contributed to their break-up? But he'd been eager to climb the ladder of success, too, albeit in a different way. His way was networking in restaurants and bars after work and she'd never complained about that, had she?

Stretched out in front of the range, Wilbur let out a little groan of contentment.

'That's his passion,' Guy said. 'Somewhere warm and cosy, lazy dog.'

'He seems very settled here,' Carrie replied. 'It's almost as if this place is his second home.'

'Hardly surprising. I did a bit of work here, getting the cottage ready to be rented out. Wilbur had a rug right there in front of the range. Dogs don't forget things like that.'

Guy checked his watch and slapped the side of his thigh.

'Time to go, Wilbur, and leave the good lady in peace.'

Wilbur raised his head but didn't move.

'Come on, lazybones. You can't take over Carrie's kitchen. She's on holiday, escaping responsibilities like having to deal with stubborn dogs.'

'I don't mind if you want to leave him here,' Carrie said, so surprised by what she was saying that her eyes widened. 'I *am* used to dogs. My parents have got a cockapoo, but I totally understand if... well, you're not going to trust him with just anyone.'

Guy laughed. The sound was deep and warm and it rang appealingly all around the kitchen.

'It's not a question of trusting *you*. It's him. He'll see you as his new best friend and have you throwing that ball, finding snacks, nudging you for a walk and...'

'I don't mind. Really. Actually, it would be quite nice to have the company. I can bring him along to the gardens later if you're going to be there – or sooner if he starts pining for you.'

He laughed again.

'The only thing Wilbur is likely to pine for is food. I'm at the gardens actually for the rest of the day. So, what's it to be, Wilbur – come with me and sit in on my meeting with the Major or stay here?'

The dog lifted his legs, his paw pads lightly touching the red enamel of the range and absorbing more of its warmth.

'No contest obviously!' Guy remarked.

He fished a tweed lead out of his pocket.

'I tend to put him on the lead when we're walking along the road. It's pretty quiet here but if he spots a rabbit, he can forget everything I've taught him.'

Carrie nodded.

'See you later then,' Guy said, turning to leave. 'I finish at around five thirty or six depending on how much there is to do. That's presuming I've survived my meeting with the Major! You don't have to keep Wilbur until then, though. Bring him back whenever. Come through the archway and into the gift shop. Heather or Jenny will track me down. If I'm not around, just leave him in their tender care.'

He waved to Wilbur.

'Have fun and be good.'

And with that he turned and left. Carrie stood in the kitchen listening to the dog's gentle breathing, the soft tweed of the lead caressing her fingertips. And then picking up Guy's mug to take to the sink, she noticed that he had filled it with a little water and floated a few daisies on the top. She smiled and felt as if something, somewhere deep inside of her had begun to shift.

CARING

'Well, wasn't that lovely?' Eliza said, with a contented sigh as she tucked her arm through Isaac's. 'Guy is such a sweetheart.'

Isaac patted Eliza's hand as they continued their stroll around the perimeter of the garden.

'Oh, Isaac!' she exclaimed, stopping abruptly and bringing both hands in prayer to her chest. 'Do you think he could be Carrie's sweetheart?'

'I think, my love,' Isaac replied with a smile, 'that you're getting rather ahead of yourself.'

'But it's not impossible, is it?'

'No,' he replied. 'Nothing's impossible, but...'

'And poor Guy has been through so much and our guest has suffered at the hands of a dishonourable man.'

'How do you know that, Eliza?'

'Female intuition, of course.'

'And...' he cajoled.

'And I might have caught sight of her diary when she left it open on the window seat and I also heard a little of the conversation she had with her friend, Jules.'

Eliza pressed herself a little closer. They had been together for so long now, but sometimes she still needed to explain how certain things worked. Isaac was a man, after all!

'Don't give me that disapproving look, Isaac. How can we help her if we don't know anything about her situation? And from what I saw of her jottings, she is still disturbingly attached to this other man. In fact, she seems to think that she might still be in love with him in spite of his betrayal.'

'We're meant to be keeping a protective eye on her, my love, not spying – and definitely not meddling.'

'I was observing closely, Isaac, not spying,' Eliza said with an indignant pout, 'and I would never meddle, not unless it was absolutely necessary.'

'We need to be careful,' he said, gently. 'It's important that our presence here is a secret. After all, we don't want to be discovered and subsequently forced out, do we?'

'Oh no,' Eliza gasped, 'that would be terrible.'

'So, no more getting too close.'

'I only wanted to check that she was comfortable on her first night. She seemed so jittery. I want everything here to be perfect for her, Isaac.'

'I know, my love, but Guy and Rita have already done their very best to ensure that's the case.'

Eliza nodded.

'Rita is an exceptionally good woman. It was so kind of her to bring Carrie the pie. I knew that she would be the right person to look after our guests.'

'It's not that I thought she wasn't right,' Isaac replied. 'I just worried that it might be too much for her, on top of everything else.'

Eliza smiled up at him.

'You're always so considerate. That's one of the reasons I fell in love with you. The thing is, Isaac,' she said, very gently, 'when you have problems which are largely beyond your control, it's better to keep busy and to follow your true nature.

Rita's nature is to give to others. She needs people and they need her.'

'If you say so, my love.'

'I do.'

'Then I trust that you're right.'

Eliza stopped walking and gazed across the gently undulating fields towards the enticing sparkle of the sea. She would never, ever tire of that view.

'If looking after this house as well as her own becomes too much, we'll know,' she reassured him. 'We'll watch for the signs and will care for her accordingly.'

Isaac turned his head slightly to look over his shoulder as Carrie gathered up her plate and cup and strolled back towards the house.

'Just as we'll care for our new friend.'

Eliza stood on tiptoes and kissed his dear cheek.

'Yes,' she said, 'precisely.'

FIVE

Carrie decided to leave the Longstone for another day. Instead, after a lunch of ham, cheese and some freshly baked crusty bread left on the doorstep by Rita, she decided to take Wilbur for a walk.

'So where shall we go?' she asked him, shrugging herself into her coat and clipping on his lead.

He looked up at her expectantly.

'This is your neck of the woods, Wilbur. Take me somewhere nice, but no rabbit holes, please. I'm not Alice in Wonderland.'

Wilbur wagged his tail enthusiastically and Carrie bent down to give him a hug.

'Oh, Wilbur,' she murmured. 'Life is so simple when you're a dog, isn't it? A ball, a cosy place to sleep, good food and plenty of fresh air. I get the feeling you have a lot to teach me!'

It felt good to walk, the sun on her face, the odd bee busying itself in the hedgerow and the dog by her side. From the cottage Wilbur had led her back up the lane, turning off after a couple of minutes onto a rutted track. Occasionally, through a gateway or a gap in the budding hedge, Carrie spotted a glimpse of the sea.

'I wonder if this goes all the way to the beach,' she said to the dog. 'I bet you like the beach, don't you, Wilbur? I haven't been there yet. Maybe we can go together.'

But the end of the track finished on a clifftop with no obvious way down to the shoreline below.

'Oh well, never mind,' Carrie said, as she sat on the grass, the dog patiently by her side. 'But I will take a photo. Do you like having your picture taken, Wilbur?'

She reached into her pocket for her phone.

'Oh, no! I must have left it in the kitchen. And I forgot to ask Guy about the best place to get a signal. Wait until I tell Jules that I forgot my phone. She'll be so full of herself. In fact, on second thoughts, I probably won't tell her. It'll be our secret. Okay?'

Wilbur thumped his tail and nudged her hand.

Carrie draped her arm around his neck.

'Who needs a camera, anyway?' she said, looking out to sea. 'Jules would tell me just to sit here and take it all in. Do you know what, I think she might be right. A picture could never do that view justice.'

It was just after five o'clock by the time Carrie headed for The Manor and the sign outside stated it was closed in emphatic Times Roman font, but the large wooden doors flanking the gateway had been left slightly ajar. Carrie eased them open just enough for herself and Wilbur to slip through the slim gap. She stepped into the small shop, which was bursting with cards and gifts. Although the light was still on, there was no one to be seen.

'Where is everyone?' she asked, leading the dog around the central display of toys and games and out through the far door which led to the garden.

As Carrie paused on the large expanse of gravel, the house

itself stood directly in front of her. With weathered sandstone walls and a clay-tiled roof, it nestled perfectly within the surroundings. Wilbur sat down, leaning into her leg, and Carrie reached down to unclip his lead. Obediently, he followed her through a gap in the wall and into a part of the garden filled with exotic plants. In the middle of the lawn was a grass maze and, around the edges, borders bursting with shrubs mixed with emerging herbaceous plants.

'No one here either, Wilbur. Where's Guy? He won't have gone home without you, will he?'

Wilbur's ears pricked up at the mention of Guy's name. He gazed up at Carrie, barked twice and suddenly he was off, bounding back in the direction she had come from.

'Wilbur, wait!' she called, swivelling to run after him and just catching sight of the tip of his tail as he disappeared around a corner of the house and out of sight. Surely, he couldn't get lost in this garden, could he? He must know it like the back of his paws. Carrie's feet skidded on the gravel stones. But what if he ran up into the woods or back on to the road? She flew up several stone steps leading to a large, terraced area flanked by wide borders. Still no sign of Wilbur. Oh, my goodness, Jules was right, she was too trusting, and obviously not just with men, with dogs, too. She really should have kept a tighter rein on Wilbur and on Mark for that matter. She'd given him too much freedom and that had allowed Paloma to move in and stake her claim.

At the far end of the borders was a tall yew hedge with an archway cut into the middle. Carrie burst through the opening and emerged in a sheltered space where an elderly gentleman was sitting on a wooden bench, eyes closed, hand resting on the top of his stick. He was dressed immaculately in a dark blue blazer with the shiniest gold buttons Carrie had ever seen, a checked Viyella shirt and a diagonally striped red and navy tie. She stopped abruptly, almost slipping on the moist grass and falling into his lap. He started, his unfriendly eyes now open and boring into her.

'We're closed. Didn't you see the sign?'

His voice was surprisingly strong for someone who looked quite frail.

Carrie gasped for breath and regained her balance.

'Um, yes, I know,' she spluttered.

'And still you chose to ignore it,' he fumed. 'That's the trouble with people these days. They have no concept of boundaries, rules. Think they can go where they like, when they like.'

Carrie raised her hand. It was a tentative gesture and immediately she felt about seven years old, sitting at the back of the class, not sure whether she should speak or not, overcome with doubt as to whether the answer she was about to give was the right one.

'Um, the gates were actually open, sort of, and...'

'Well, they shouldn't have been,' he shot back, before she had the chance to continue. 'You'll have to come back another time. Although I should have you blacklisted.'

'Oh, believe me, I'd like to – come back, I mean. Not be blacklisted. Oh no! That would be awful. I've never been blacklisted from anything although my brother did ban me from his birthday party once, but Mum made him change his mind.'

She pressed her lips together.

'Sorry!' she whispered. 'Irrelevant.'

'Totally,' he snapped. 'Although your sibling has my profound sympathy. Perhaps he thought you were going to talk his friends to death.'

'Embarrassing...' she gulped. 'Little sister... cramping his style.'

She looked away from his bushy eyebrows which seemed capable of expressing his extreme belligerence all on their own. Briefly, she took solace from the intimacy of the enclosed space with its four, square planting beds arranged around a small central pool. No wonder he liked to sit here. Alone. She should go.

'Hmph!' he replied. 'I have a younger sister. She was always tagging on to my coat tails. Infuriating.'

'I can imagine. Sorry.'

'Why are you apologising for my sister?'

'I don't know.'

He narrowed his eyes.

'You look like the sort of person who apologises a lot.'

Carrie felt her breastbone cave a little.

'Do I? Yes, I suppose I do. I mean, not that I look like that sort of person, but that I do apolo—'

He waved his hand dismissively and she stopped.

'Sorr...' she started to say again while taking a few backward steps. 'I'll leave you in peace.'

She swivelled, looking up over the hedges to where the ground rose steeply, the ridge fringed with a variety of trees, some evergreen, some deciduous. It gave the whole garden a secretive feel. Briefly she half turned back towards him.

'This is a very peaceful place.'

'In an ideal world, yes.'

She glanced down at the rose border where her foot had knocked one of the labels off kilter.

'Oh, Desdemona! That's one of my favourite roses. I bought my granny one just before she died. I've dug it up and put it in a pot although it's not very happy. We've got a small shared garden at the back of our house but it's a bit shady. One day I'd like to have a garden all of my own and plant Desdemona. Are all these the same variety? They must look stunning when they're in flower.'

'They are and they do. I thought you were going.'

'I am. I really *am* sorry to have disturbed you.'

He twisted his hands on the top of the stick, his signet ring glinting in the fading sunlight.

'So you keep saying. We're open tomorrow – from eleven o'clock. I presume that you can find your own way out?'

'Yes. Thank you. But before I go, I just have to find...'

She was interrupted by the sound of heavy breathing and a rush of air as Wilbur dashed past her, tail wagging furiously. He stopped in front of the man and rested his head on the tweed checked trousers.

'Wilbur!' Carrie exclaimed. 'There you are. I thought I'd lost you.'

'No chance,' a rich, warm voice chuckled and suddenly Guy was beside her. 'He's never far from people – always worried he'll miss out on a snack. Isn't he, Major?'

The elderly man was busy reaching into his jacket pocket and producing a dog biscuit which Wilbur took gently from his fingers.

'I see you two have met,' Guy said.

'Well, yes,' Carrie replied, 'although we hadn't actually got around to introducing ourselves.'

She stepped forwards and held out a hand.

'I'm Carrie. I've been dog-sitting this afternoon. I was just returning him, but he ran off and...'

The Major stood up with surprising alacrity and tipped his Panama hat before returning her grasp.

'Andrew Fox-Patterson.'

His eyes flashed.

'You might have explained,' he said accusingly, and Carrie wasn't sure whether he was addressing her, Guy or both of them. 'Thought you were another of those damnable intruders.'

'You think everyone's an intruder,' Guy said, teasingly, 'even the ones who have paid good money to admire your beautiful garden.'

Andrew didn't reply, just sat back down and hunched himself over to fondle Wilbur's ears.

'Sorry!' Guy whispered to Carrie.

'I can hear you,' Andrew said. 'I may be old but I'm not deaf and I don't need you apologising for me as well as the rest of the world. I'm quite capable of doing it myself.'

'Except you never do,' Guy said, shooting Carrie a wry grin and rolling his eyes slightly.

'And I can see, too,' Andrew said.

'Please don't fall out over me,' Carrie said. 'It was a misunderstanding.'

'Perhaps I was a bit hasty,' the Major retorted.

'And that,' whispered Guy, 'is the nearest thing to an apology you're likely to get. Actually, you're pretty honoured.'

'To be honest, I wouldn't want people wandering around my home, especially not when it's meant to be closed. You can't have much time to enjoy it on your own.'

Beside her she heard Guy give a little groan.

'Don't encourage him,' he murmured. 'I'm convinced that one day I'll turn up for work and he'll have barricaded everyone out.'

'And if I want to, why shouldn't I?' Andrew retorted. 'All you're worried about is your job.'

Guy gave a deep sigh.

'We've been through all of this, Andrew. Many times. And it's not appropriate to drag Carrie into our discussions.'

He took her elbow.

'Come on. I'll show you out and I'll see you tomorrow, Andrew.'

'There's really no need to see me off the premises,' Carrie said, following Guy down the steps. 'I can find my own way.'

'Actually, I've got to head off myself. I promised my gran that I'd pop in and see her tonight. If I don't go soon, we'll miss visiting time. Come on, Wilbur. You know how much all of those ladies at the home love you.'

As they left the sanctuary of the rose garden a sudden flood of emotion coursed through her.

'You okay?' he asked, as she stumbled over her own feet.

She was acutely aware of his hand hovering to steady her. *He could steady Jules, too,* she thought. *Get her to see that she didn't have to take fright every time someone started to get serious.*

'Fine. It's just we were talking about roses, and it reminded me of my granny. I spent a lot of time with her when I was little.'

She couldn't speak for a moment. Her life felt as if it was full of loss – Granny, Mark, her job, her brother moving abroad. The sense of loneliness was overwhelming even in this beautiful place. And then there was the Major sitting on his bench. Alone.

'It's hard when you lose someone you love,' Guy said, 'and it can be hard to know how to help those who are left behind. I've tried to help Andrew but since Honoria, his wife, died five years ago he keeps everyone at arm's length.'

Carrie felt her breath settle, relief course through her at the opportunity to change focus.

'Does he live here all by himself?'

'Yes.'

She glanced up at the house and did a quick tally of the leaded windows, trying to guess how many rooms were contained inside. *Twenty, at least,* she thought.

'What about children?'

'Just one. It was a second marriage for Andrew. Honoria's first and she was quite a bit younger than him. Sebastian lives in Hong Kong.'

'Does he visit?'

Out of the corner of her eye she noticed Guy's jaw tense.

'Occasionally.'

'And the Major said he has a sister. What about her? Is she nearby?'

'He told you that, did he? You are honoured. Actually, he

fell out with Margaret a long time ago. He's fallen out with a lot of people, especially since Honoria died.'

They had reached the archway, and Guy pulled the heavy oak door towards them.

'Don't take Andrew's rudeness personally,' he said. 'This was Honoria's garden. She basically made it what it is today and opened it up to the public in order to help with the upkeep of the house. Andrew never liked people traipsing around even back then but now she's gone he resents it even more. He just seems to want to be left completely on his own here with only his memories.'

'That's so sad.'

Guy shrugged.

'Fortunately, or unfortunately, for him, depending how you look at it, he can't afford such a luxury. Not if he wants to hang on to the place.'

'Will his son come back and take over?'

'That's what Andrew hopes, but...'

Guy bit his lip. Carrie sensed that he felt he'd said too much. She crouched down and patted Wilbur.

'Thank you for letting me hang on to him,' she said. 'We've had a wonderful afternoon.'

'If you want to come back one day and visit the gardens then you won't be charged,' he said. 'I'll tell Heather and Jenny that you're a VIP visitor.'

'There's no need. Really.'

'It's the least I can do to make up for Andrew's rudeness and for you putting up with Wilbur.'

'I would like to come back.'

She smiled at him, and he smiled back. It was suddenly an awkward, shy smile. She hoped that he didn't think she was after him. That would be awful. Perhaps he thought she was desperate for a relationship. Perhaps she ought to make it clear if they met again that she wasn't. But perhaps he wouldn't even be here if she came back to visit the gardens and there would be no need to say anything at all.

'See you around then,' he said.

'Yes. Maybe.'

And as she walked up the drive towards the church with its banks of lemon-yellow primroses and late afternoon sun turning the windows to liquid gold, the gate closed firmly behind her.

The Major sat down slowly and cursed under his breath at the pain in his knee – and the pain in his heart. As he had watched Carrie and Guy walk away, he could hear Honoria's voice ringing in his ears.

'You're a silly old thing, Andrew,' she would have said.

And she was right, of course. He was. Even sillier without her here beside him to put him right.

SIX

Carrie paused for a moment and listened to the birdsong. She took a deep breath; grass, tree pollen, primroses, the sea, the cooling air turning warm as it entered her nostrils. Crossing the road a stone in her shoe caused her to stop by the church. Reaching out, her hand rested on the moss-cushioned wall as she balanced on one leg. There was something about moss that was incredibly calming, and Carrie was instantly transported back to making an Easter garden at Sunday school; remembering the satisfying smoothness of small pebbles between her fingers as she arranged them alongside spring flowers. And then there was the moss – a vibrant green carpet which needed to be sprinkled regularly with water and the endearingly named moss piglets that lived within it, some of the most resilient creatures on earth. That's what she needed, to develop more resilience, and coming here would be the starting point.

A high-pitched wailing interrupted her thoughts and, turning around, Carrie spotted a vision in white. For a brief moment she could have imagined that it was a ghost returning to the churchyard but as the apparition moved closer, she recognised the whirr of wheels on tarmac and the soft 'shushing' of a flesh and blood voice. The wailing rang out from one side of a double buggy.

'Sorry,' the woman said, her straight blonde hair swinging with an almost impossible fluidity as she stooped to push a pearly pink dummy into a petulant mouth. 'Talk about disturbing the peace and quiet. The trouble is, if one sleeps the other invariably doesn't. Sometimes I think they have a secret pact!'

Carrie gazed at the baby with her soft blonde curls and furiously pink face. Next to her, another baby, almost identical, was fast asleep, long lashes resting on milky, cherubic cheeks.

'They're beautiful,' Carrie said.

'Aargh!' the woman groaned, as the angry child spat out the dummy and exercised her lungs even more vigorously. 'That's not the word I'd use at the moment, especially when Olivia's like this.'

Carrie's bare foot was still poised in mid-air, her trainer dangling from one hand.

'Gosh, are you okay? Have you hurt yourself?'

'No, not at all. It's just a bit of grit,' Carrie replied.

'Sorry if we startled you.'

'My fault. I was miles away,' Carrie said with a rueful smile. Olivia sounded as if she was about to spontaneously combust.

'Go on then, you win,' the woman said, leaning over once more and lifting the baby into her arms. Olivia gulped and then hiccupped.

'See, she stops crying as soon as I pick her up, but I can't hold her all the time. I thought she'd dropped off to sleep at home but the minute I put her down she woke up again, which is why I've walked halfway around the island. I think tonight is going to be yet another sleepless one.'

She smiled at Carrie.

'I don't suppose you could do me a favour, could you? If you're heading back to Hideaway Cottage, I'd love the company. My husband's away so I've had days on my own with these two monsters. A bit of adult conversation would be just bliss. Also, you could push the buggy for me. It's not that easy to steer with one hand on these lanes and then I can stroke Olivia's head while we walk. She does love that and sometimes it does the trick.'

'Oh!' Carrie couldn't hide her confusion. How could she explain that pushing a buggy containing a sleeping child was an incredibly difficult thing to do?

The woman grinned, obviously totally misconstruing her reluctance.

'That must sound a bit creepy, the fact that we haven't even introduced ourselves and I know where you're staying. I'm Cressie and I promise that I'm not a serial killer!'

'Carrie,' she replied, replacing her trainer as slowly as she could to give herself time. *It's just a buggy, Carrie, and you won't be pushing it for long. You don't have to let this send you into a meltdown.*

'You'll soon learn that news travels faster than the speed of light in a tiny place like this,' Cressie said. 'There's not much else going on here, not on the surface anyway. Someone coming to stay at Hideaway Cottage caused great excitement. It was in a bit of a state, so it's nice to see it brought back to life. You don't really have to walk with me, by the way. I won't be offended if you want to wander back on your own. I would in your shoes.'

'In Manchester most people avoid eye contact, let alone start a conversation with a complete stranger. I barely know my neighbours. In fact, I've never seen the people who live in the flat above us. I'm sure it's as much my fault as theirs. We're all working long hours, shifts, you know the thing...'

She suddenly felt another form of wistfulness, not just for the baby she and Mark had never had but for connection. How remote she had become from everyone, not just the people she could have known if she'd made more effort, but from friends, too. And all because of a job she thought she loved but which would never love her back. She smiled at Cressie and lightly rested her hands around the handle of the buggy.

'It's nice to have the company,' she said, falling into step.

'It won't bite,' Cressie said.

'No,' Carrie said, tightening her grip. 'Sorry. I'm not used to babies.'

'Not many people are until they have their own,' Cressie replied. 'You won't be short of company here. Everyone loves a chat, which has its pros and cons. On the whole it's good, though. It's one of the reasons we moved from London. I really wanted to belong to a proper community, especially with Jack being away so much. He's a jazz musician so he travels a lot. This is a great village. If you want to keep yourself to yourself, that's fine, but also if you want company, then people are there for you.'

'Which is your house?' Carrie asked.

'It's the barn just on the outskirts. You must have passed it on the way in from the ferry port. Probably almost ran over one of our chickens. Just about everyone does!'

'Yes, I did. Sorry!'

'Don't apologise. It's their stupid fault for wandering over the road when they've got a perfectly nice garden.'

Cressie patted Olivia on the back, and she burped loudly. 'Please God, that might help,' she said. 'Freddie isn't nearly so windy but then he's much the easier baby. Olivia takes after her daddy. She just loves to be the centre of attention. How long are you here for? Guy did tell me, but I've got the most awful baby brain. I suppose it lasts for twice as long with twins.'

Carrie frowned. She didn't remember telling Guy how long she was staying but perhaps Rita had mentioned it to him.

'Two weeks.'

'And are you settling in? Sorry, I've spent far too much time talking about me. One of the downsides of spending so much time with two little people who can't talk back. When you meet someone new you tend to offload.'

'You haven't offloaded at all and yes, absolutely. I'm settling in fine. It's just beautiful here. I was worried it would be a bit quiet but I'm starting to realise that's probably just what I need.'

'That's what I love about it,' Cressie said. 'The peace and quiet, at least until these two came along.' Her face softened. 'I shouldn't moan. Some people would give anything to have what I've got.'

She glanced at Carrie.

'Oh, I'm sorry. Have I put my foot in it? I do that quite a lot.'

She reached out and touched Carrie's shoulder. They both shifted on to the grass verge as a car went past. Carrie raised one hand to cover her trembling lips.

'It's okay really. It's just my ex fiancé and I tried for a baby for quite a time but it didn't happen and then we split up because he said he needed some space and on top of that he proceeded to steal the job which should have been mine and started a relationship with Perfect Paloma who he's now engaged to and she's s roughly eleven weeks pregnant and supposedly they've only been together a bit longer than that and...' She gasped for breath and leaned a little harder on the buggy for support. 'You didn't need to know all of that or even any of it!'

'Oh, my goodness. Poor you! I'm so sorry. That's awful. Jack's always telling me I need to think before I speak.'

'It's not your fault. You weren't to know. Anyway, that's why I'm here,' Carrie said, 'to try and come to terms with every-thing, to try and sort out my life. At least, that's what my friend Jules says I am here for.'

'She sounds like a good friend, and you won't find a better place than this. People here are very kind. They have time for you.' Cressie stroked Olivia's head. 'Are her eyes closing?'

Carrie nodded, at which point Olivia's lids snapped open and the baby's big, blue eyes stared straight at her.

'Um, at least they were.'

Cressie bit her lip.

'I knew it was going to be hard but... I mean, I do love them really, but I just get so tired sometimes. Jack doesn't understand how exhausting it is.'

'Well, men don't have to give birth, do they?'

'I reckon the human race would die out pretty quickly if they did,' Cressie replied with a laugh.

'I can't imagine how hard it must be managing on your own.'

'Jack does what he can when he's here, but in the meantime, you just have to get on with it, don't you? People are always offering to help but I don't like to take advantage.'

They stopped outside Hideaway Cottage. Carrie could see that Olivia was fighting sleep with all of her being.

'I can help while I'm here.'

Why did you say that? Carrie thought. *You're here for yourself, remember, not other people* – but there was something about this place which made her want to get involved. To give back. Cressie touched her arm.

'That's *so* sweet but I wouldn't dream of interrupting your reinvention in such a way. If you would like a coffee one morning, though, that would be lovely. Although if you've got plans...'

Reinvention – she'd not thought of it like that until now. Did she really want to have coffee with a complete stranger, even one who seemed really nice? It was one thing walking along the road and having a brief chat but quite another going to someone's house and...

'Sorry,' Cressie said. 'There I go again making inappropriate suggestions.'

Carrie looked at Cressie's face and for the first time registered the fine lines around her eyes, the slight quivering at the corners of her mouth.

'I don't have any plans at all,' she said. 'Coffee would be great.'

Cressie's eyes lit up.

'What about tomorrow? Gosh, that makes me sound a bit desperate, doesn't it? Won't blame you if you want to run a mile!'

'Tomorrow is good,' Carrie replied. 'Shall I bring cake? I've got this massive carrot cake from Rita. I'm never going to eat it on my own.'

'Ooh, yes, please. Rita's cakes are heavenly. Eleven-ish okay? I try to get the monsters to have a nap around that time.' She raised a hand with both fingers crossed. 'We should be able to have a proper chat.'

Cressie twisted her head to look at Olivia's face.

'Are her eyes completely closed?' she whispered.

Carrie nodded.

'Then I'd better get home and try to sleep while I can.'

'Will you be okay walking back on your own?'

'I'll be fine,' Cressie replied, and as she headed off up the lane, pushing the buggy, Carrie got the feeling that was a phrase she used quite a lot.

SEVEN

Carrie snuggled down beneath the duvet and turned out the bedside lamp. She lay there studying the darkness and realised that she felt a little different, as if there was a tiny and tentative bubble of happiness inside her. She put her hand to her stomach as if to protect it and thought about that article she'd read in one of Jules's magazines about the benefits of talking to strangers – how it was good for your overall wellbeing. *Who has time for that*, she'd thought, *when I barely get the chance to check in with my actual friends?* But maybe there was something in it. She'd only been here for a few days, and she'd been trusted with someone's beloved dog and a complete stranger had asked her round for coffee. She turned on her side and closed her eyes. When she got back to Manchester she was going to knock on her neighbours' doors and properly introduce herself. She might even ask them around for drinks. She must mention it to Jules. She'd send her a message tomorrow morning if she could find a spot where her phone would pick up a signal. And her parents, too – she'd send them a message to let them know she was fine just in case they'd been trying to get in touch.

In the meantime, all of that fresh air had made her really tired, too tired to even bother about spiders.

Something woke her. Suddenly. Breath held, limbs taut, senses blaring, eyes struggling to adjust to the gloom. Nothing... except for thick silence. But it felt as if someone was there. In the house. *You're being ridiculous, Carrie. You checked both of the doors before you came to bed, and the only window that is open is this one.* She propped herself up slightly and directed her gaze towards the curtains which she could just make out were still firmly drawn. Maybe the noise had been outside. She was sure now that it had been something like a door closing. Sounds travelled so mischievously, especially at night, especially if you were alone.

She longed to stretch out a hand and feel the reassuring arm or shoulder of someone special, someone who would whisper sleepily that there was nothing to worry about, or even better, someone who would get out of bed without any hint of reluctance and check every nook and cranny. *If only Mark was here instead of lying next to Paloma.* But he wasn't so she would have to face this herself because there was absolutely no way she was going to get back to sleep until she made sure that she was alone. Turning on the lamp, Carrie shivered and reached for her dressing gown strewn across the end of the bed. Wrapping it around her, standing up and pulling the tie tightly around her waist, she scanned the room for some sort of defence. If she hadn't gone completely organic with her toiletries and got rid of all her aerosols, she could have at least sprayed any intruder in the face. An aloe vera roll-on deodorant was hardly a lethal weapon! In the end she secreted a pair of nail scissors in her dressing gown pocket and tiptoed on to the landing.

Flicking on the lights as quickly as possible, one hand ready to pounce with the scissors, she could barely breathe. But the bathroom and the other bedroom were totally undisturbed. She was going to have to go downstairs and hope the creaky boards didn't alert any intruder. On the other hand, they'd have heard her moving about up here anyway. Would they make their escape or stay silently waiting, ready to grab her when she approached, a hand over her mouth to stifle her screams? She should have accompanied Jules to those self-defence lessons, then she wouldn't feel as weak as a kitten and totally unable to fight anyone off. If the bedroom had been lockable, she'd have bolted straight back in there and stayed until daylight, but it wasn't, so there was no alternative.

Carrie paused at the top of the stairs and placed one hand on the banister rail to steady herself. *Get a grip, Carrie. Go downstairs, check everywhere, make yourself a drink and come back to bed.* She reached for the switch that turned on the wall lights downstairs, the steady tick of the grandmother clock giving her courage to descend. At the bottom she paused, braced herself, tried to regulate her breathing. Nothing seemed different and yet if she allowed herself to be over-fanciful, there seemed to be a frisson of something in the air, a trail of incongruity spooling its way across the room.

'You and your imagination!' her mother used to say when she'd made up one of her stories to get herself out of trouble or avoid going to school.

The sitting room looked the same as when she'd left it and gradually Carrie's breathing became more regular. She approached the door to the kitchen and placed her thumb on the shallow teaspoon-shaped latch. As softly as possible she depressed it. The handle was smooth from years of use, but it still clicked, the sound outwitting her attempts at stealth. Pushing open the door, a shaft of light rushed in over the limestone floor. Shadows split the room into a geometric study of inkiness. The smell of the pizza she had cooked for supper invaded her nostrils and the fridge hummed reassuringly. Then the tap dripped, making her jump.

Turn on the light, you idiot. Light always makes things better. Now she could almost see the entire room except for the space behind the door so she pushed it back as far as it would go. *Even the skinniest man in the world couldn't fit behind there. You're such a drama queen, Carrie. There is no one here, nothing to worry about at all.*

It was then that she spotted it, just as she was about to lift the kettle from its trivet next to the range. Her slippered foot came into contact with something soft and unfamiliar – a purple checked blanket carefully arranged on the floor. Carrie blinked, one hand on the kettle handle, the other flying to her chest. *How had that got there?* She took a step backwards. Someone *had* been in the house. She reached towards the pine block and extricated a knife. Legs trembling, retracing her steps, she double checked all the doors and windows, the cupboard under the stairs and the wardrobes. No sign of anyone or anything missing. Just the addition of the blanket. It must be someone who had a key. Someone had let themselves into the house when she was sleeping and, although they were no longer there, if they had got in once, they could do it again.

There was no point in going back to bed. She sat in the kitchen drinking camomile tea and trying to calm her thoughts. But everything crowded in. Mark, Paloma, her job or lack of it, her inability to conceive, her parents' expectations. So many feelings of failure and regret jostled for attention: not making contact with her brother often enough, not being a good enough auntie, sister-in-law, friend, colleague... She could on and on. Within the space of a few hours all of the guilt and shame and disappointment and loneliness from her whole life played out before her. All because of a purple blanket.

Three large mugs of camomile tea later Carrie's adrenaline levels were still sky high and she had to do something, go somewhere instead of just pacing around the kitchen. She showered, dressed and put on her running shoes for the first time in months. It was as if some sixth sense had made her chuck them in the back of the car at the very last minute. She didn't plan to go far but she needed to do something to send the self-flagellatory gremlins packing.

Closing the front door quietly behind her she headed out into the awakening day. The damp earthiness from the hedgerows was grounding and, as she crossed the village green, smoke was already curling out of one of the tall chimneys of The Manor. Less than a minute later, already settling into a surprisingly easy stride, she spotted a sign pointing to the Longstone. Turning into the sunken path, she almost had second thoughts. The centre of the track was thick with mud and the overhanging trees blocked out much of the light which was beginning to permeate the sky. She must have been mad coming out at this time on her own in a strange place, but she didn't want to go back, not yet. And if anyone did leap out at her she was fast, at least she used to be.

Zig-zagging from one side to the other to avoid the more prominent tree roots and dense mud, she placed her fingertips on the banked-up earth with its fascination of plants, stones and moss. She remembered reading that some of these holloways and sunken paths went back to Iron Age times. Sometimes they were used to drive cattle or livestock and sometimes they were part of a pilgrimage route.

'This is your pilgrimage, Carrie,' she panted. 'This whole holiday is part of your pilgrimage to a better, more balanced life.'

After a few minutes of gentle incline, the path opened out into a clearing of trees which overlooked the rear of The Manor gardens. It was getting lighter by the minute and as Carrie paused to catch her breath and rub her aching calves, she caught sight of the Major picking flowers from one of the camellia bushes, placing them meticulously in a small trug. She was ready to wave if he looked towards her, but he turned resolutely back towards the house without raising his head. Passing through a small wooden gate she continued to ascend, slowing to a walk to admire the tiny ferns and violets growing out of the bank. There were holes, too, leading to some small animals' homes, buds on overhanging branches ready to burst forth and a clear, cleansing light filtering through the trees. And then, before she was really ready, the path opened out and she was right at the top, the wind tugging at her hair, landscape and sky outspread before her, the Longstone to her left.

Carrie was unprepared for the strength of her emotions. Suddenly she felt as if it was extra important, coming up here, and she had no idea why. She desperately didn't want to be disappointed, so she avoided looking directly at the stone, instead taking in the wider view across the valley, birds swooping beneath scudding clouds, light, shadow and beguiling colours creating an ever-changing mood. This felt a lonely, unsettling place but worshipful, too. And she sensed the Longstone, just within her field of vision, waiting for her to turn and give it her full attention.

An apology was on her lips. How ridiculous was that. She was ready to apologise to a rock for not understanding its meaning, to explain how she'd enjoyed history at school but never got into ancient history. She was ready to say sorry for not seeing more than just a lozenge-shaped piece of iron sandstone, rooted firmly in the ground and pointing heavenwards. But her words were whisked away on the wind and, as she moved towards it, Carrie realised that this monument had a presence that was so much more than the sum of its parts. Beside it was another stone now lying on its side, providing somewhere to perch. Beyond that, half-covered in brambles, she could make out the raised terrain of a long barrow. She shivered slightly. This was a place of death but of life, too. Ten thousand years ago people had used this place in reverence, and it felt as if their spirits were here still, swirling and dancing in the air. She pulled up the hood on her sweatshirt, acutely aware that with each step she was following in the presence of so many who had gone before.

Carrie pressed her palm against the rough-hewn surface and moved around the stone, keeping her hand in contact. Inserted into some of its weather-worn pockets were small crystals, amethyst, rose quartz and turquoise being the ones she instantly recognised.

The footsteps, although too soft to be deemed intrusive, were enough to make her jump. A woman glided into view from the same path she herself had taken. Carrie guessed her to be in her late forties or early fifties, her greying brown hair twisted carelessly into a coil on the top of her head and her waxed jacket blowing open. She obviously didn't feel the cold.

'Sorry, I didn't mean to disturb you.'

She looked as if she was about to retreat.

'You didn't really. It's fine. Please don't go. I was just lost in thought for a while, that's all.'

The woman smiled knowingly.

'It does that to you, this place. Sometimes another person, however quiet, can feel like a gatecrasher.'

Carrie's gaze fell to the amethyst crystal which the woman caressed between her thumb and forefinger.

'To be honest it feels as if it's me who's gatecrashing. I wasn't aware that I intended to come up here today, at this hour, but I came out for a run and...'

She let the sentence fall away.

'This place calls to people,' the woman said, gazing around almost as if listening to voices in the ether. 'Some people are funny about it because of its association with death. It does have its turns but on the whole it feels good. It must be or it wouldn't have been a meeting place for thousands of years. It wasn't just our Neolithic ancestors who met here. The Saxons and Jutes possibly used it as a local parliament, too. Maybe that's why it feels like somewhere to come and make decisions.'

The woman gazed affectionately at the stone.

'Anyway, history apart, it's quite something, isn't it?'

Carrie nodded.

'I'm Jo,' the woman said, stepping forwards and holding out a hand, which was surprisingly soft and warm. 'And I can easily come back later.'

'Please don't let me chase you away. I'm Carrie. I'm staying in the village.'

'You're the lady who's staying at Hideaway Cottage.'

It was definitely a statement, not a question. *Does everyone on the whole island know who I am?* Carrie thought.

'Now there's a special place as well,' Jo continued. 'How are you finding it?'

'Good. Lovely. At least it was until...'

Jo was as still as the Megalithic monument beside her. Her whole being possessed an air of well-cultivated serenity. It was impossible not to confide in her.

'...something happened last night,' Carrie continued. 'Something strange. It's left me feeling a little edgy.' She shrugged. 'But I'm sure there's a logical explanation.'

Jo's expression didn't betray an ounce of curiosity.

'Not everything can be explained,' she replied. 'Sometimes it's better not to look for reasons.'

Carrie frowned. Clarity was important to her. She wanted, needed explanations for things. Hadn't she spent the last few months trying to work out why Mark had needed some space? She'd been convinced they'd get back together, never for one minute thought he'd go off with someone else, let alone someone like Paloma?

'Maybe,' she said, aware that her doubt was blatant. 'Maybe

I'm overreacting. My best friend says I'm prone to doing that and I'm not used to being on my own.'

'I can see that.'

Carrie's eyes widened.

'Can you?'

Jo chuckled, her kind laughter enveloping Carrie like a warm cape.

'Don't worry. You don't come over as needy, but we can all benefit from time alone, even those of us who think we can't bear it. With practice we find that we can.'

'I've been so busy, and I've had a bit of a disappointment recently, actually more than one, so I've come away to reflect and part of me thinks that it's the best thing I've ever done, coming to the island, but another part of me thinks I should be *doing* something.'

'We all expect everything to happen instantly these days, don't we? Switching off takes time. It's an adjustment, that's all. Don't try too hard.'

She pressed the tumbled amethyst into Carrie's hand.

'I knew that I picked this up for a reason as I left the house. It's for healing and cleansing. It will help you to find a positive solution to your problems.'

'It's beautiful,' Carrie said, feeling the cool smoothness of the stone nestled in her palm. 'Thank you.'

'And now I'm going to leave you in peace, to let this place speak to you.'

'I'm sorry. I don't normally bare my soul to complete strangers. Feel free to avoid me like the plague from now on.'

Jo smiled.

'I'm up here most days. Sunrise is the best time but I'm sure we'll bump into each other again if it's meant.'

'But if we don't, where can I return the amethyst to you before I go?'

Jo shook her head.

'No need. It's yours now.'

'But I'd really like to give you something in return.'

Jo paused and looked Carrie straight in the eyes.

'Then let the past go, Carrie. Look forwards. That can be your gift to me.'

She turned and headed back down the path, but Carrie was still aware of her energy and the weight of her words long after she had disappeared from sight. Carrie walked rather than ran back down the track. She would call Rita and tell her what had happened. Or maybe she wouldn't have to. Maybe when she got back to the cottage the blanket would have gone and the whole thing could be chalked up as a ridiculous dream. Stress could do that to you – make you imagine things.

Rather than going right to the beginning of the holloway she cut through a little opening, which led into the carpark for The Manor. Skirting along the track she realised that behind the hedge on the left was a garden. Stopping to peer through she could see the back of Cressie's house. Lights were on in a couple of the rooms. A strong cup of coffee and some company would be good, but Cressie probably wouldn't thank her for knocking on the door at just past dawn. Besides, as the back door opened and the murmur of voices drifted over the damp air, it was obvious that someone else was there. Jack must be back. She carried on walking and was almost back at the road when a stitch needled the side of her waist. She bent double just as the rumble of an engine started up, followed by tyres crunching on gravel. Headlights flared towards the sheep in the opposite field as the old Land Rover edged out of the driveway.

She had no idea why, but Carrie instinctively shrank back towards the hedgerow, a bramble snagging at her top. Even from a distance she could see that Guy's hair was tousled, his face relaxed with a just-got-out-of-bed air. Carrie's breath caught at the back of her throat. Cressie and Guy? Surely not. But there she was in a pale grey velour dressing gown, hair tied in a plait, closing the gate behind him. Carrie stayed where she was as the Land Rover disappeared around the corner.

Her thoughts were a complete jumble. Cressie was happily married. At least, that's the aura she gave off. And Guy had seemed so straightforward, so honourable, definitely not the type to have an affair with a married woman, let alone one with twins. Carrie stood up and disentangled herself from the bramble. It was nothing to do with her. It really shouldn't matter. But somehow it did. It was ridiculous how betrayed she felt. No, it was more than that. She felt completely foolish. Granny had always told her that first impressions were important, to trust your gut. Look where that had got her in the past. She'd made a judgement about Guy and Cressie, and it was wrong, totally and utterly wrong.

'Heavens above,' Rita said over the phone. 'You mean someone has broken in?'

'No, that's the thing, the doors and windows apart from in my bedroom were and are all firmly closed.'

'Well, I never,' Rita gasped. 'That's very odd. Did you hear anything?'

'Something woke me, but I don't know what. The house does have its little aches and pains which it lets you know about, especially in the middle of the night but I've quickly got used to those. This seemed to be something else.' She hesitated. 'I had this feeling that someone had been here. Does anyone else apart from you have keys to the house?'

'I have two for the front door, one of which I left under the pot just before your arrival and the other one is hanging on my hook in the pantry. Of course, the owner has one too. And there are two keys to the back door, both of which are kept in the cottage. Do you still have those?'

'Yes, those are still here. I thought that you were the owner.'

'Oh, goodness me, no, although it belonged to my great-aunt so I'm very attached to the place. As you know, you're the first person to stay there and the present owner certainly wouldn't come into the house without asking.'

She went quiet for a moment. Carrie glanced through the doorway towards the kitchen where the purple checked blanket was still lying in front of the range.

'I just can't explain it. I'm not making it up.'

'Oh, Lordy!' Rita exclaimed. 'I never for one moment thought you were. And nothing else has been moved or taken?'

'No. Guy did say that Wilbur used to have a blanket in front of the range when he was working on the cottage, but I hadn't seen it anywhere so it's not as if I went and got it in my sleep and put it there. At least, I don't think I did.'

Suddenly she felt overcome with panic. What if she had done that?

'I'm really sorry to bother you, Rita,' she said, her voice quavering. 'I was just beginning to settle in and relax and now this.'

'You stay exactly where you are, deary,' Rita said firmly. 'I'll be round in a jiffy. We need to get to the bottom of this.'

Rita was as good as her word. She also produced a small bottle of whisky from her cardigan pocket.

'What you need is a good, strong cup of tea with a splash of this in it.'

'I'm all right, really,' Carrie protested.

'Nonsense. You look as white as a sheet. Sit down before you fall down. My George said this amber nectar is as good as many medicines.'

Carrie sank onto the kitchen chair while Rita stepped deftly around the blanket, which was still on the floor, and busied herself with filling the kettle and being particular about choosing two mugs.

'I've asked Guy to pop around and double check the locks, perhaps add a couple of bolts to the doors. Would that make you feel a little better?'

'Yes, I suppose it would, thank you,' Carrie replied.

'And if you're still feeling uneasy you can always come and stay at the farmhouse with me tonight if you like. I've got plenty of space and always keep a bed made up for unexpected guests.'

'That's so kind,' Carrie said, 'but I'm sure I'll be okay.'

'If you want to pop around for a cup of tea, the kettle's always on, day or night. I'm not a good sleeper, not since my hubby died, so there's no need to worry about waking me if you need to phone in the night. I can almost see the chimney of Hideaway Cottage from my kitchen window so I can be with you in a couple of minutes. I can grab a pitchfork from the yard on the way round!'

Carrie had a brief image of Rita, hair in rollers, nightie billowing, wielding a pitchfork to deal with any intruders. It was a comforting image. No one would dare mess with Rita in battle mode, she was sure.

'Guy will be here mid-morning. I can wait with you until then.'

'I was meant to be having coffee with Cressie but I'm not sure that I'm up to it.'

'Nonsense!' Rita said, pouring a good dose of whisky into Carrie's mug of tea. 'It will do you good. Her, too. She's a wonderful girl and such a lot on her plate but always a smile on her face. She'll take your mind off things.'

Carrie nodded. She didn't have to stay long and at least it would mean she could avoid seeing Guy and feeling more of a nuisance than she did already.

'Now, drink up.' Rita reached out and touched her arm. 'Remember, dear, I'm always here.'

Carrie looked at the thick gold band glistening on Rita's wedding finger. George had been a lucky man.

'Thank you, Rita. I really appreciate that.'

And she did. So many people said the words, 'I'm always here' and didn't really mean them but she was pretty certain that Rita wouldn't let her down. If *she* wasn't all she appeared to be, there really was no hope for the world.

PATIENCE

'Now look what you've done,' Isaac said. 'I thought that we agreed – no meddling.'

Eliza pulled at the lace on the edge of her handkerchief.

'I'm so sorry, Isaac. I was just thinking of Wilbur. I wanted him to be comfortable when he came back. He loved that blanket when Guy was working on the cottage. It had been pushed to the back of the cupboard under the stairs and I'm sure that he's forgotten it's there so...'

Isaac placed his hands on her delicate shoulders and gently turned her towards him with a frown on his face.

'You've frightened our guest, Eliza.'

'I know, I know. I really didn't mean to.' She hesitated. 'It wasn't just Wilbur I was thinking about. I was thinking about Bonnie, too. I thought that maybe if I put the blanket by the range Bonnie would return to us. I look for her in the garden all the time, but she isn't there and I don't understand.'

'Maybe she's in the fields chasing rabbits,' he said, with a sad smile.

'She was the first dog we had together, Isaac. I never thought she would leave us.'

'And one day, my love, we'll be reunited. I'm sure of it as I'm sure, in spite of your kindness to animals, you weren't just thinking of Wilbur and our beloved Bonnie when you put that blanket by the range.'

Eliza tipped her head to one side.

'Well, maybe I was thinking of our two young people, too. I was just trying to help things along a little. I knew that Carrie would contact Rita, and she would get in touch with Guy. I thought that when Guy returned to check on the security that Wilbur would see his blanket, settle down straight away and then Carrie might invite Guy to linger for a cup of tea and...'

Isaac placed a finger to her rosebud lips.

'Except Carrie won't be here when Guy comes back because she's visiting Cressie.'

Eliza smiled. 'Even the best laid plans can go awry.'

'I suppose,' Isaac said, with a teasing tone, 'that I should be relieved by that admission. At least it means that you're not following our guest around constantly.'

'Of course not,' Eliza protested. 'How can you think such a thing? Carrie has come here for some respite from the world and deserves a degree of privacy.'

'And sometimes, my dearest, we have to allow nature to take its course.'

Eliza felt a chill run through her. The hem of her dress rippled as she pressed her feet together for comfort. What was that feeling she had? That chasm which opened up and she felt might swallow her into its darkness. But Isaac was still speaking and she must hang onto his words, to his wisdom, to stop herself falling away from the light that he brought to her, to the strength he gave her.

'I want Guy to be happy just as much as you do, but you can't force these things. The right person for him will come along at the right time.'

'But what if he doesn't recognise the right person?' Eliza

asked. 'Our guest is only here for a few days. What if that isn't enough time? He's not exactly a fast mover.'

She threw Isaac a coquettish look.

'Not like some people I could mention.'

'That was different,' he said. 'I saw you on the beach that day, the wind blowing your beautiful chestnut hair this way and that, and I just knew. That's the woman I'm going to marry, I thought.'

She placed a hand against his cheek.

'And you've never regretted it?'

He turned to kiss her fingers.

'Do you really have to ask that? Not for a day or an hour or a minute have I ever thought that you weren't the one for me.'

Eliza looked into his eyes, so full of love, even more so now than when they first met, despite or maybe because of all that they had been through together.

'We had such opposition, though, and... your family. I've always felt guilty about that.'

'I had free will, Eliza. Just as Guy has free will. And we have to remember that Carrie is here to recover from a relationship which didn't work out. She may not be ready to meet someone new. She and Guy may not be suited.'

'I want everyone to be happy,' Eliza whispered, 'as happy as we have been.'

Isaac was quiet for a moment. She fancied she saw a shadow play across his face.

'We have been happy, Isaac, haven't we? In spite of not being blessed with children, we have been happy?'

He drew her closer and watched the sparrows hop across the hedgerows.

'There are sadnesses in all lives, Eliza, but we were lucky that we found each other.'

'And I give thanks for that, every single day,' she said. 'I just want Guy to have someone special to go home to. Have I ruined everything, Isaac? I can't think why it didn't occur to me that she would be so upset. You don't think she'll depart early?'

'I hope not but what is meant to be is meant to be, Eliza,' Isaac said. 'That's one of the hardest lessons we have to learn. And patience,' he added.

'I'm not very good at that,' she said, with a sigh.

'No, you're not,' he replied. 'And your desire to make the world a better place is delightful but if you're not careful it will get us into trouble.'

She leaned away from him, her muslin dress billowing around her ankles.

'I can go and put the blanket back in the cupboard.'

'No! You must leave well alone. No more interfering. It's hard, I know, but we just have to watch, wait and protect. That's what we're here for.'

Eliza nodded. Isaac was so wise. She could manage the protecting, but she wasn't very good at watching and waiting. She would have to try her best.

EIGHT

Cressie opened the door even before Carrie had the chance to press the bell.

'Shh,' Cressie said in a low voice, 'the monsters are asleep, and I couldn't bear it if they woke up. I've been looking forward to some uninterrupted adult company.'

Carrie did her best not to raise an eyebrow. She really shouldn't have come. She was feeling too judgemental, but Rita had been adamant and Carrie had thought it would be easier facing Cressie than Guy. Now as Cressie wafted away a chicken who was trying to sneak over the threshold, she wasn't sure she'd made the right decision.

'Sorry,' she added, ushering Carrie inside, 'there are so many distractions here – babies, chickens, idiosyncratic rescue cats.'

A man who isn't your husband, Carrie thought. She really must stop this train of thought. 'I bring cake,' she said, holding out a tin.

'You don't know how fortunate that is for both of us,' Cressie chuckled. 'The last time I tried to bake some biscuits they looked like a suitable exhibit for the Turner Prize. In fact, my cooking's rubbish full stop at the moment. Even if it's not burnt it tastes awful.'

Carrie followed Cressie down a long narrow hall with several roof lights, the walls lined with black and white photographs of a band and a good-looking man who she assumed was Jack. The kitchen had a double height roof, brilliant white walls, glossy units and a lime green sofa at one end.

'What a beautiful room,' Carrie said, looking out of the bifold doors towards the back garden where the disgruntled chicken was peering back at them with an accusing eye.

'Thank you. The barn was a complete wreck when we bought it. We actually lived in a tent in the garden for the first summer – at least, I did, while Jack was swanning off around the world. Someone had to stay here and project manage. When Jack came back, we had to borrow friends' bathrooms from time to time. He's such a diva! Can only slum it for so long.'

She placed two large pottery mugs on a tray.

'Tea or coffee?'

'Coffee, please.'

'I'll join you. I shouldn't really. I'm meant to keep my caffeine intake down while I'm breast-feeding but to be honest sometimes a good strong coffee is the only thing that keeps me awake and I definitely need that this morning. Mind you, I don't want to lead you astray, so I've got decaf if you'd rather?'

Carrie avoided direct eye contact.

'If you want a rest,' she said, 'we can always rearrange.'

Cressie's eyes darted backwards and forwards in alarm.

'No, no, I don't. I'm sorry, that didn't come out right and it must have sounded rude. I've been looking forward to you coming so much. This village is darling and the neighbours are amazing, but there aren't many people my age.'

'Except for Guy,' Carrie said.

'Oh, you've met Guy?'

'He came to mow the lawn.'

'Well, he's wonderful, of course,' Cressie said, placing the tray on the coffee table and gesturing to the sofa, 'but I want to hear about you. I love living here but sometimes it does feel a long way from the real world.'

Carrie couldn't help but admire the artfulness with which she changed the conversation. *Who am I to judge?* she thought. *I'm only here for another ten days. I need to just go with the flow.* Cressie was one of those people you couldn't help liking, whatever her morals.

'That's what my friend Jules said that I needed,' Carrie replied, cradling the steaming mug. 'To be a long way away from the real world.'

'Ah,' Cressie replied, looking sympathetic. 'We've all had moments like that. You certainly chose the right place. Hideaway Cottage is perfect for a pick-me-up.'

Carrie took a sip of the coffee. It was dark and delicious.

'It's the weirdest thing but I almost felt that the cottage chose me. I was completely at home the minute I walked in.'

She hesitated. She really didn't want to tell Cressie about the blanket. She'd probably think that she was completely unhinged. Cressie beamed.

'I'm so pleased. I think that's what the owner was aiming for.'

'Who does own it?' Carrie asked. 'Is it someone local?'

'What am I thinking of!' Cressie said, placing her mug on the shiny white table and leaping up. 'We haven't got anything to eat. Some days I can barely remember who I am.'

She flitted across to the island unit and placed two generous slices of cake on blue and white plates.

'Mmm!' she said. 'Rita makes the most gorgeous cakes. She's a real treasure in the village, totally embraces everyone. I couldn't cook a thing when I moved here – barely even boil an egg – but she took me under her wing and showed me how to bake, well, almost. She's been like a mother to me, better than a mother actually, and she's always offering to help out with the twins, but I don't like to impose.'

'Haven't you got any family nearby?' Carrie asked.

'No, I'm from Surrey originally. What about you?'

'Norfolk.'

'Happy childhood?'

'Mostly,' Carrie replied.

'That's what I want for my two,' Cressie said, glancing over towards the baby monitor. 'Stability. It's so important, don't you think? My mum's on husband number three and my dad's on wife number four. I was packed off to boarding school when I was eight because that was *their* idea of giving me some stability or that's how they justified it. Of course, I think they just wanted me and my brother out of the way. There's nothing like recalcitrant children to put the kibosh on a new relationship! And they both had plenty of dalliances in between the marriages. That's probably too flattering a term, actually. Anyway, I want my two to come home every afternoon to find me here, healthy snacks ready and waiting, not wondering if I'm in bed with some stranger.'

She took a bite of cake.

'Sorry, too much information.'

Carrie shook her head. She had to hand it to Cressie. There was absolutely not a hint of hypocrisy in either her body language or her delivery.

'Sounds idyllic,' she said, hoping there wasn't a slice of sarcasm book-ending her words. 'The dream for your life, I mean, not the other stuff.'

'That's me,' Cressie said, raising an eyebrow, 'always chasing the dream.'

She slid her finger across the plate to gather up the remnants of frosted icing and put it in her mouth.

'See,' she chuckled. 'There's a sign of a neglected child. Bet your mum would never let you do that in front of a guest! No chance of losing my baby weight at this rate.'

'You look great to me,' Carrie said, trying not to stare but intrigued to know where the excess baby weight was. Cressie looked as sleek and toned as her old yoga teacher.

'Thanks,' Cressie said gratefully. 'It's really hard to find time for myself. Some days even brushing my hair is an effort and I feel like I'm turning into a slob.'

Carrie thought she had never met anyone in her whole life who looked less likely to turn into a slob.

'Jack's always surrounded by all of these glamorous people when he's recording. It can be a bit intimidating, especially when you're not feeling your best!'

'I'm sure he isn't comparing you to them,' Carrie replied.

And presumably Guy was helping her to get back into shape...

'Everyone says that you need to be kind to yourself when you've had a baby,' Cressie said. 'At least, that's what my sister-in-law said after she had hers, but she didn't have two at once and a husband who was away all the time.'

Cressie's eyes suddenly filled with tears.

'I'm so sorry,' she sniffed, reaching for the box of tissues. 'Bloody hormones. I try not to feel overwhelmed and sorry for myself, but they make you so unpredictable. I go on Instagram and there are all these pictures of yummy mummies, and I feel like an absolute pig.'

'Don't apologise. It must be really hard. I'm not surprised you get upset sometimes. Instagram's great for some things but for others, well, it's just a lot of pressure.'

'Jack says I shouldn't look at it. He says that I get upset too easily. He's probably right.'

Carrie filled her mouth with cake so she wouldn't have to respond. She was beginning to think that she wouldn't like Jack much if she ever met him. Maybe this was why Cressie needed Guy.

'Jack's home this weekend and I'm counting down the days. You must meet him. We'll have a barbecue. Get a few people together and then you'll feel as if you really belong here. Who knows, you might never want to leave!'

Carrie gazed out of the window at the lush greenness of the garden. One of the chickens had just laid an egg at the edge of the flower border.

'When I first arrived, two weeks seemed such a long time but now it doesn't seem long enough.'

'Ah ha!' Cressie said, clapping her hands together. 'It gets to you, this place, doesn't it? Originally, we only came here for a long weekend to visit Guy, and we ended up buying a house. He persuaded us that it was the perfect place to settle, and he was right.'

Cressie leapt up to pour more coffee.

'Guy is one of my favourite people in the whole wide world and I've travelled most of it, so I know what I'm talking about.'

'That sounds interesting.'

'To be honest, yes, and no, but mostly yes. I was cabin crew for a major airline. I just loved it. I met Jack on a plane. He was flying to LA for some meetings and I had a couple of days free, so we spent some time together. He's really into old films so we went around Warner Studios which was great and the next day he took me to The Getty Museum. I'd been before but I never tire of it. You can do a mindfulness session in front of one of the paintings, which is just amazing. That day it was Van Gogh's *Starry Night*. Do you know that painting? I love Van Gogh. Jack's not into the whole mindfulness thing. I didn't think he'd keep in touch afterwards. You know how it is – lots of men say they'll call but they don't.'

Carrie couldn't imagine that Cressie would have had any problem holding on to men.

'In fact, Guy says that Jack pursued me relentlessly. It probably helps that he thought Guy and I were an item. Jack likes a challenge.'

'So how long have you known Guy?'

'Oh, ages. Before I was married, he was my chaperone.'

She laughed at Carrie's confused expression.

'That sounds really old-fashioned, doesn't it, and I haven't explained properly. Guy and I worked together.'

'Oh, so Guy was cabin crew, too?'

'Goodness, no! Guy was a pilot, ex-Royal Air Force and then a commercial airline pilot. He could have been a real high-flier, if you'll pardon the pun. We started to pretend to be a couple because drunken passengers were often hitting on me. Mind you, it suited him, too. He looked pretty hot in his uniform so he was a bit of a babe magnet, but he hated all the attention.'

She looked at Carrie over the rim of her cup.

'He's just one of the nicest men in the world, apart from Jack, of course. Actually, Jack thinks I'm a bit in love with Guy and he doesn't mind. But then everyone falls in love with Guy. I suspect Jack has a bit of a man crush on him himself! And then there's the wonderful Wilbur. If you want to keep the girls at arm's length, you don't get a gorgeous dog like Wilbur, do you? I did warn him.'

'Is that what he does then?' Carrie asked, trying to sound casual. 'Keep girls at arm's length?'

'He does have his reasons. But just because you've had a couple of bad experiences doesn't mean that all women are—'

Cressie paused and inclined her head towards the baby monitor.

'Oops! I reckon my time is almost up. That's Freddie doing his little snuffling thing just before he wakes which means Olivia won't be far behind. She snaps her eyes open, fills her lungs and bawls "come and get me this instant."' She pulled a face. 'I'm sorry, we haven't had much time to chat at all.'

Carrie drained her cup and stood up. 'Don't worry about it. Thank you for inviting me. It's been lovely.'

'You don't have to go. Actually, you'd be doing me a favour if you could wait while I feed Fred. If Livvy wakes you could go and get her before she sends herself purple. That's if you wouldn't mind?'

'Well... I'm not sure. I mean, pushing a buggy is a bit different to...'

She imagined lifting Olivia out of her cot, holding her close, smelling her hair, trying in vain to soothe her.

'You'll be fine,' Cressie beamed. 'She's as robust as anything and if she carries on crying, don't worry. It won't be you. She does that with me, too.'

Carrie checked her watch, which was ridiculous because she hadn't got anywhere else to be.

'And she'll probably be so surprised and delighted that it's not her boring old mama getting her out of the cot that she'll stop instantly and coo away at you. She does have the ability to be charming.'

'Okay,' Carrie said with a laugh. 'You've convinced me I'll cope.'

Cressie beamed.

'You're an absolute star. You *must* meet Jack. He'll love you to bits. We'll definitely do a barbecue at the weekend, whatever the weather.'

And with that she disappeared towards the stairs as Freddie's snuffles turned into small cries. Carrie washed up the coffee mugs, studied some of the paintings hanging on the walls, which all seemed to be by local artists, and then settled back down to read the *Island Life* magazine from cover to cover. Twenty minutes later Cressie reappeared, Freddie nestling contentedly in her arms.

'Thank you,' she said. 'Livvy must have worn herself out from being awake half the night.'

Just at that moment a shrill, high-pitched cry blared through the room.

'Spoke too soon,' Cressie said, with a rueful smile. 'Don't worry, you don't have to stay any longer. I will release you! Fred's an angel. He's quite happy to lie on his mat while I feed Olivia.'

'Perhaps I ought to get back,' Carrie said, apologetically.

'See you at the weekend then, if not before. You're welcome to call in, anytime. Or we could go to the beach together. Have you been yet?'

Carrie shook her head.

'Oh, you must. Brook Beach is beautiful, and the dinosaur footprints are amazing.'

'I will,' Carrie said. 'Thanks for the coffee. I'll let myself out. You'd better get Olivia, she sounds desperate.'

'Sometimes,' Cressie replied, 'she's not the only one.'

And for a moment, just before she shifted Freddie up against her shoulder and turned away, Carrie thought how vulnerable she looked.

Guy was perched on the front step eating a sandwich when she got back to the cottage, Wilbur's head inclined hopefully against his shoulder. Carrie hadn't expected him to be there, and she felt ridiculously flustered, not that he seemed to notice.

'Early lunch,' he said, standing up. 'I had a meeting with the Major which held me up and Rita had to dash off when I got here. She said you'd only gone out for coffee so you probably wouldn't be long.'

'I was with Cressie.'

She waited for a reaction, but he just folded up the greaseproof paper which had contained his sandwich and stooped to place it in the Tupperware container by his foot.

'I was keeping an ear out for one of the babies or I'd have been back sooner.'

'That's kind of you. She needs the help. I thought I'd take the opportunity for a short break here before heading back for another debate, no, more of a battle about dahlias.'

'I'm sorry to be such a nuisance,' she said, avoiding eye contact.

'You're not.'

Did he sound curter than before or was she imagining it?

'Let me show you what I've done.'

He took his boots off in the porch and she followed him through into the hall. There was a sudden springiness in the air, a featherlike brush against her cheek, as if someone had danced past unseen. She looked at Guy. Did he feel it, too? But he was already closing the front door behind him and pointing to the heavy duty bolts top and bottom.

'They're easy to use,' he said, sliding one across, the resounding clunk as it engaged meant to signify safety.

Carrie wasn't sure that she would ever feel safe, not even here. Paloma, Mark, grief for her grandparents, had all taken away her trust in life. She blinked. Or perhaps that was unfair. Perhaps she lost it long before when she realised as a small child that whatever she did, in her parents' eyes she would never be good enough.

'I've put two on the back door as well,' he said, 'and the windows already have locks.'

'Yes, yes, thank you.'

She followed him through to the kitchen where his head almost touched the ceiling.

'This one's a bit stiff but it should ease with use,' he said, pulling the bolt backwards and forwards.

'Thank you.'

She glanced down at Wilbur, who was now lying on the purple rug.

'I'll take it away if you like,' Guy said. 'Wilbur has blankets all over the place. I'd forgotten it was still here.'

Does he have a blanket at Cressie's? she wondered. *Why was she obsessing over this? It was nothing to do with her.*

'No, it's fine. Might as well leave it here now. Wilbur can use it if you need to come back for anything else.'

'I hope there won't be anything else.'

She really was a problem guest.

He frowned.

'I'm very sorry, Carrie. I can't explain it any more than Rita.'

He didn't believe her, maybe thought she had put the rug there deliberately to get him back here or gain attention. He thought she fancied him! He was probably one of those men who thought all women fancied him just because he was vaguely good looking.

'I do understand that it's very unsettling,' he said, and the sudden softness in his voice brought a lump to her throat. Carrie moved to sit on one of the kitchen chairs, her legs suddenly shaky.

'You okay? You've gone pale.'

He did look genuinely concerned.

'Fine. Just a bit wobbly.'

'Do you need a glass of water or a cup of tea with lashings of whisky? That's what my gran would prescribe.'

'I've already had some whisky today,' she replied. 'Rita's prescription. Maybe a glass of water.'

Anything to stop him looking at her like that. *Maybe she did like him a little bit! No, she was sworn off men. She was never going to fall for anyone again.*

Wilbur plodded over and leaned against her leg which made her feel a little better, as did the sip of cool water. She fondled Wilbur's ears to cover her embarrassment at the question she had to ask.

'This is going to sound really ridiculous, but do you know if the cottage is haunted?'

Oh, my goodness! She knew she shouldn't have asked it. He was staring at her as if she was completely mad.

'It would be all right. I wouldn't mind. As long as it's not a malevolent spirit. I'm not afraid of ghosts and I'd rather the blanket had been moved that way than by a complete stranger.'

She paused, waiting for him to say something, but he didn't. *Fill the void, Carrie, although more words will probably make his opinion of you even worse.*

'You must think I'm insane. My ex-fiancé would.'

'Which is presumably why he's an ex,' he replied, with a wry twist of his lips.

'Actually, that's more to do with the fact that he went off with someone else when we were having a "relationship sabbatical". His idea the sabbatical. I really thought it was just a temporary blip.'

'That's tough.'

She blinked back tears. *Don't cry, Carrie. Don't cry.*

'Yes. Yes, it is. It's been six months since he suggested we could do with a bit of space and then three months ago he got together with Paloma.'

She wiped her eyes with the back of her hand.

'I really should be getting over it. At least, that's what everyone else says.'

'People can be very good at advising others how they should feel. In my opinion, three months, even six months, isn't very long.'

She glanced up at him. He was leaning against the work surface, completely still, in no apparent hurry to leave. She wished he would go and leave her alone but then she didn't want to be alone. She didn't know what she wanted anymore.

'Thank you for saying that. It makes me feel a bit less pathetic because I'm not putting it behind me and "moving on".'

'Often said by people who have never been dumped.'

He passed her a tissue from the box on the dresser and she wiped her eyes.

'You're right. Or people who've not had to work with their exes and see them every day. I got a job there first so I didn't see why I should be the one to leave.'

It sounded really childish saying it out loud.

'Although that might have been decided for me now.'

She took a moment and dropped her forehead on to the top of Wilbur's before straightening up again. She needed to change the conversation for both their sakes.

'I'm beginning to wonder if I found that blanket and put it there myself. I bet stress can cause sleepwalking. It can cause most other things. On top of the job and the relationship going pear-shaped, and losing Granny. I lost my granny recently.'

She rubbed the eternity ring on her right hand.

'She and my grandad were devoted. I thought Mark and I would be like that.'

She managed a weak smile.

'Life can be a bitch, can't it? And I'm really over-sharing.'

Guy studied her for a moment and Carrie felt herself beginning to blush. She had revealed far too much.

'Sometimes we all need to talk,' he said.

She glanced out of the window at the burgeoning clouds.

'And sometimes we need to shut up! You'd better get back for your dahlia debate before the rain arrives.'

He checked his watch.

'You're right.'

'Thank you for coming around so quickly.'

'No problem. You're still nervous?'

'Of myself as much as anything!'

'I hope you'll stay.'

She felt startled. How had he known that she was thinking of leaving?

'Sometimes you need to give things a chance, Carrie.'

She felt so guilty. It wasn't fair.

'This place is pretty and peaceful and quiet but I'm not sure it's what I need at the moment. I haven't had this much time to think in years. Everyone's been really kind but perhaps the timing wasn't right. Timing's so important, isn't it? It's not just the blanket.'

He didn't look convinced.

'I can get the ferry in the morning, try and get an appointment with the partners at work to sort things out. At least to find out where I stand. Jules will be furious, of course. She's a nurse and says I don't know what's good for me but...'

'Maybe she's right.'

She looked up at him. He seemed so steady and capable, probably just what Cressie needed. Pity about Jules, though. He'd have been good for her, too.

'Would you like a job while you're here?'

Carrie opened her eyes wide.

'What?'

'A job? Would that help?'

'What sort of a job? You barely know me, except for the fact that I'm a complete emotional wreck.'

'Plants don't judge you like that,' he replied with a smile. 'They're very accepting. Besides, I don't think you're an emotional wreck at all.'

'You're just being kind, too,' Carrie said, as the tears welled up again. 'I wish everyone wouldn't be so kind.'

'In my case, I do have an ulterior motive,' he said, with a smile. 'One of my volunteers developed appendicitis last week. She won't be back for a while and it's such a busy time. We're getting really behind with planting out the beds and potting up for the shop.'

'I might be one of those people who kills plants on sight.'

'You might, but I doubt it. Besides, haven't you heard about the benefits of getting your hands in the soil? It's a great de-stresser.'

Carrie thought back to helping Granny in her garden, pricking out seedlings, winding beans up canes, dead-heading roses, all totally absorbing tasks.

'Come for a couple of hours to see if you like it.'

He was very persuasive. It felt as if she was the only person he really wanted for this job. That's how she'd wanted Ian and the other partners to feel about her.

'If it doesn't make you feel better,' he continued, 'then I promise to come and help you pack the car for your journey back to Manchester.'

She hesitated. Would a few hours in a garden really clear her head? Surely the only thing that could achieve that was sorting out the mess she had left behind.

'Look, you don't have to make a decision now,' he said. 'Sleep on it. If you'd like some plant therapy when you wake up, just head along to the gardens when you're ready.'

He took a piece of paper out of his pocket and scribbled something down.

'This is my landline and my mobile number if anything else goes bump in the night. I live in the next village so it's only five minutes away. I'm going to visit my gran tonight for a couple of hours. She's champing at the bit to get out of respite care and I'm trying to persuade her to stay in for a little longer. I usually turn my phone off when I'm with her, but I'll leave it on – although the signal's pretty poor here, as you may have realised, which can be a mixed blessing.'

'You really don't have to...' Carrie protested. 'I'll be fine.'

'No,' he said, gently, 'I don't, but we look after each other here, Carrie, whether you're a permanent resident or just visiting.'

'I didn't mean to sound ungrateful.'

'You didn't. But believe me, you're not being a nuisance, even though you think you are. Now, come on, Wilbur, let's get some more planting done before this rain turns up.'

The dog sloped reluctantly to his side.

'I don't suppose...' Carrie began.

'...that I could leave him with you? Normally I'd say yes, of course, but my gran loves to see him. It gives her and the other residents a real lift.'

'Of course.'

'But I could bring him back later if you like. He may look like the soppiest dog in the world, but he'd protect you in an instant if you needed it. Eight o'clock okay? He can stay the night, and you can drop him back in the morning before you leave.'

Carrie looked up into his deep blue eyes and thought she had never met a more considerate man in her entire life. No wonder Cressie described him as wonderful.

NINE

Finally, Jules picked up. Carrie had been trying her phone all afternoon.

'Where have you been? I thought it was your day off?'

'It is. I've been shopping.'

'All day? You hate shopping. Jules, something really odd has happened. You couldn't come over for a couple of days, could you? I need some company.'

As Carrie explained about the blanket there was a silence at the end of the phone.

'Jules? Are you still there?'

'Yes. I'm still here.'

'It's a wonderful place, really relaxing.'

'Apart from a potential poltergeist,' Jules quipped. 'Aren't dogs meant to sense these things?'

'Wilbur's very chilled and, if there is such a thing, I'm sure it isn't malevolent. Besides, you don't believe in ghosts so I can't believe that's putting you off.'

'No,' Jules replied slowly, 'it's not that. The thing is, I've met this amazing man.'

Carrie stifled a groan. All Jules' men were 'amazing', at least for the first fortnight.

'I know what you're thinking,' Jules said, breathlessly, 'but he's the one, Carrie. I just know it this time.'

What could she say? How many others had Jules described as 'the one'? For someone who was so practical in other areas of her life, Jules was a hopeless romantic when it came to her relationships. The trouble was the heady heights never lasted much more than a month and most of her relationships no longer than six weeks. But one day she was going to meet the right person and maybe this was it.

'I'm thinking that I've only been gone for four days,' Carrie said.

'Well, you never know what's around the corner,' Jules replied, and Carrie could hear the smile in her voice. She must swallow her misgivings, be optimistic.

'No, that's true and I'm really pleased for you.'

'Gavin's got these tickets to the football...'

'Football! He must be special. You hate football.'

'No, no, hate's too strong a word. I may have been ambivalent in the past but I'm sure I can learn to appreciate the beautiful game's finer qualities. It's an England match at Old Trafford and he says it'll be really exciting. Then he's booked us a table at that swanky new restaurant in the centre of town. Tonight, we're going to see the Ibsen at the theatre. He's got such a wide variety of interests.'

'I can tell,' Carrie replied, hoping she didn't sound too wry.

'You'll love him. I can't wait for you two to meet. If I'm going to spend the rest of my life with this man, he's got to care about you as much as I do.'

Jules was silent for a moment.

'And I do care. You're like the sister I never had, so what am I thinking of? If you need me, I'll see if I can get some time off and come over even though we're really short-staffed. Gavin will understand about the other stuff.'

'No,' Carrie said. 'No, you won't come over. I'll be fine. You concentrate on those mums and babies and especially on gorgeous Gavin. I want you to be happy, Jules.'

'And I am. Right now, I'm deliriously happy, but you need me and I want to be there for you, especially as I was the one who sent you to this haunted house in the first place. Besides, you're right about the football and that restaurant will probably be horrendously busy. It would be better to go in a few days when the novelty's worn off. I'll see if I can get a train down and then the ferry later on tomorrow. That means I can go to the Ibsen tonight and explain to Gavin. Will you be all right tonight?'

'Yes, I'll be fine. I'll have Wilbur the Labrador here to defend me.'

'What about this chap, Guy? Could he stay with you tonight until I get there tomorrow?'

'He hasn't offered, and I don't want to ask.'

'You should. He sounds pretty decent. Is he single? Oh my God, is he hot? Maybe he fancies you like mad but doesn't want to appear too pushy? Come on, he must like you to leave his dog with you.'

Carrie laughed.

'He's just very kind and I think he might be sort of attached but I barely know him. As for being hot, I have no idea. I've lost all sense of perspective on what's hot and what's not. It's irrelevant, anyway, because he's just not my type.'

'Oh!' Jules said, emphatically.

'What does that mean?'

'It means that if you don't think he's your type, then he probably is!'

'Says the woman who thinks that almost everyone is her type!'

'I'm open-minded. Sometimes love appears when you least expect it and with a person who you wouldn't necessarily include in your hall of handsome heroes. This Guy person might be just what you need to get over Mark.'

'I'm over Mark.'

'Really?' Jules replied, disbelievingly. 'In that case, what's holding you back?'

'The fact that he hasn't shown the least bit of interest in me in that way, and I think he might be seeing someone.'

'That shouldn't stop you.'

'Jules!'

'Well, it shouldn't. Maybe it's not serious with this other person. Maybe he's shy around you and needs a little encouragement. I bet you haven't been flirting, have you? A holiday romance is good for the soul, Carrie.'

'Not for this soul,' Carrie retorted. 'I can't believe you're encouraging me to throw myself at the nearest eligible man when you told me only last week that I virtually needed to go into purdah.'

'Situations change! Is he eligible as well as hot? That would be perfect, really rub Mark's nose in it. Does Guy have a country estate or a villa in the south of France or one of those really sleek and gleaming yachts?'

'I doubt it. He's a gardener.'

'Mmm. A man of the soil. It has certain attractions. Gavin's got his own property company. We'll be able to build our own house. Isn't that exciting?'

'Jules, do you think that perhaps you're getting a little bit...'

'I'm sorry, honey, I've got to go,' Jules said. 'Gavin will be here soon, and I look like the back end of a bus. I'll call you in the morning to check you're okay and let you know what time I'm arriving.'

'I feel as if I'm really messing you around. Maybe it would just be better if I came back to Manchester.'

'No, you're not messing me around at all.'

'You're amazing, you know.'

'I do!'

Carrie grinned down the phone.

'Enjoy the Ibsen.'

'I'll try but really, it's after the Ibsen that I'm going to enjoy. Gavin's got the builder's in so he's stopping over for a few days. Just until you get back. You don't mind, do you?'

Carrie leaned back in the chair. What could she say? If she went back to the house, she'd have to play gooseberry to Jules and Gavin, but if Jules came to Hideaway Cottage, it sounded as if she was going to do her best to set Carrie up with Guy which was the last thing she wanted.

'Make sure you lock up well tonight,' Jules said, 'and I'll see you tomorrow.'

Guy knocked on the door at exactly eight o'clock.

'Wilbur is ready for his sleepover,' he said, with a grin. Wilbur looked as if he was grinning, too.

Guy held up a hessian bag.

'Food, bowls and a spare blanket are all in here.'

Carrie ushered him in.

'How was your gran?' she asked, as he placed the bag on the floor by the fridge.

'Not so good today. She really wants to come home but I'm not sure she's up to it.'

'Where does she live?'

'With me or, rather, I live with her. That's one of the reasons I moved back to the island, to look after her when she needed it. I had my own place to start with but then she had a fall and broke her wrist, so I moved in with her temporarily. She was slow to recover so I rented out my house. She feels very guilty, says she's ruining my life, which isn't true at all.'

'She's lucky to have you.'

'Not as lucky as I am to have her. After all she did for me when I was growing up, it's the least I can do, and she won't be here for ever. You have to make the most of the moments you have.'

Suddenly the shutters came down as if he had opened up too much about personal stuff. Carrie saw the tiredness and worry etched around his eyes.

'Now,' he said, in a much more business-like tone, 'let me tell you about Wilbur's routine and then I can go and leave you in peace.'

'You don't have to rush off,' she said, softly. 'I mean, Wilbur's good company but his vocabulary's a bit limited. Have you eaten?'

He shook his head. 'I have some pasta and half a jar of pesto waiting at home if I can be bothered to cook it.'

'I've got eggs, mushrooms and cheese. Why don't I make you an omelette, then you can just sit and relax?'

She sensed his hesitation, almost wariness.

'I've drunk the wine that was left, I'm afraid, but there's still some beer in the fridge. Local ale, I think.'

'Well, in that case,' he said, 'perhaps I will take you up on your offer. I'm pretty whacked, to be honest. It's amazing how being one volunteer down at this time of year can make such a difference.'

Carrie took the chilled beer out of the fridge and poured it into a glass. As she put together some salad and cut a couple of hefty slices from a fresh loaf of Rita's wholemeal bread, Guy settled on the sofa in the living room, Wilbur at his feet. She turned on Classic FM so that he wouldn't feel the need to talk to her through the open door to the kitchen and hummed as she sliced mushrooms, grated cheese and cracked eggs.

'That looks so good,' he said, as she placed a tray in front of him. 'And no, Wilbur, it isn't for you.'

The dog put his head back down on his paws.

Carrie settled onto the other sofa with a glass of apple juice and picked up the *Island Life* magazine.

'Which would you recommend?' she asked. 'Osborne House or Carisbrooke Castle?'

Guy looked up. She sensed slight surprise.

'Both are fantastic.'

'Then I shall visit both,' she said.

'So, you're staying?'

'Yes. The decision has really been made for me.'

She told him a little of her conversation with Jules.

'She's "deliriously happy".'

'Ah!' Guy said, pulling a face.

'Exactly!' Carrie replied. 'I'm not sure I can cope with that right now. I'll message her later and tell her not to come. It's not fair to rain on her parade and the last thing she'll want is me turning up back in Manchester to hamper her fledgling romance. I know what Jules is like in the first stages of a relationship – it's pretty intense. I'd have to stuff my ears with cotton wool, if you get my drift.'

'Not one for taking things slowly then.'

'I love her to bits but when it comes to life partners, she's got no idea.' Carrie raised her eyebrows. 'But then look at me. I can hardly talk. And who knows, Gavin might be "the one", if you believe in that sort of thing.'

'Don't you?'

'I used to. I was a complete hearts, flowers and happily ever after girl, but now I'm not so sure. Mark always used to say there wasn't just one person destined for you. That used to hurt, to be honest, but maybe he was right after all.'

She gave herself a little shake.

'But I'm not going to indulge in self-pity any longer and I'm basically stuck here so if your offer still stands, I would love to take you up on it.'

He studied her for a moment and then dipped his head in agreement.

'My plants await,' he said. 'They are ready when you are.'

Guy had said that Wilbur wasn't allowed upstairs at home, but she couldn't bear to leave him on his own in the kitchen. And it was reassuring to have his solid presence on the floor at the end of the bed.

'Wilbur,' she said, straightening his blanket and giving him one final pat before taking off her dressing gown, 'I'm really glad you're here.'

Carrie woke a couple of times in the night but despite straining her ears, the only sound she could hear was Wilbur's snoring. The house had felt still and serene. In the morning, although she felt a little apprehensive leading Wilbur downstairs, nothing had been moved.

Carrie opened the door to the garden and let the dog out. She breathed in deeply. Today was going to be a good day. She could just feel it. Thank goodness for Gavin, after all. If it hadn't been for him, she'd have been getting ready to welcome Jules or packing up to leave. She wasn't ready to go yet. How could a place steal a piece of you so quickly, especially when you didn't have anything spare to give away? Working in the gardens could be just what she needed. A few more days would make all the difference and then she'd be ready to go back to her old life feeling rested and optimistic and determined, whatever the future held.

Just after eight thirty, Carrie strolled up the lane trying to quell her misgivings. What had she let herself in for? She was on holiday, for goodness' sake. But she'd said she'd help out and she wasn't one to go back on her word. It was ridiculous to feel so nervous. She'd been gardening since she was a toddler when Grandad had bought her a miniature trowel, fork and rake. But what if she mistakenly dug up some rare and precious plant? Wilbur tugged at his lead, oblivious to her doubts. He sniffed at everything he possibly could in the hedgerow as if it was the very first time he'd ever been out for a walk.

'You'll make sure I'm all right, won't you, Wilbur?' she murmured. 'And if it's a disaster, well, it's only a few hours out of my whole life. I don't have to go back. I might not be allowed back!'

Carrie paused to inhale the lemony scent of the primroses scattering the grassy bank before slipping through the half-open gate and into the stone archway. Over to the left she could see Guy's Land Rover already parked up. Stooping a little, she let Wilbur off the lead and he gazed up at her questioningly.

'Go on,' she said. 'Go and find him. You know you're dying to.'

Wilbur didn't need telling twice. He skirted the table, which was already laid out with a smattering of herbaceous plants ready to tempt the paying public, and scooted across the gravel in search of his master. In the small gift shop, a petite woman of about her age was totally absorbed arranging a pile of books into neatness while another older lady stood behind the counter dunking a piece of shortbread into a mug of coffee.

'Oops, caught me!' she said to Carrie, through a mouthful of crumbs. 'Good thing you're not my mother – she still slaps my hand when she sees me doing that and I'm nearly sixty.'

Carrie smiled.

'Mine, too, but dunking makes it taste so much nicer.'

'If I could, I'd give you free entry to the gardens for that comment alone,' the woman said, 'but you're more than a bit early. We don't open until ten.'

'I know. I'm Carrie and I'm actually here to work.'

'Oh dear, nobody told me. Jenny,' she said, turning to the woman in the corner, 'do you know anything about Carrie coming to work here?'

Jenny turned towards them.

'Sorry, I was miles away. You must be Guy's friend.'

The very words made Carrie feel ridiculously warm inside.

'You are expected. I just forgot to mention it to Heather.'

'Nobody tells me anything around here,' Heather joked, holding out a hand which Carrie shook.

'Don't listen to her,' Jenny shot back. 'She's usually the first to know everything.'

Carrie smiled and shook Jenny's hand, too.

'Welcome to the gardens,' she said, with a beaming smile. 'We're so pleased to have you here.'

'We can't thank you enough for offering to help out,' Heather interrupted, brushing some shortbread crumbs away from her lips. 'We certainly need it. There's so much to do at this time of year and the weather hasn't been helpful. Poor Guy's been getting more and more stressed.' She took a neat sideways step and peered beyond the doorway towards the house.

'The Major can be a bit difficult at the best of times,' she said, lowering her voice, 'but at this time of year, with the Season building, he's even more curmudgeonly than usual and Guy bears the brunt of it. He might seem calm on the surface but underneath I can tell that he's feeling the pressure.'

'Well, there's his gran as well,' Jenny countered. 'He's been beside himself with worry about her.'

Carrie opened her mouth to speak but didn't get a chance.

'She virtually brought him up, you know,' Heather said. 'He really didn't get on with his stepfather. Mind you, hardly surprising. What sort of person sends a seven-year-old to boarding school when he's already lost his father? And of course, his last relationship broke up because of his devotion to Irene, but I expect you know all about that.'

'Um, not exactly.'

'His ex wanted him to choose between them. Suggested he put Irene in a home so he wasn't "tied to the island" and he wasn't even living with her then, just popping in most days to check she was all right. That was before the fall, of course. That's when it all came to a head. Jen can tell you all about it.'

Carrie got the distinct impression that Jenny would rather have put her hand over Heather's biscuit-sprinkled lips if she'd been within arm's length distance but, before either of them got the chance to say anything else, there was the sound of footsteps on the gravel outside the door.

'I see you three have met.'

All of them started slightly and Carrie was mortified as she felt herself beginning to blush. She really didn't want Guy to think she'd been indulging in idle gossip.

'I hate to interrupt your no-doubt fascinating conversation,' he said, and there was definitely a touch of sarcasm shredding the surface friendliness of the words, 'but perhaps we'd better get started?'

She wondered whether to say anything as she almost ran to keep up with him. If he hadn't been so tight-lipped, she might have let it go but the last thing she wanted was an atmosphere. She was meant to be here to enjoy herself.

'I'm sorry. I hope you don't think I was prying.'

'No need to apologise,' he replied, his tone definitely more clipped than usual. 'Heather isn't known for her tact but she's excellent at running the shop. No problems last night, I take it?'

She was relieved that he had changed the subject and sensed he was, too.

'None at all. Everything was totally serene – except for Wilbur's snoring.'

'Ah yes. Forgot to mention that.'

'I did feel much better with him there, though, and the extra security on the doors was reassuring, too. I do appreciate you doing that so quickly and the owner agreeing.'

He stopped next to a couple of cold frames.

'It wasn't a problem. You're here to make sure everything is running smoothly for future holiday guests. Perhaps it was something which should have been looked at a bit more closely. It's easy to get lulled into a false sense of security around here.'

'I'm beginning to think I imagined the whole thing. It's so odd.'

He shrugged.

'Some things just can't be explained but I'm glad you're feeling a bit better about the cottage.'

'Oh, I am, much better.' She wiggled her fingers. 'And I'm really looking forward to getting my hands dirty. I've only got a small shared scrubby garden in Manchester and it's quite shady, so I've had to resort to hostas and ferns mainly, but one day I'd love a big garden with a sweeping herbaceous border.'

He smiled, and Carrie realised that she only had to mention plants to take his mind off other things and change his mood.

'That's serendipitous because that's where you're working first, on the herbaceous border.'

Carrie couldn't resist clapping her hands and virtually jumping up and down on the spot. He laughed.

'That's the first time anyone's ever done that when I've set them to work.'

He picked up a couple of trays of cuttings with fresh limey green fern-like leaves and a few buds on the point of opening.

'These are Jamaican daisies. They're such good value. Once they start flowering, they really don't stop until the frost comes. Generally, it doesn't get really cold here but you can't be too careful, so I've been holding them back a bit. We've had some colder nights than usual over the last few weeks, and they are tender, but we're quite protected here so I think they'll be okay to put out now.'

He produced a pair of pink gloves from his pocket.

'I got you these so you don't get your hands too dirty. If they're not the right size or the right colour, go and get a different pair from Heather.'

She slipped them on and flexed her fingers.

'Absolutely perfect. Thank you.'

He thrust the two trays of daisies into her hands and picked up two more himself.

'Right, let's get going.'

Guy introduced Carrie to a couple of the other volunteers and then showed her where he wanted the planting doing. When that was completed, there was some weeding further down the herbaceous border and, if she got that finished, some potting in the greenhouse. Coffee and homemade cake was served at ten thirty, provided by the ladies in the tearoom. Just before lunch Guy came to find her.

'You're still here,' he said teasingly.

'I am,' she said. 'I haven't had time to even think about running away!'

'You've made a really good job of that,' he said, admiring the pile of weeds in her barrow and the freshly forked over soil. 'And those daisies look really good over in the blue and yellow section of the border.'

'Thank you,' Carrie said, feeling herself expand with the praise. She stood up and stretched. 'I'd forgotten how it gets to your back.'

'Time for a break, I think. Go and get some lunch. Then you can go home.'

She lifted her face to the sun and crinkled up her eyes.

'I'm happy to stay longer if you like. I've enjoyed it so much and I haven't finished weeding the border,' she said. 'My grandfather made me a little plot of my own when I was about two years old and every year I grew vegetables and broadcast marigold and cornflower seeds. I'd forgotten how amazing it is, to be out in the fresh air, listening to the birds singing, turning over the soil. There was a robin which came so close I wouldn't even have had to stretch out my arm to touch it. That's such a privilege.'

'I told you it was better than therapy.'

'Cheap, too,' she said. 'Just the price of a pair of gloves.'

'Oh, you don't have to pay for those,' he said. 'They come with the job.'

'Or the price of a meal?'

Why had she said that? She regretted it as soon as the words left her mouth.

'You've been so kind, loaning me Wilbur, inviting me here – I'd like to repay you in some way.'

'You don't have to.'

Carrie sensed that he wanted to take a step back but was stopping himself from doing so. She could leave it at that, let him rebuff her gracefully.

'To paraphrase a certain person,' she said, keeping it as light as possible, 'no, I don't have to, but I would like to. You'd be doing me a favour. I haven't been out for a meal since I got here because I'm one of those really sad people who doesn't want to eat on their own for fear of what people will think – basically, that I'm a billy no-mates.'

'I can't imagine that anyone would think that.'

'They wouldn't be far wrong. I've spent so much time on my job recently that I've neglected my friends.'

'If they're true friends they won't mind being neglected for a while. They'll understand.'

'I hope so. Anyway, think about the meal thing. No pressure. I promise. And I won't mention Mark once. We can just talk about plants and food. I'm absolutely starving! I'd forgotten how being out in the open air does that to you, too. I'm going to get a salad with one of those humungous homemade sausage rolls that I've seen in the tearoom. Then I'm coming back to finish weeding. Grandad wouldn't like it if I left it half done.'

At the mention of a sausage roll, Wilbur's ears had pricked up.

'Coming, Wilbur?' she said, turning away, sensing that she needed to give Guy some space.

The dog was by her side in an instant and together they strolled in the direction of lunch. But she was aware of Guy standing very still and watching them go.

Carrie was hand forking the last few weeds from the border when a shadow cast across her back.

'The interloper,' a gruff voice said.

She twisted to look up at the Major.

'That's me. Here again. Good afternoon, Major.'

'Be careful of that poppy. It's one of the last things my wife planted.'

Carrie shielded her eyes and blinked up at him.

'I'm a bit concerned about it actually. It doesn't look that well.'

'It's in the perfect place. Honoria was always very careful to make sure her plants had the right conditions.'

'I'm sure she was but look, it's struggling.'

'And you're an expert on Papaver Orientalis, are you?'

Carrie stood up and brushed herself down. Her neck was aching, and she had a slight headache from all the bending over and the heat of the sun. She wished that she'd gone and bought a hat from the shop.

'No, no, of course not. But my granny used to say that if something wasn't doing well, even if it was in supposedly the right place, you'd be better to move it.'

'Hmmph! Well, I've never met your granny, but I do know that Honoria wouldn't want it moved by someone who's barely been here for five minutes and who probably doesn't know the first thing about gardening.'

His frown deepened and Carrie rubbed her forehead.

'I do know a little.'

'A little knowledge is a dangerous thing, they say.'

'So you'd prefer it if I didn't know anything?'

The Major narrowed his eyes. His face had turned an angry shade of red. He was probably about to have her escorted off the premises. Another job she'd made a mess of.

'I've been very careful.'

She did her best to keep her voice even.

'If I'm not sure whether it's a weed or a plant I've left it alone.'

'It's very sudden,' he said, 'your being here.'

Carrie felt herself sagging a little. Perhaps she'd done a bit too much.

'That's my life at the moment, sir. Everything is very sudden and...'

She looked back along the border, at the herbaceous perennials that came up year after year, reliably, faithfully.

'...I've realised this afternoon, kneeling in the sunshine, in this beautiful place which has had a house here for so long and has been loved for generations, that I'm not very good at change, especially when it's sudden.'

Next to her she fancied that his body language softened slightly but perhaps she was imagining it. Perhaps he was just getting tired, too.

'Yes, well. Not many of us are.'

She didn't dare look at him in case the severity of his features made her want to weep again. But she wanted him to know how good this garden had made her feel in such a short space of time.

'But being here, doing this, *has* been like an unexpected gift.'

Now, she cast him a shy glance, her voice uncontrollably dropping to a mere whisper.

'Only yesterday I was planning on leaving the island. So, change isn't all bad, is it?'

He didn't reply, just studied her carefully as if she was an unusual specimen of plant.

'I'm sorry if you don't like me being here, Major.'

His head moved back a fraction.

'Why on earth would you think that?'

She didn't reply.

'Perhaps I was a bit ungracious,' he said. 'Whether I like your being here or not is immaterial. My opinions don't count for much these days.'

'Well, they should,' Carrie replied. 'This is your home. You're in charge.'

'It doesn't feel like that most of the time.'

'Perhaps,' she said, warily, 'the people who are working here are just trying to help.'

He wavered slightly, leaned a little more heavily on his stick. Standing still for too long was obviously not easy for him. Suddenly the fight seemed to have gone out of him. Carrie was desperate to go back to the cottage and get in the shower, to lie down on the bed with a book and a cup of tea by her side. He had done nothing to make her feel welcome so why should she bother to try and cheer him up? She really needed to put herself first but...

'Can I ask you a favour?'

He looked suspicious.

'Do you need money? Because I haven't got any of that and...'

Carrie gave a short, half-shocked laugh.

'Really? You think I'd ask you for money?'

'People do. They think because I live in a big house that I'm, what's the expression, loaded.'

Carrie shot him a sympathetic look.

'Believe me, I've learned the hard way not to make assumptions about anyone or anything.'

'What is this favour?'

'I wondered if you would walk me around the garden and tell me about its history and some of the plants. Guy has put me to work but I haven't had time to really appreciate everything that's here. I've read the guidebook but it's so much nicer to learn about a place from someone to whom it all means so much.'

The Major was totally still, apart from his eyes which appeared to get smaller and more watery.

'It doesn't have to be now,' Carrie added, 'if you're too tired or haven't got the time.'

'I've got plenty of time. Too much of the blessed stuff.' He shot her a slightly concerned look. 'You won't get into trouble with Guy?'

'I was planning to clock off at about four anyway.'

'Does *he* know that? If not, *I'll* probably get into trouble with him for dragging you away.'

Carrie grinned at him.

'I think between us we can handle Guy, don't you? Besides, I can always come back and finish off tomorrow. I'm not going anywhere now, not for a few days anyway.'

The Major seemed to be weighing up her proposal. Carrie waited.

'You'll be the very first interloper to get a guided tour,' he said at last.

'I'm honoured,' Carrie replied, and she offered up a small, wobbly curtsey.

The Major held out his arm and she eyed up his immaculate blazer.

'And also a bit grubby.'

'My dear interloper,' he said, 'clothes can easily be cleaned. At my time of life, soil on the Savile Row is the least of my worries!'

At which she linked her arm through his and they strolled slowly back along the border together.

TEN

'Well, you've certainly cheered him up,' Guy said, as an hour later he accompanied Carrie towards the exit. 'I haven't seen him so chipper for ages.'

'He's been good company.'

'And he actually took you around the whole garden?'

'Yes.'

'Not into the house, though?'

'No. I get the impression that he guards that quite fiercely.'

'You're not wrong there. I'm barely allowed in. There's a study not far from the front door and if the weather's bad we meet in there, but he much prefers to discuss things in the greenhouse or the potting shed. Did he say I bullied him about the garden?'

'Not at all. Just that you didn't give up in trying to get him more involved. Mostly he was telling me about the plants and how his mother and then his wife had laid out the gardens as they are today. He told me something about the history of the house, too, how he was born in that room up there and the responsibility of it all; how his son doesn't feel the same sense of obligation...'

'He talked about that?'

'A little.' Carrie paused and looked around, breathed in the scent of the early evening, the sun softening everything around them. 'He's so full of sadness, for the loss of his wife, at having a son who lives so far away, for the slipping away of something which has been cherished for generations.'

'I do know that – even if he thinks I don't.'

She looked up at him.

'You love it here, too, almost as much as he does.'

Guy stared over the top of her head, into the distance.

'I used to come here as a boy. I played in those woods. We climbed trees, built dens, camped out. It was, is, a magical place.'

'You and Sebastian?'

'Yes.'

'So, if you're friends, can't you persuade him to come back or at least get them together so a plan can be devised for the future?'

'I'm afraid not.'

'Because...?'

'Because we're not friends any longer.'

He spoke in such a way that the topic was definitely closed.

'Well, I'll see you in the morning then,' she said, and bent down to rub Wilbur under his chin.

'If you like,' Guy replied. 'As I said, it's not compulsory.'

And with that he turned on his heel, slapped his thigh for Wilbur to follow him and headed back up the path towards the potting shed.

Carrie was still feeling put out when she got back to Hideaway Cottage. Even the blue tits darting in and out of the apple tree in the front garden couldn't soften her indignation. Rita had pinned a note to the door asking her to pop around for a cup of tea when she got back. Carrie sighed. She felt incredibly tired, but it would be rude to refuse. Besides, she wouldn't have to stay for long and it would take her mind off Guy. He'd seemed so open and uncomplicated when she first met him.

Rita was looking out of the window and waved as she saw Carrie approaching. Carrie waved back, suddenly overcome with a huge surge of gratitude and a small degree of guilt for not wanting to come. There was something about Rita which always made you feel better. She'd sensed it from the very first time she spoke to her on the phone. Rita wasn't one of those people who blew hot and cold, and right now she needed someone down to earth, someone who would stop her from feeling responsible for the change in Guy's mood. The smell of baking greeted her even before the back door was opened.

'Tradesman's entrance, I'm afraid,' Rita said, with a laugh. 'Mind the wellingtons. I stand them up every day, but they seem to have a mind of their own. I often wonder what the collective name for a group of wellington boots should be – something like an insubordination of wellingtons, at least in this house, anyway.'

Carrie laughed and felt her shoulders drop by at least an inch. Obviously, she didn't want to offend Guy but, in a few days, she would be away from here and probably never see him again so why was she worrying? It felt good to settle at the old pine table while Rita unhooked three mugs from the crammed dresser and filled a very large brown teapot.

'Cake?' Rita asked. 'It's apricot and almond, Tasha's favourite, so I treat her every now and again, don't I, Tasha?'

Carrie hadn't noticed the teenage girl curled up in the large leather armchair looking out of the bay window towards the farmyard.

'You treat me a lot,' the girl replied, 'probably too much.'

'Nonsense,' Rita tutted. 'You need treats. We all do. You ask Carrie here.'

'Hello, sorry, I didn't see you there and yes, treats are definitely good. Don't turn them down.'

The girl looked up from her book. 'I'm not allowed to, am I, Gran? Especially if they're food.'

'Certainly not,' Rita replied, placing a mug of tea next to her and a slice of cake on the pile of *Farmer's Weekly* magazines that weighed down the rickety side table.

'Now you eat all of that, Tash. It'll do you good.'

Rita dropped a kiss on the top of the girl's head and bustled back over to Carrie.

'I'm the luckiest woman alive to have my grandchildren living next door,' she said.

'And lucky for them to have you so close,' Carrie said.

'I try to help where I can,' Rita said, lowering her voice, 'especially with Tasha. Who'd be fourteen again, especially in this day and age with all the extra pressures? Things were much less complicated in my day.'

'And even in mine,' Carrie said.

Rita cut two more generous slices of cake and placed them on the table along with the tea. No sooner had she sat at the table opposite Carrie than a tan and white Jack Russell scuttled over from its basket next to the range and jumped up on to Rita's knees.

'This is Hercules,' she said, scratching the dog behind his ears, 'my tower of strength.'

'He's gorgeous,' Carrie said, pulling a mug of tea towards her.

'We think so, don't we, Tash?' Rita said, breaking off a small piece of sponge and popping it into the dog's open mouth. 'I know I shouldn't. He's a bit on the heavy side already and he's only five. I'll have to get William to take him for an extra-long walk tomorrow to burn it all off. Anyway, enough about us, tell me about you. Is everything all right now? I spoke to Guy earlier and he said that things had settled down. No more strange happenings?'

'No, thank goodness, and I've had a perfect day working at the gardens. It's really done me good. Then just before I left the Major showed me around.'

Rita coughed slightly and took a sip of her tea.

'Well, I never. That's a turn-up. He doesn't particularly take to strangers. In fact, he doesn't take to anyone these days, even people he's known for years. It's grief, of course. Makes it easy to withdraw from the world. I suppose that might have happened to me when my George went, if it hadn't been for Tasha and her brother, William. My salvation, they have been.'

Carrie glanced over at the blonde-haired girl, totally absorbed in her book, the cake untouched beside her. Did she know how blessed she was to have this kitchen to escape to whenever she needed it? A room where love seeped from every threadbare hand-embroidered cushion, from each of the photographs jostling on the windowsill, but most of all from the woman at the heart of it.

'Completely floored Andrew when Honoria died,' Rita continued. 'She knew he wouldn't cope well without her. Hung on as long as she could, poor love. She was desperate for Sebastian to come back from Hong Kong, preferably with a beautiful wife in tow. That was her dream, for the house to be secured for the next generation and to see grandchildren playing hide and seek in the shrubbery.'

'It might still happen.'

Rita shook her head.

'I doubt it. Not while Guy's there.'

'They were obviously friends once?'

'Inseparable as boys, but after Seb did what he did – well, Guy might have got over it but he's not one for forgiving easily.'

Rita settled back in her chair and blew on her tea.

'There was this girl, you see, prettiest little thing she was. Louisa, she was called, and Guy had liked her for ages but just couldn't pluck up the courage to ask her out. Sebastian knew about it, of course. Then Guy went off to university and Seb took a gap year. He was meant to be spending time in the garden, learning about the plants before going off to do a degree in business studies. The minute Guy had gone, Sebastian made his move. By the time Guy came home a few weeks later the two of them were an item and flaunting it around the whole island. The boys' relationship was never the same after that. But then Sebastian was always a bit sneaky. I was surprised the friendship with Guy lasted as long as it did. I could see they'd outgrown each other years before but Honoria and Irene, Guy's grandmother, were very close. They got on like a house on fire, raised money for the same charities, and I think that made it more difficult for the lads to admit that they didn't have much in common any longer.' Rita dropped an extra lump of sugar into her tea which sploshed over the side of the mug and on to her pale pink apron.

'We can all find it difficult to face up to things,' Rita continued, dabbing at the tea stain. 'We carry on hoping that something will turn out for the best...'

She stared out of the window to where a man was sitting on his tractor talking to a tall, slim woman with a sharp face. The conservation looked tense, and Carrie noticed that Tasha had shrunk further into her chair.

'Some things come into our lives that are just hard to deal with,' Rita murmured. 'But deal with them we must. It's absolutely no good burying our heads in the sand.'

'No,' Carrie replied. 'I suppose you're right.'

The older woman's eyes swivelled to fix Carrie with a penetrating stare.

'Oh, I am, dear. I may be wrong about a lot of things but not about this. Facing up to the truth about ourselves and others is really the only way to go if you want to be happy.'

She turned to her granddaughter.

'Now, Tasha, sweetheart, you're not eating that cake, and I made it specially for you. Remember your promise?'

'It's delicious,' Carrie said, watching as Tasha stretched out a thin arm and took the tiniest bite from one corner.

'Tasha hasn't been very well,' Rita explained. 'But you're on the mend now, aren't you, pet?'

The girl smiled at her grandmother and Rita went over and perched on the edge of the chair, pulling her close.

'There's nothing that can't be solved by tea, cake and lashings of love, is there, sweetheart?'

Carrie watched as they leaned into each other, and she knew that if anyone could save Tasha from whatever it was that was troubling her then Rita could.

'This is my son, Alastair,' Rita said, returning to the table, as the man Carrie had seen on the tractor strode into the kitchen. She wafted one hand through the air, picked up a polka-dotted plate and reached for the knife, poised to cut a slice of cake. 'Everything all right, love? Would you like a piece of apricot and almond loaf?'

'No, no thanks, Mum.'

Rita sat down heavily.

'Meet Carrie. She's staying at Hideaway Cottage. You remember me telling you?'

'Yes, yes, of course. Hello. Welcome.'

'Thank you.'

He turned away from her.

'Tasha, Mum wants you home.'

The girl lifted her chin. 'Why?'

'Homework.'

Tasha raised the book from her lap and waved it at him.

'Doing it.'

'There must be more than that?'

'Nope, done it.'

'Well, I think it's time you came home anyway.'

'I am home.'

'Tasha, don't be difficult. You know what I mean.'

'Perhaps it's time I went,' Carrie said.

'Nonsense,' Rita replied. 'You've only just got here.'

And as if Rita had subconsciously instructed him to keep her there, Hercules came and got on her knee, pinning her to the chair.

Rita's breath stuttered. She knew how this was going to go. Maybe this time she could change the outcome. Maybe Carrie being there would help.

'She's all right here, sweetheart. Leave her a little bit longer. She hasn't had a chance to chat to Carrie yet and they both like books.'

She cast a desperate glance at Carrie who nodded in agreement, but Alastair didn't look in the mood to be appeased.

'She spends far too much time here, Mum.'

Rita bit her lip. If George had been here, he'd have had something to say to that. She could hear his voice as clear as day.

'And why do you think that is?' he'd have said.

She'd have tugged at his shirt sleeve, the checked one which had been washed so many times that it was as soft as a lamb's tail. She kept that shirt on her bed for Hercules to sleep on. She might have been able to stop George exploding or she might not. You never could tell with George. Alastair was just like him. Stubborn. Sometimes he'd insist that Tasha went home; once he'd even tried to drag her out of the chair. She'd fought back, of course, kicked her father in the shins. Rita had had to step in then, calm them both down, but something had changed that day. She'd tried to explain to Tasha the pressure Alastair was under and not just with the farm, but she always had to pick her words so carefully. Christabel was the girl's mother, after all.

George had seen through her straight away, of course. Knew that she was marrying their boy for the wrong reasons.

'How many clothes does one woman need?' George had said, when she'd been staying with them that first time and worn something which looked brand new every single day. 'Not a woollen jumper in sight,' he'd chuntered. 'What good are silk blouses and strappy shoes in a place like this?'

Rita had defended her then. 'She's young, George,' she'd said, 'and she comes from a different world. She's a city girl. Anyway, I wouldn't worry. It probably won't last.'

But it had lasted.

'I know you don't approve of her, Dad,' Alastair had said one day, when they were putting the new collie through her paces. 'But I love her. She's the one.'

Rita remembered that day well; the day she knew that Christa, as Alastair called her, was going to become part of the family, that everything was going to change. She'd been rolling out sweet pastry for an apricot tart. The espaliered tree on the back of the barn wall was dripping with fruit. She'd already made jam and sauce for ice cream. She was worried the tree was going to exhaust itself, that over the winter it would turn up its toes and die. That tree had been there since she was a child. It was like a friend. She would save some of the kernels and try to get one to germinate in case the worst happened. She was contemplating loss and how to come to terms with it when George had blown into the kitchen. He had marched in, taken the bottle of whisky from the cupboard and poured himself enough for three good gulps. It was only half past two in the afternoon. Rita had stopped rolling her pastry and watched him.

'What is it, love? What's happened?'

'He's going to marry her,' he'd said.

'No,' she'd said, 'not yet. He barely knows her.'

'He's blind,' George replied. 'She's bewitched him. She'll

change this family, Rita. You mark my words, she'll change it and not for the good.'

And he'd walked back out again to busy himself on the farm while she was left with a growing sense of dread. Could she have done more to stop the marriage? Rita wondered. Alastair wouldn't have listened. Look what had happened with his brother. Robin had tried to talk to him, advised him not to rush into anything and there had been a massive fall-out. She'd lain awake that whole night after Robin left, listening to George breathing beside her. He wasn't asleep either but neither of them spoke. That had been the start of it. Maybe the upset had been the start of George's illness, too. From that day on their family unit, which had been so strong – unbreakable, she thought – was cracked beyond repair. If Christabel hadn't come into Alastair's life, would they all be here together now, running the farm as she and George had hoped? They'd done their best, of course, tried to welcome Christabel with open arms but it was never enough. In Rita's opinion, first impressions were rarely wrong. She'd got a good first impression of Carrie and look at her now, sitting at their table, trying to hide her embarrassment while giving out vibes of sympathy and compassion. If only Christa had Carrie's softness. Oh, she could be very charming when she wanted something, like a big wedding reception in a marquee on the top field, but very difficult when she didn't get her own way, like moving into the old farmhouse the minute George died. But God threw challenges to everyone, and the test was how you responded to them. And without Christa there wouldn't be Tash and William, so how could she wish away the marriage? What was that quote in the bible: *Whoever pursues righteousness and kindness will find life, righteousness, and honour.* Proverbs, she thought it was. She must look it up later and put herself back on the right path. She was forever falling off it but sometimes you had to prioritise your kindnesses. This was one of those times. She stood up, plucked

Hercules from Carrie's lap, tucked him under her arm and moved to stand next to Tasha.

'Let her stay a bit longer, Al. Please. She's not doing any harm. She'll go back in a bit, won't you, Tasha, darling? Look, she's still got her cake to eat.'

Alastair threw a glance from one to the other. Rita could see the desperation in his eyes. What could she do? She really didn't want to make things more difficult for him, but Tasha needed her, too.

'Ten minutes and not a second more,' he said, waving a finger at both of them and storming out.

Rita dropped another kiss on to her granddaughter's head.

'I'm sorry,' she said, looking over at Carrie.

'Please don't apologise. Families are complicated.'

'You can say that again,' said Rita. 'Some more than others.'

One thing she knew for sure. They'd all pay the price for that extra ten minutes.

ELEVEN

The beach was only five minutes' drive from the cottage. Carrie parked in the small carpark, pulled on her warm coat and took the path down towards the sound of the waves. The tide was going out and there were a few people walking behind a couple of dogs chasing sticks. Carrie turned left and picked her way across the small stream of water which ran into the sea. Her shoes made imprints in the wet sand, and she sauntered along the shoreline picking up shells and pebbles.

Rita was right. She had to face up to the truth about herself, about Mark, about her fear of letting down her parents. They weren't going to change. Their opinion of her career success wasn't going to alter. In trying not to disappoint them she was constantly doomed to not feeling good enough. Did she really want to go through the rest of her life like that? She placed her seashore treasure in her pockets and stopped to stare into a rock pool searching for signs of life. It took her straight back to family holidays and the competition between herself and her brother as to who could fill their buckets with the most creatures before putting them back into the water. He always won. He'd been better than her at everything, sport, music, academic work; it just seemed to come so easily whereas she had to work hard.

'It's good for you,' Deborah used to say to her, as Carrie had vented tears of frustration at being beaten yet again at Cluedo or badminton or grades on her school reports. 'It will spur you on. Give you a competitive edge.'

But all it had done was made her feel inadequate, especially when she knew that sometimes her brother tried not to do as well just to make her feel better. And then he got into trouble for not trying hard enough, for letting everyone except her down. It didn't matter that she was younger, she still got the blame.

'The trouble is, you're a bad influence, Carrie. A distraction.' Sometimes it had felt as if everything was her fault. But now she had nothing to prove. Charlie had opted out of his high-flying city job and was living in a caravan in New Zealand with his beautiful bohemian wife and two free-spirited children. How she admired and envied him for having the courage to admit that he was on the wrong track and putting happiness ahead of status or financial reward.

Some salt spray hit her in the face, startling her, almost causing her to slip over on the seaweed-laden rock. Where had that thought come from? She wasn't on the wrong path, was she? She loved PR, or did she? Wasn't it something she had fallen into after university because she wasn't sure what else to do? She was going to have to tell her parents what had happened. She'd already picked up a message on her phone when she was out and about and managed to put them off from Zooming this week. If she did it again, her mother would know something was wrong. Besides, if she was going to be unemployed, better to break them in gently. Poor parentals! She was their last hope after Charlie had 'become a bum', as her mother called it.

'He *is* working, Mum,' Carrie had said.

'Carpentry,' Deborah had replied. 'That's not what we had in mind when he graduated with a first from Oxford in Classics with French.'

Carrie had made some joke about him becoming an expert in French polishing but had been berated for her flippancy.

'But he's happy,' Carrie said. 'Isn't that what parents want most of all, for their children to be happy?'

Deborah had said of course she wanted that, but she had turned away as if to hide her face. Carrie knew that what her parents really aspired to was for Charlie to be happy doing a job which earned him a shedload of money and was something they could boast about to their competitive friends. 'At least you're still doing a proper job, Carrie,' her father had added. 'We're so proud of you, darling. And if you play your cards right, you'll be a partner at Winterson's before too long.'

But she hadn't played her cards right and very, very soon she was going to have to own up about it all, which wasn't something she could cope with thinking about right now. A firm nudge at the back of her knees made her stagger forwards, flailing her arms, sure that she was about to land face first in the rock pool.

'Wilbur!' she said, as soon as she'd regained her balance. 'What *are* you trying to do to me?'

Damn, that meant Guy was nearby and he was the last person she wanted to see. Could she saunter away and pretend that she hadn't seen him, that the brown Labrador was someone else's? No chance of that, Wilbur was now licking her hand and Guy was striding up the beach towards them.

'Wilbur,' he called, and the dog turned his head. 'Leave the lady alone.'

The lady! As if she were a complete stranger. Why did that sting?

'I'm sorry,' Guy said. 'He's a law unto himself when he likes someone. Takes no notice of me whatsoever.'

'It's okay,' she said. 'It's nice to be popular.'

She fancied he almost blushed or perhaps his cheeks were just attractively pink from chasing after the dog.

'I think I was a bit rude earlier,' he said. 'I'm sorry. You touched a nerve. Stupid after all this time.'

Carrie wrinkled up her nose.

'It's meant to be a great healer, isn't it?'

'So they say.'

'I think they lied.'

'I suppose it depends what you're talking about, but for the important things...'

'...the things which break your heart,' Carrie whispered.

'Yes, for those things, I think they lied, too.'

They stood for a moment looking at each other and she had the disconcerting urge to give him a hug, but she'd probably slip on the seaweed and fall into his arms which he would totally misconstrue.

'Have you seen the casts of the dinosaur footprints?' he asked.

'No.'

'Would you like me to show you? I was fascinated by them when I was small.'

'Yes, please,' she said. 'I'd like that very much.'

He held out his hand to help her down from the rock. And as he wrapped strong fingers around hers, she couldn't help smiling at how good it felt. It was the next best thing to him giving *her* a hug and suddenly she realised that was what she needed at this moment: a great big hug to make her feel safe and warm and cherished.

'That's amazing!' Carrie gasped, placing her small size-four foot against the three-toed lump of rock.

'It's about one hundred and twenty-five million years old,' Guy replied.

'That's almost too much for me to get my head around,' Carrie said with a laugh. 'What did it belong to?'

'An iguanodon or a theropod, perhaps. This area may have been on a dinosaur migration route. The herds would have been following the muddy banks of the river looking for plants to eat.'

Carrie looked up at the cliffs and along the beach, imagining the huge creatures roaming the landscape.

'You can find fossilised bones all over the place,' Guy said. He bent down and picked up a piece of black rock which looked just like coal.

'This is lignite which is fossilised wood,' he said, handing it to Carrie. 'If you look carefully, you can see the grain. And over there is a petrified forest. It's only visible at low tide.'

She followed the sweep of his arm towards what looked like more lumps of coal, some of them spun with gold.

'They actually look as if they're glowing.'

'That's the iron pyrites reflecting in the last of the sunshine.'

'It's stunning.'

He looked at her and for a moment she imagined what it would be like to kiss him. She hadn't kissed anyone but Mark since she was about eighteen. What would it feel like? She blinked, stunned by the way her thoughts were running away with her. Thank goodness for Wilbur, who charged out of the sea back towards them, standing next to her and shaking himself vigorously.

'Wilbur!' Guy admonished. 'That's not very gentlemanly.'

'I don't mind,' Carrie said with a laugh. 'I'd love to have a dog of my own one day. Mark never much liked animals. Said they were too much of a tie. He and Paloma are much better suited in that respect. I can't imagine she's an animal person.'

The sun was dropping fast now, and they began to walk back along the beach.

'Shall I see you tomorrow?' Guy asked, as they reached the carpark and Wilbur jumped in the back of the Land Rover.

'I think so,' she said. 'If you still want me?'

He gazed down at her and Carrie was aware that he was standing quite close. She could smell the garden on his clothes, earthy and strangely appealing.

'I want you to do what you want to do, Carrie. I'm aware that you're not here for much longer and this is a beautiful island. There's so much to see. I don't want to stop you exploring.'

'I've still got a few days. Besides, it's better for me to work in the gardens when they're closed and spread my wings when you're open for visitors. That way I can get more done. So, weather permitting, I'll come over tomorrow and then head off to Osborne House the day after. Is that okay?'

Suddenly his reply felt important. She knew that if it was ambivalent she would feel disappointed.

'Yes,' he said. 'I'll look forward to it.'

'Me too,' she said.

And Wilbur threw his head back and barked twice as if he was looking forward to it as well.

Carrie was repotting some cuttings when Cressie came running up the path towards her. She was wearing a white linen shirt and some well-washed jeans.

'There you are. I went to the cottage and then I saw Rita, who said you might be here. What are you doing? I thought you were meant to be on holiday?'

'I am but this is good for the soul.'

'Jack got home last night for a flying visit,' she said breathlessly, 'and he bought me this.'

She fingered a single diamond on a delicate chain hanging around her neck.

'It's beautiful.'

'He's so good with presents. I always tell him not to buy me anything, but I think he feels guilty for going away. Anyway, he's dying to meet you and we're going to have that barbecue on Saturday evening. Please say you're not doing anything.'

Carrie laughed and brushed compost from her gloves.

'Strangely enough, I'm not doing anything, so yes, I'd love to come.'

'Wonderful,' Cressie said, flinging her arms around her. 'Just bring yourself. No need to worry about food or wine. We'll do all that. Now I must find Guy and tell him and then get back in case the twins wake up. Jack can only cope with one of them at once.'

'What time?' Carrie called, as Cressie flew back in the direction she had come from.

'Five-ish,' she called, 'so we can spend some time outside before it gets dark. And pray for this weather to hold but if it doesn't, we'll just decamp inside. See you then.'

And with a wave and a flick of her hair she had gone, leaving Carrie with a warm glow.

That evening Carrie walked up to the Longstone again. She was tired and her back ached, but she couldn't make this call from the cottage. It would have cost a fortune on the landline, and she really couldn't put it off any longer. It was starting to prey on her mind too much. With any luck her parents would still be asleep and she could just leave a message, let them know where she was so that they didn't worry. She settled at the base of the Longstone, sheltered from the wind, and pressed the short dial.

'Hello? Carrie, is that you?'

'Oh, Mum. Yes. I wasn't expecting you to pick up. It's early there.'

'Is everything all right, darling? I spoke to Jules when you said that you couldn't Zoom and she was very mysterious. Just said that you'd gone away for a few days and didn't have much signal or any internet. That must be very inconvenient, darling. What if work need to contact you? Didn't you look into it properly before you booked? You've always been a bit slapdash with that sort of thing. I've always been amazed that you've done as well in that job as you have. You know how Dad and I always tell you to double check the detail. And you're on the Isle of Wight, Jules said. That doesn't sound like you either. I have the feeling that there's something going on that I don't know about. We should be FaceTiming. I want to see your face.'

But I don't want to see yours, Carrie thought, *not when I tell you that I'm about to quit my job, if I haven't already been sacked.*

'We can't FaceTime, Mum. I don't have enough signal. It's a bit random here and I've had to come right to the top of a hill to call you as it is.' Carrie took a deep breath. Where did she start? 'The Isle of Wight is very beautiful, and it's turned out to be just what I needed. No, I didn't know about the internet but that's turned out to be a blessing in disguise as well. It's given me space to think about things instead of constantly being in contact with a world that I don't really need to know about a lot of the time.'

There was silence at the end of the phone.

'Mum? Are you still there? I can't stay on for long. This call is costing a fortune.'

'Are you ill?'

'No, why?'

'Because you sound different and you're saying things which are worrying me. Oh my God, Carrie, you haven't joined a cult, have you? They can totally brainwash people into thinking all sorts of things about their earlier lives.'

The ground felt exceptionally hard beneath her. Carrie

shifted her pelvis slightly and watched a kite circling on the air currents.

'No, Mum, I haven't joined a cult. I'm just staying in a gorgeous cottage in a small village populated by some lovely, genuine people.'

'People who obviously are happy living in their island bubble,' Deborah pronounced, 'which is probably absolutely fine for them. I'm not one to judge. But you're in PR, Carrie. It's part of your raison d'être to be in touch with the wider world.'

Carrie swallowed hard and leaned back against the Longstone, feeling its weathered surface almost massaging her spine.

'Maybe not anymore.'

Another silence. She could almost hear the cogs turning in her mother's brain.

'Have you got another job? A better one? Oh, my goodness, have you been head-hunted? That would be amazing.'

Carrie stifled a laugh. She had no idea why. It really wasn't a laughing matter. Hadn't she spent the last week crying about the job and about Mark?

'No, Mum, I'm afraid not. The thing is... are you sitting down? Because if not, you'd better be. You're not going to be very pleased with what I've got to say.'

There was a sharp intake of breath at the end of the phone.

'I knew there was something wrong. Said so to your father after you didn't reply to my texts and I had to call Jules to find out if you were all right. Is it to do with Mark?'

Her mother's voice was getting more and more high-pitched. She was going to over-react. Carrie could see it coming.

'Sort of. Now, Mum, I don't want you to get upset because it will probably all turn out for the best.'

She blinked into the distance. Not only was she saying that, she actually believed it. She kept her voice calm and steady as she gave her mother a brief, sanitised version of events.

'So you're going to lose your job?' Deborah said, when

Carrie finally ran out of steam. 'Mark's been made a partner instead of you?'

'I might not lose my job.'

There was a harrumph at the end of the line. Carrie marvelled at how a harrumph could travel so far, all across the world, and still have the same effect. She felt like Alice in Wonderland after she'd drunk the potion which made her shrink. She sat up straighter against the Longstone trying to absorb some of its power.

'You will if you spend any longer mooching about on the Isle of Wight. You shouldn't have just bolted like that.'

'Jules said I needed a break to think things over and she was right.'

'I've always thought that girl was a bad influence,' Deborah shot back. 'And how are you going to get another job in PR if you haven't got decent references?'

Carrie bit her lip. Don't snap, she told herself. She doesn't mean to be unsupportive.

She's just coming to terms with the fact that her daughter isn't living up to expectations, yet

again.

'Jules is a good friend, Mum. She has seen how stressful the last few months have been.'

'Stress is good, Carrie. If you use it constructively, it can drive you on. How do you think Dad and I have got where we are, being able to retire early and travel the world? It's because we worked jolly hard and coped with stress. And I had two children as well. And you weren't an easy baby, Carrie.'

Carrie rolled her eyes. How many times had she heard that reproach?

'Your father is going to be so disappointed. Are you sure there isn't something you can do to salvage this situation?'

'I'm not sure that I want to.'

She had spoken out loud without intending to.

'What do you mean? What have you been working towards for all these years?'

'I'm beginning to wonder,' Carrie replied. 'Perhaps it's time for a change.'

'Not you, too,' Deborah replied. 'Have you been speaking to your brother?'

'No, actually, but perhaps I ought to. He seems to have got his priorities sorted.'

'That's a matter of opinion,' Deborah said dryly. 'Listen, darling, I'm not saying that holidays aren't good when you've had a lot to cope with, but they can play tricks with the mind, you know. They can make you think things which aren't true.'

'Or they can help you to find the truth. Look, Mum, it's been good to talk but I've got to go now. Give my love to Dad and tell him I'm sorry. I know that you'll both be disappointed in me.'

'I don't want you to do anything rash until I've spoken to your father, Carrie. If necessary, we can fly back and all put our heads together to see if there's a way around this.'

Carrie sighed.

'Please don't, Mum. I need to sort this out myself. I know what I'm doing.'

But Deborah wasn't listening and as she finally extricated herself from the conversation, Carrie could already tell that her mother's mind had gone into overdrive in an effort to solve 'the problem'.

She rested her head on her knees. It was done and it was a relief. When she finally looked up, Jo was tiptoeing up to the Longstone with a bunch of wildflowers in her hand.

'Sorry,' she said. 'I didn't mean to disturb you. I just wanted to leave these here.'

'It's fine,' Carrie said. 'Just recovering from a difficult conversation. They're beautiful flowers.'

'For my daughter,' Jo said softly. 'It's her sixteenth birthday today.'

'How exciting,' Carrie replied. 'What are you doing to celebrate?'

Jo didn't move, just stared down at the bouquet tied with yellow ribbon as the wind ruffled her hair and tugged at her skirt.

'This is my celebration for her,' she murmured. 'We're not in touch, you see.'

'Oh, Jo, I'm so sorry,' Carrie said. 'That's tough. How long is it since you've seen her?'

'Two years,' she whispered, her face crumpling. 'She lives with her father on the mainland.'

Carrie stood up and put her arms around the older woman, being careful not to crush the flowers.

'Both of my girls took their father's side when our marriage was breaking up.'

'Don't you have any contact with either of them?'

The older woman shook her head.

'They don't even know where I am.'

'Can't you let them know? I'm sure they'd want to see you if—'

'I daren't.'

Her eyes were wide with fear.

'I can't risk my ex finding out.'

'Gosh, I'm sorry,' Carrie murmured but it felt as if any effort to convey some comfort was hopeless.

'I had to leave. I couldn't stay a moment longer or...' Jo said, swallowing hard. 'Or something dreadful would have happened.'

'You don't have to explain.'

'But I want to. I never talk about it, and it's locked in here.' She put a hand to her breastbone. 'It's not good for me. I miss my girls so much, but they wouldn't have come without making a fuss and if he'd discovered us trying to leave... well, suffice to say we wouldn't have got away unscathed, if at all, so I made the hardest decision of my entire life and just scooped up Daniel. I didn't even dare go into the girls' rooms and give them one last kiss in case they woke up. I was petrified that Dan would make a noise, but he was as quiet as a mouse. Didn't even stir as I lifted him out of his little bed. He was the child who was meant to save our marriage but of course he didn't. If anything, he just made things worse. My husband was jealous of him from the moment he was born. I knew he'd never hurt the girls, but he got so impatient with Daniel that I couldn't be sure he'd control himself. One day I found bruises, all over the top of Dan's arms. I knew my husband had grabbed him too hard because he'd done that to me – always on places which wouldn't show. I couldn't risk that happening to my boy because it would only get worse, especially after the drinking.'

She caressed the petals of the ragged robin.

'Most days I can live with myself but sometimes, when it's a birthday or I hear a piece of music they liked or see a mother and daughter out shopping together, then it gets too much.'

She leaned away a little.

'Are you close to your mother?'

Carrie stared at her.

'That was her on the phone. She's in New Zealand with my dad. They're visiting my brother. My mother – in fact, both of my parents – think that I'm a complete failure so, no, I wouldn't say we're particularly close.'

'I'm sure they don't really think that.'

'You don't know my parents. I'm sure they really do.'

Jo looked right into her eyes which made Carrie want to look away, but she couldn't.

'People expect so much of us, don't they? And we expect so much of ourselves. I was not the person my husband wanted me to be.'

'But that wasn't your fault.'

'No, no, it wasn't, and I can see that now, although for a long time I didn't. Likewise, dear Carrie, it isn't your fault if you're not the daughter your parents hoped for, and you need to forgive yourself for that. It's hard enough to be true to ourselves, let alone transform into something which is against our nature just for the satisfaction of others. That, in my experience, is impossible to sustain in the long term without it leading to abject misery.'

'I hate disappointing them, though.'

'Instead, you're prepared to disappoint yourself? You're prepared to look back in twenty, thirty or forty years' time with regret and unfulfilled longings at not following your true path?'

Carrie didn't answer.

'Sometimes, Carrie, we have to put ourselves first. As women, we're not taught that and it can be hard to go against the grain. I know better than most. It broke my heart to leave my daughters, but I got to a point where I had to think of myself and my son before all else. I have no idea of the details of your life, and I don't need to, but it strikes me that you're at a turning point. What you choose to do next or not do could determine your whole future.'

Jo broke an ox-eye daisy from the bunch and handed it to Carrie.

'But you have already made the most important decision and that was to come to this island.'

She smiled at Carrie.

'If there is anywhere in the world that can help you to find your focus, it is here.'

'Do you really think so?'

'I know so. I also know that letting go can't be forced. It has to evolve, Carrie, be given time.'

'But you haven't let go of your daughters.'

'Of course not, and I never will. I'm their mother before

everything else even if I'm not with them. What I've learned to do is to let go of the family life I envisaged. Let me rephrase that. I'm still learning. And now I'm going to leave Willow's flowers and get going. I have a client coming for a crystal treatment early tomorrow and I want to prepare my room.'

'This probably sounds ridiculous but are you friendly with Beulah? She's my housemate's mum and she told us about the cottage. Actually, no, that can't be right. Ignore me! It's ludicrous how people assume that just because it's a small island everyone knows everyone else and, anyway, I'm sure her friend was called Claudia, not Jo.'

Jo swivelled to look behind her for a moment before taking Carrie's arm and moving her around to the far side of the Longstone, away from the path.

'I'm Claudia. At least I was in a previous life,' she said, in a voice barely above a whisper. 'I had to change our names when we moved here so we couldn't be traced. I've only kept in touch with a few people and Beulah's one of them. We've been friends forever which I suppose is why she sometimes forgets. I can't afford slips of the tongue, Carrie. That's how he'll find me.'

Carrie clasped the older woman's arm and could feel her trembling.

'Your secret is safe with me. I promise. I think you're incredibly brave to have done what you did. It's going to be dark soon. Why don't we walk back down together? I could certainly do with the company, and I think you could, too.'

She stepped to one side to give Jo a few moments of solitude while placing her flowers. Then the two women fell into step together and trod in companionable silence down the narrow path through the woods as a soft and gentle rain began to patter against the emerging leaf canopy.

TWELVE

On the Friday morning Carrie got up late, made herself some soft-boiled eggs and buttery toast soldiers before having a long, luxurious shower. She had been here almost a week and her life in Manchester seemed a lifetime ago. She pulled on a pair of jeans, a pink and white striped Breton and some canvas shoes, locked up the cottage and headed off to Osborne House.

'Are you really going on your own?' Jules asked, as Carrie locked the car and strolled towards the entrance. 'Yes, of course. Who else would I be going with?'

'Gorgeous Guy!'

'He's not particularly gorgeous...'

'You're lying. I can always tell when you're lying. I bet he's like some Greek god of gardeners. Apollo – he wore a crown of laurel leaves. I can picture Guy now, all rippling muscles and tanned skin, wearing some skimpy loincloth and...'

Carrie laughed.

'I think you're getting a bit carried away and aren't you meant to be working?'

'There's a lull," Jules replied. "I'm having a break and don't try to change the subject. It's good to get carried away. 'You should try it.'

'One step at a time, and, for your information, I *am* on my way to being a new woman. I'm actually looking forward to sightseeing on my own.'

'Well, that's a turn-up,' Jules joked down the phone. 'Hideaway Cottage is a true miracle worker.'

'Yes, it is. But it's still not enough to placate my mum. I finally spoke to her last night.'

'I know. She called me straight afterwards.'

'What?!'

'I've always thought that she didn't really like me, you know. Anyway, in spite of that she wants me to "knock some sense" into you. I think she's even trying to convince herself that getting you and Mark back together would be the answer. Then she can bask in the glory of her son-in-law being a partner at Winterson's if not her daughter.'

'No!'

'Is that "no" you can't believe she's thinking that or "no way" would you get back with Mark?'

'Both.' Carrie paused. 'And don't say I told you so.'

'I don't know what you mean. I haven't said a word.'

'You can say it silently.'

'I admit it's a special skill. Do you mean it?'

'Yes,' Carrie said, and for the first time she actually did feel as if she meant it. If Mark came crawling and wanting her back, the chances were, unless he got her in a very weak moment, she would tell him to get stuffed. Hideaway Cottage wasn't just a sanctuary; it did indeed seem to be working miracles.

The Isle of Wight had been Queen Victoria's sanctuary, too, Carrie thought, as she wandered around the impressive building. At Osborne House she could relax and be herself, if you could ever be yourself when you were the Queen. Carrie supposed the children would have helped her to forget the affairs of state, all nine of them. Nine! Just the thought of that made her eyes water. Imagine giving birth that many times back in the nineteenth century even if you did have the best possible medical care. She wouldn't want to give birth nine times in this day and age with Jules at her side and every painkiller known to humankind! No, twice or three times would be more than enough for her, but would she even get the chance for one? For goodness' sake, Carrie, you're only in your early thirties, the biological clock isn't sounding an alarm just yet. All the same, it took time to meet someone, get to know them, settle down and then she might not get pregnant. Of course, she could always look into getting a sperm donor and IVF.

She paused in the drawing room with its beautiful yellow satin curtains and drank in the paintings, the furniture, the whole atmosphere of it reminding her of Paloma. She was probably going to be one of those irritating women who looked amazing throughout the whole pregnancy. Carrie wandered from room to room, each one glorious in its own unique way: vivid colours, intricate plasterwork, fascinating ornaments and family mementoes. It seemed fitting that Victoria had died in the home that her beloved Albert had designed, and which still transmitted the love they had felt for it. Carrie's favourite part of the house was the area that contained the family rooms with their chintzy upholstery and personal photographs. She could imagine the royal couple standing on the balcony of a summer's evening, arms entwined, listening to the nightingales.

She stopped for a pot of tea and a prawn sandwich in the orangery before exploring the grounds. Her niece and nephew would love the Swiss Cottage, which had been specially brought over from Switzerland for the children and contained child-sized pieces of furniture, and the miniature fort built by

Princes Bertie and Affie. She must bring Charlie, Lucy and the children here next time they managed a trip over.

Carrie stood still and stared at a pure white rhododendron flower. She was thinking as though she'd still be on the island, and it would just be a day trip which was ridiculous. But she had a feeling that she'd return. If there'd been a fountain to throw a coin into like the Trevi in Rome she'd have done it just to be doubly sure. Instead, she had to be content with strolling down to the private beach and dipping her toes in the chilly Solent. Ferreting in her bag she extracted a ten pence coin and buried it in the shingle where the water lapped over her feet.

'I will be back one day,' she said. 'I promise.'

It was just after five o'clock on Saturday evening when, freshly showered and changed, Carrie stepped into Cressie's garden. The trees were strewn with fairy lights, candles in jam jars flickered on every flat surface and the sound of light jazz music drifted out of the open patio doors. A handful of people were already there, including Heather who was holding Freddie and Rita who was entertaining Olivia by pulling funny faces at her. The woman who Carrie had seen in the farmyard that day was sitting on the swing seat next to Tasha and studying her reflection in her phone screen.

'Carrie,' Cressie called, stepping out of the kitchen and looking incredibly glamorous in a pale pink jumpsuit. 'I'm so glad you could make it. Jack is dying to meet you, but I must warn you he's a terrible flirt.'

Carrie smiled warily as a handsome man in a black shirt and dark jeans bounded towards them. He reminded Carrie of a cocker spaniel puppy with his loping gait and earnest eyes.

'You must be Carrie. I've heard so much about you.'

He kissed her a little too warmly on both cheeks and over his shoulder Cressie gave her a knowing smile.

'Drinks are in the kitchen. What would you like? We've got some white wine, rosé and the amazing Mermaid gins which are distilled on the island. They do a vodka and a rum now, too.'

'I'll have a gin and tonic please,' Carrie replied.

'Sea air, strawberries or citrus?'

'Ooh, they all sound delicious but strawberries, please. I'll come and give you a hand.'

'It's all right,' Jack said, almost standing in her way and definitely too close for comfort. 'Cress can manage on her own. In the meantime, you can tell me all about yourself.'

His breath was warm, and she was grateful when he intermittently leaned back slightly and swigged from a bottle of beer.

'Not much to tell really,' Carrie said.

'I can't believe that.'

Jack smiled lazily. He was attractive and he knew it.

'How are you finding Hideaway Cottage?'

'It's wonderful.'

'No trouble with the residents then?'

Carrie frowned. 'Sorry?'

'The resident ghosts.'

Carrie half laughed. Jack moved closer and ducked his head towards hers. 'You think I'm teasing but there have been sightings and things move. Have you gone to find something and it's not where you left it?'

'Well, actually...'

'Ah, Guy, I was just telling Carrie about the ghosts at Hideaway Cottage.'

Carrie half turned to see Guy standing just behind her, wearing a mint green linen shirt loose over navy chinos.

'That's just the way to make a visitor feel at ease,' Guy said.

'She might like ghosts,' Jack retorted. 'She might be a ghost hunter.' He grinned at Carrie. 'Do you like ghosts?'

'I'm not sure. At least, I don't think I mind them as long as they don't mean any harm.'

'Oh, I don't think these mean any harm, do they, Guy?'

Guy took Carrie's arm more firmly than she was expecting.

'I have no idea why you're asking me.'

She glanced up at him just as he appeared to be sending Jack what she could only construe was a warning glance.

'But I can see that Carrie doesn't have a drink so I'm going to take her into the kitchen and find her something.'

'You don't need to worry. Cress has got it all sorted. You might like to tell Carrie about all those strange happenings when you were doing up the house,' Jack continued.

Guy paused and glanced around. 'And perhaps you might like to give your wife a hand. There are more people arriving.'

Jack raised an eyebrow and lifted his bottle of beer higher into the air almost as if proposing a toast.

'Always trying to remind me of my duty,' he said, dryly. 'See you later, Carrie, if I'm allowed.'

Carrie was suddenly aware, as Guy steered her across the lawn, that she'd been holding her breath. There was a definite tension between the two men.

'Sorry about that,' he said. 'Jack can be a bit of an idiot. You looked as if you might need rescuing.'

Carrie felt herself bristling. Did she really look like some wan maiden from yesteryear who couldn't cope with a bit of over-the-top flirting? 'He's very...' She just didn't know how to describe Jack without causing offence.

'Jack's "very" everything,' he said, pulling a face. 'Bit of a man child. Not helped by the way Cressie panders to him.'

'I thought you two were friends?'

'We are. Don't you have friends who behave idiotically sometimes?'

Carrie thought of Jules and nodded. She looked over to where Jack was now flirting with the woman on the swing seat.

'I'm sorry to disappoint,' Guy said, 'but he does it with everyone under fifty. Just can't help himself.'

Now she *was* bristling.

'Why would I be disappointed?'

He shrugged. 'A lot of women would be flattered to get the undivided attention of Jack Demur.'

'Well, I'm not a lot of women.'

He studied her for a moment.

'No,' he said, 'I can see that now.'

'I'm not the sort to get involved with someone who's already attached.'

She watched his face, waiting for some reaction, but he looked impassive.

'And I certainly wouldn't want anyone, least of all Cressie, to think that I was encouraging him.'

She had raised her voice a little and was aware that it had an angry tinge but fortunately the music meant her words could only be heard by Guy.

'Cressie knows he doesn't need any encouragement.'

'I don't think I could cope with a partner like that.'

She thought of Mark. He may have had many faults, but he was never a flirt. She couldn't even remember him flirting with Paloma when she first came to redesign the office space.

'I suppose it's a good thing we're all different,' he said.

'You're very fond of Cressie, aren't you?'

She was treading on dangerous ground here and she knew it. He was bound to shut her down. Instead, his whole face softened, his mouth giving way to a generous smile.

'You'll never meet a better person. Cressie is the epitome of goodness. She won't hear a word said against anyone, least of all Jack.'

'Did I hear my name mentioned?' Cressie asked, as they stepped into the kitchen. Her hands, which were holding a pristine white muslin, flew to her face. 'Oh, Carrie, I'm sorry. I went upstairs to get this for Rita. Olivia's a bit of a sicky baby and I don't want her vomiting down the back of that gorgeous dress

Rita's wearing. I completely forgot about your drink. Has Guy been looking after you?'

She threw him a grateful and, Carrie thought, loving look.

'Remind me what you wanted and I'll do it straight away. I'm such an airhead at the moment.'

She glanced over Carrie's shoulder and towards the garden.

'And oh my goodness, I don't think Jack's even started the barbecue even though I asked him to get it going ages ago. It's the one job he had to do.' Her lips quivered. 'Maybe this wasn't such a good idea, after all.'

'Hey, hey,' Guy said, putting an arm around her shoulders and pulling her close so that her face was buried in his shoulder. 'Don't worry. I'll go and get the barbecue started as our host seems to have got distracted.'

'Got your arms around my wife again, Guy.'

Jack's voice made Carrie jump. Slowly, deliberately slowly, Carrie thought, Guy loosened his grip on Cressie.

'She needs a bit of support, that's all.'

'And you're always the one to give it, aren't you?'

For a couple of seconds, the two men stared at each other.

'Jack, don't be stupid,' Cressie said. 'I was just upset about the barbecue.'

'You're always upset about something.'

Carrie thought Guy was about to explode but Cressie clung to his arm as if restraining him.

'You know it's the hormones,' Cressie said, tears now trickling down her face. 'I'll be better soon, I promise. I'm sorry. I thought this would be a nice thing to do. I know you like a bit of socialising so...'

Carrie reached for a box of tissues and handed a clump to Cressie. Someone needed to intervene here or it was going to turn into a full blown domestic and heaven knows what secrets would be revealed. On the island unit was a packet of firelighters. She grabbed them out of desperation and chucked them at Guy who caught them deftly with his free hand.

'People are bound to be getting hungry so why don't you two men do your hunter-gatherer thing and get the barbecue going?' she said. 'I'll give Cressie a hand setting out the salads.'

Guy looked at her slightly belligerently while Jack had his feet planted widely as if rooting himself to the spot.

'Go on,' she said, firmly. 'We'll bring some food out for you to cook in a few minutes.'

It was Guy who reacted first, removing himself from Cressie's grasp.

When they had both sloped outside Cressie picked up a tall tumbler from the island unit and took a large gulp of water.

'Gosh, I wish that was gin,' she said with a half laugh. 'Sorry about that little scene. Jack's ridiculously jealous.'

'At least it shows that he cares about you,' Carrie said.

'It does. I'm very lucky and Guy's such a gem, too. I really don't know where I'd be without him.'

'I'm surprised he's not attached,' Carrie said, casually following Cressie to the fridge and taking packs of sausages, lamb koftas and chicken wings from her. She placed them all on a waiting tray alongside a small bowl of oil and a couple of pastry brushes.

'Oh, I'm not sure that Guy will ever marry.'

She offered Carrie a canapé, crimped rounds of cucumber topped with herb cheese and a sprinkling of toasted sesame seeds. Carrie popped one in her mouth and wondered whether she should let her curiosity get the better of her.

'He's very wary of getting hurt again,' Cressie said, solving Carrie's dilemma for her, 'and I think he likes his independence. Some women can be very clingy, can't they? Guy doesn't like that. Then there's his gran. She really comes first at the moment.'

'His gran must be a very special lady,' Carrie said, deciding not to pry further.

'She is. Absolutely amazing.'

'Who's absolutely amazing?' Guy asked, wandering into the kitchen, rummaging in one of the drawers as if it was his own personal domain and extracting a large pair of tongs.

'Irene,' Cressie replied.

'I'm lucky enough to have two amazing women in my life,' Guy said to Carrie, gripping Cressie around the waist and planting a kiss on her cheek. 'Not many new mums would throw a barbecue and get everyone together like this when they're coping almost singlehandedly with twins.'

Cressie blushed and something twinged in Carrie's stomach. She felt almost embarrassed to be there. They were so close, almost impossibly, improbably so, and he knew his way around this kitchen too well. No wonder Jack was jealous. There was a really sour taste in her mouth. Perhaps it was the cucumber and not the fact that she felt a teeny bit jealous, too. No, absolutely not. It was definitely the cucumber.

'I've got an idea!' Cressie said, bobbing up and down on the spot.

'Uh oh!' Guy said, burying his head in his hands but Carrie could see him making eye contact with Cressie through slightly open fingers.

'You should take Carrie to meet Irene. It's doing her head in at that home. She'd love someone new to talk to and she grew up near Manchester.'

'She grew up in Bakewell,' Guy corrected, revealing a mock serious face.

'Now you're just being pedantic,' Cressie said. 'Even I know that's not far from there. She and Carrie could talk all about the area.'

She shot Carrie a beaming smile.

'You must have been to Bakewell?'

'Um, well, yes, I have. It's very pretty.'

'And lovely cakes,' Cressie added.

'Tarts,' Guy said.

'I know that!'

Cressie threw a tea towel at him and Carrie began to feel distinctly like a third wheel.

'I can never stay that long on visits because one of the twins starts playing up and our conversation ends up being all baby related which I'm sure she gets bored with. Also, she looks so abandoned when I leave.'

She was still addressing Guy and Carrie wondered if they'd almost forgotten she was there.

'Carrie's on holiday,' Guy said. 'I'm sure she's got better things to do with her time and Gran isn't abandoned so she shouldn't make you feel guilty. She has loads of visitors. She just needs to stay there for a little bit longer until she gets her strength back.'

'But Carrie would be a fresh face and she'd get on so well with Irene,' Cressie said. 'She could go when you're at work. You've said yourself what a long day it is for her, and she doesn't have visitors every day, apart from you and you don't count.'

'Thanks very much.' Guy chuckled.

'What do you think, Carrie?' Cressie said, swivelling so fast her hair followed her head in a golden swirl across her chest and under her chin. Carrie started. She'd been thinking about whether to slink out of the kitchen with the tray of meat and if they'd even notice she had gone.

'Well...' she demurred.

'You see, she really doesn't want to,' Guy said to Cressie. 'You must stop trying to solve everyone else's problems. It can put people in embarrassing positions.'

Cressie stuck her tongue out at Guy.

'No, no, it's not that, at all,' Carrie protested. 'I mean, I'm not embarrassed.' Actually, she was, although not at the thought of visiting Guy's grandmother. That would be quite a welcome escape at the moment. 'I do love older people. They have such interesting stories to tell, and I adore the Peak District. I used to go running there but your gran's never met me. Wouldn't it be weird if I just turned up on my own and if we go together, wouldn't she jump to...'

Now she was even more embarrassed. She wished she had hair like Cressie's that would swish across her face and hide the redness which she felt beginning to burn her cheeks.

'...the wrong conclusions,' he agreed.

'Then come with me,' Cressie said. 'If I have to leave for feeding or nappy changing you can stay on.'

Guy fixed his lips in a firm line before stooping so that his forehead almost touched hers.

'Cressie,' he murmured, 'sometimes you can really be too pushy.'

'No, no, I'm not being pushy. This is a good idea!' Cressie said, backing away. 'She'll love meeting Carrie. You know she will. After all, you just talk about gardens and I tell her how many times the twins have vomited. She must be desperate for some intelligent conversation.'

Guy held up his hands and smiled. 'Okay, okay. I'll mention it tomorrow.' He threw Carrie an apologetic smile. 'If you really don't mind.'

'I don't mind one little bit.'

'When Cressie gets an idea into her head there's not much that will stop her.'

'And isn't it for your own good?' she teased.

'Not always,' he said. 'Now let's get this stuff on the barbecue before those gathering clouds release their rain and everything gets soaking wet.'

. . .

'Did you enjoy that?' Guy asked several hours later, as he closed the gate behind them.

'Very much. Everyone was so friendly. I didn't feel like an outsider at all.'

If she was honest, she'd never felt completely at home in Manchester. She'd always had to make an effort to fit in with city life and convinced herself that the sacrifices she was making would all be worth it when she got her dream job. *Sometimes*, she thought, *it took going away to make you realise that you'd been conning yourself for a very long time.* She shivered. The rain had finally arrived, and they'd all had to scurry inside to finish the barbecue. Now, even though it was barely ten o'clock, the temperature had dropped by several degrees and the dampness was seeping into her bones.

'You're cold.'

'I'm fine.'

She really hadn't wanted him to walk her home, but he'd insisted.

'Aren't you needed here?' she'd said, trying not to sound pointed.

He'd glanced over to where Cressie and Jack were giggling together on the swing seat.

'I don't think so. Anyway, I might have already overstayed my welcome. Sorry about that incident earlier. Jack's always been a bit resentful of the friendship Cressie and I have.'

'I suppose,' she said, carefully placing some glasses in the top of the dishwasher, 'you can't blame him. I mean, you're here all the time and he's not.'

He stopped drying one of the large salad bowls and stared at her.

'And your point is?'

The edge in his voice was unmistakable.

Carrie bent low, rearranged the glasses.

'I just meant,' she said, racking her brains for a way out,

'that the babies are very small and he's missing so much by being away. You probably see more of them than he does. Perhaps he's worried that they'll get more attached to you than him.'

She was gabbling. *Call yourself a PR person, Carrie,* she thought wryly. She cast him a glance, but he didn't say anything.

'Stop that clearing up, you two,' Cressie said, sauntering into the kitchen. 'I can finish it off in the morning. Jack says he'll walk you home, Carrie.'

'Oh no, really, that's very kind, but I'll be fine. It's not far.'

The thought of Jack walking her down a dark country lane made her feel quite queasy. She'd spent the whole evening trying to avoid him.

'I insist,' Jack said, swaying into the kitchen.

Carrie swallowed. He'd been over-attentive when he was sober and now he was obviously drunk, there was no telling what he might do.

'Unlessh, of course, the sharis-sharishma-tic Guy ish going to ride to your reshcue,' he slurred, slumping onto the sofa.

'I don't need rescuing,' Carrie said, forcing a smile.

'I left the Landy at The Manor so I'm walking back in your direction anyway,' Guy said.

'There,' Cressie said, 'that's sorted.'

She glanced at the baby monitor.

'If I'm lucky I can get this big baby up to bed before one of the others wakes up.'

'Will you manage?' Guy asked.

'Yes,' she said, softly punching his arm. 'I'll manage. You two go. You've done enough already.'

They walked in silence for several minutes until close by an owl hooted and something rustled in the hedgerow. Carrie felt as if all her senses were heightened by the darkness, the scent of the earth and the water dripping from the trees, Guy by her side, Wilbur padding ahead of them. From the direction of Rita's farm, a cow lowed.

'People think the countryside is quiet,' she said, 'but it really isn't.'

'It's better than the sound of traffic, though, isn't it?'

'Infinitely. I often wonder if those cows you see in fields next to the motorway find it stressful with all those cars rocketing past and if they produce less milk.'

'I would think so. Rita plays music to her cows when they're inside in the winter.'

'That's nice. What sort of music?'

'Slow stuff, I believe. Bridge Over Troubled Water, a bit of Beethoven's Pastoral Symphony. Although I believe they respond well to some heavy rock, too.'

'Perhaps Jack could contribute some slow jazz,' she suggested, stopping as the road forked. She shouldn't have mentioned Jack. He had definitely tensed at the sound of his name.

'Goodnight then,' she said. 'It was an amazing evening.'

'I'll walk you all the way back.'

She felt flustered all of a sudden. This wasn't the deal, if there had been a deal. She glanced up at him in the dim moonlight. His jaw was set in a determined way, and he had taken hold of her elbow.

'I'm fi—'

'I know you are, but it would just make me feel better if I saw you to your front door.'

'In case the ghosts are waiting to ambush me in the front garden?' she joked to cover her confusion. The touch of his elbow had sent little electric shocks up her arm and now her heart was beating faster.

'You *are* cold,' he said.

'A little, but I'll be home in a minute. I should have brought a warmer coat.'

'Here.'

Before she could stop him, he'd whisked off his waxed jacket and draped it over her shoulders, his fingers just brushing the back of her neck which sent tiny charges of electricity through her body. *Too much island gin, Carrie,* she admonished herself, *and not enough tonic.*

'Thank you but...'

'I know, I know, it's not necessary.'

He sounded a bit put out, so she pulled the coat more closely around her. The lining was soft and warm and she felt guilty that she'd sounded so ungracious.

'It's very gentlemanly of you.'

He shrugged. 'I try to maintain some old-fashioned values, unlike some people.'

'Despite your protestations I don't think you like Jack very much.'

'He can be good company.'

She shot him a sideways glance. 'That's not what I said.'

'I don't think he treats Cressie very well sometimes.'

'You seem very close.'

'We are. She's like the sister I never had.'

Carrie wasn't sure she believed him.

'Have you got siblings?'

'One brother, in New Zealand. He's married with two children.'

'What does he do?'

'He's got a small carpentry business. He did all the tradi-tional things, went to uni, then got an MA, planned a high-powered job in the City earning lots of money but then he met Lucy. She makes jewellery and it turns out that Charlie had secretly always wanted to work with his hands so eventually they decided to follow their dream.'

'And ended up in New Zealand.'

'She has relatives there, so they went for a short visit, loved the lifestyle and decided to stay. They've been there for over ten years now.'

'Do you miss him?'

'Yes. The older I get the more I miss him.'

'You could have gone out there for your great escape.'

'It did cross my mind, but my parents are visiting him and no doubt telling him that he should be making more of his life.'

'He might have valued your support.'

She laughed. 'I don't think I'm in a position to support anyone else at the moment, not successfully anyway, and certainly not with my mother as judge and juror. I'm having enough trouble supporting myself.'

'You seem to be doing pretty well to me, and you've done wonders with that herbaceous border.'

'Thank you, that's kind of you. Perhaps that could be an alternative career when I get dropped from my current one. There's a growing demand for female gardeners, I believe.'

'Definitely.'

Rounding the corner, she could see the outline of Hideaway Cottage just coming into view. From an upstairs window the lamp which she had set on the timer glowed welcomingly.

'What Jack was saying, about the cottage being haunted. Is that true?'

'Who knows? I suppose quite a few very old houses have ghosts.'

'What were these strange things that happened when you were doing it up?'

The jacket slipped off one shoulder and as she lifted her hand to right it, he did the same thing, their knuckles catching.

'Sorry,' he said, almost jumping away from her.

They were both on edge and she had no idea why. Perhaps he was thinking about Cressie having to cope with Jack and the twins on her own.

'Sometimes doors would be closed that I was convinced I'd

left open. Maybe the wind had blown them or I was mistaken. I was pretty tired by the end of the day.'

She turned to look at his profile as he walked steadily beside her, at her particular pace. 'Anything else?'

'Nothing unpleasant.'

'But there was something?'

'Once or twice my toolkit would have moved. It was odd actually because it would always turn up in a room where something needed doing more urgently than I had realised.'

'As if someone was trying to help you.'

'Maybe. I do think that the cottage has an aura of calm.'

'I do, too. They must have loved the cottage very much.'

'They?'

'Oh yes. I think there's more than one of them. When I've heard the whispering, it sounded like two people.'

'And presumably love it still,' Guy said.

They had reached the little gate and by now the moon had emerged fully from behind the clouds.

'And who wouldn't?' Carrie said, looking at the house she had come to think of as home. 'I didn't want to come here, you know. Jules persuaded me.'

'You said.'

'It's the strangest sensation, being here. It's like rediscovering who I am. It's as if I've been living the wrong life all these years.' She looked up at him. 'How can that have happened?'

'You might change your mind when you get back to Manchester. Holidays can play tricks with your mind.'

'My mother said that on the phone,' Carrie said, 'but somehow I don't think so.'

Her words sounded startlingly emphatic in the darkness.

'This place is beautiful,' he said, softly, 'but it doesn't solve problems, Carrie. To you everyone might appear to be living an ideal life, but they are still struggling under the surface.'

She looked up at him, the moonlight catching the golden

strands in his hair and emphasizing one side of his face. He *was* a bit like a Greek god, she decided, with those cheekbones and that strong chin. Pity he was spoken for.

'I do know that. I'm not stupid. Wasn't it Thoreau who said that the mass of men lead lives of quiet desperation?'

'I believe so. Perhaps they need to spend more time with plants. Anyway, I'm sorry. I didn't mean to imply that you were stupid.'

He sounded a little put out. Perhaps she had been sharper than intended.

'I'm well aware that you can't run away from your problems. They will follow you. I'm not just going to forget about Mark and our life together or my lost job opportunities. You don't work at something for a long time and then get over it in an instant.'

He didn't say anything and she wondered if she'd struck a nerve, but his face was inscrutable. In fact, she realised that her initial impression of him had been completely wrong. He may have acquired the art of appearing open and uncomplicated but in fact he was anything but and suddenly she was feeling needy and unsure of herself. When would this seesaw of emotions ever end?

'Sometimes a new start can help, can't it?' In her own mind she sounded as if she was almost begging.

He looked down at her.

'Yes, of course,' he replied, which should have enabled her to take a deeper breath except he didn't avert his gaze and she had the strangest inkling that he might be about to raise his hand and caress her cheek. She stood very still. She really, really didn't want that but her limbs felt so heavy that she was unable to move. At last, he looked away, over the garden towards the sea.

'Do you want to come in?' she asked, her voice small and floaty in the darkness. 'I could make coffee.'

He shook his head, and she felt a ridiculous surge of disappointment.

'Better not.'

Why not? she wondered. *Would Cressie be jealous?*

'About my gran,' he said. 'You don't have to. Cressie did sort of box you into a corner.'

'Why don't we leave it up to her?' Carrie said. 'Unless you'd rather I didn't visit.'

'Why would I think that?'

He sounded offended.

'Because I'm just a visitor and may never pass this way again, to quote a famous song.'

'Sometimes people we only meet once can make a great impression on us, though, can't they?'

'Sometimes, yes.'

'I think you might make quite an impression on my gran,' he said.

'In a good way, I hope.' She took his jacket from her shoulders. 'Thank you for this.'

He nodded.

'And for walking me back.'

'You're welcome.'

'I'm not sure I'd have felt' – she searched for the right words – 'so comfortable with Jack.'

His eyes glinted. 'And I'm not sure that I'd have been comfortable with that either.'

What did he mean by that? Did he actually want her company or, more likely, was it because he didn't trust Jack and he wanted to protect Cressie? She opened the gate, a shower of raindrops dancing across her face from the honeysuckle arch.

'Do you want to keep Wilbur?' he asked.

Carrie leaned down and fondled the dog's ears before standing to look up at the cottage.

'No. I'll be absolutely fine, but thanks anyway.'

'We'll pop by in the morning then to check you're okay.'

'You don't have to.'

'It would set my mind at rest.'

'In case the ghosts have caused havoc in the house?'

'I was thinking more about you than the house.'

And suddenly Carrie felt protected and cared for by someone in a way she hadn't for a long time.

'That's nice,' she said. 'Thank you.'

'And Carrie,' he said, as she fished her key out of her bag, 'I do hope that being here gives you what you need for your new start.'

He leaned down and brushed her cheek with a gentle kiss before turning briskly on his heel and disappearing into the darkness. And Carrie stood, looking up at the stars, annoyed at the way her skin tingled from the touch of his lips.

JOY

Eliza was beside herself with joy.

'Isaac! Isaac! Where are you?' she called, rushing up the stairs.

He emerged from the spare bedroom, his hands outstretched.

'What's the matter?' he asked, his face rippling with alarm. 'Is the house on fire?'

'Of course not,' Eliza scoffed, 'not with us here to protect it.'

She spun on the spot, her muslin dress spiralling around her ankles, and finished with a clap of her hands.

'Oh, Isaac, it's happened. He kissed her. I knew he would!' She pouted at little. 'It was only on the cheek but it's a start,' Eliza continued with a girlish laugh.

Isaac took her hands between his in an effort to hold her still.

'How do you know this, Eliza? Whereabouts were they when you saw this?'

'Why, just outside the front door. I was peeping out of the window, very discreetly, and looking at the moon and feeling a bit sad and trying to remember why when I saw them walking down the lane. Isn't it exciting?'

Isaac placed a finger to her lips.

'Shh! She'll hear you.'

'No, no, she's still outside, gazing at the stars, dreaming of Guy.'

'Except,' Isaac whispered, tilting his head to one side, 'I don't think she is.'

'Oh!' Eliza gasped. 'She's coming up the stairs. Quickly, Isaac, we must hide in case she sees us.'

'She's more likely to hear us than see us,' Isaac murmured, leading Eliza into the little front bedroom where they melted into the shadows.

Carrie had stopped at the top of the stairs and looked around. For one moment Isaac thought she would come through the door. Was she able to see them? More than likely not, but he couldn't take that risk. Some people were more sensitive than others, children in particular, although adults tended not to believe children and thought they were making things up. No, it was the adults to be wary of. They were unpredictable and could cause trouble for those who had not yet crossed over. The last thing Isaac wanted was trouble. There had been enough of that in the past. Carrie seemed like a nice person but... he tried not to think of the consequences. Sometimes he believed it would be for the best if they left this house, but Eliza must not be forced. She had to be ready, for both of their sakes.

He pulled Eliza close and shushed gently in her ear. She nodded in acquiescence and they melded back into the wall as Carrie hovered outside the room. How Isaac wished that they could permeate that wall and disappear completely but that was an art they had not yet perfected. Maybe with practice it would come – if they remained here for long enough. Carrie seemed to stand there for an age and Eliza found it difficult to be still or quiet for long. They'd be discovered, he was sure of it, and they'd be removed one way or another. No one wants to stay in a house with unexpected residents, so they'd have to go. His mind was in turmoil at the thought of Eliza's anguish if such a thing came to pass. And then he heard their guest's bare feet twist on the carpet and pad across the landing to her own room. Isaac closed his eyes for a moment and said a silent prayer of thanks before dropping a kiss on the top of Eliza's head and releasing his grip on her. The danger had passed – for now.

THIRTEEN

Carrie was sure she had heard the whispers as soon as she entered the cottage again, one high-pitched voice and another lower, but she couldn't make out what they were saying. She had paused at the bottom of the stairs and wondered briefly if there was someone living in the loft. She'd read about that, people living in the roof space without the owner's knowledge, or perhaps she'd seen it in a film? She couldn't remember and the whispering sounded joyful, not threatening or claustrophobic. The waft of air that streamed down the stairs and wrapped itself around her felt as if it, too, was speckled with joy.

She had followed it up to the spare room, but something stopped her from pushing the door fully open. Instead, she stood outside and listened. She wondered whether to say something like 'It's okay, I won't harm you' or 'There's nothing to be afraid of' but it felt so ridiculous and fanciful. Maybe she just wanted there to be something or someone here protecting her. Maybe it was all a figment of her imagination and all that stuff Jack had said was just attention seeking.

Guy didn't seem like the type to make things up, although

he'd probably made that up about having brotherly feelings towards Cressie. How dare he kiss her! At least he hadn't gone for the lips. Maybe he was a smooth mover. Maybe that would be next time. Maybe he wasn't a one-woman person. Maybe, maybe, maybe... *Maybe, Carrie,* she said to herself, *you ought to go to bed and give your head a rest.*

By the time Carrie finally got into bed she was convinced that all the lavender scented sheets and hot chocolate in the world wouldn't send her to sleep. Her limbs were tired, but her mind was still in overdrive, shining a torch beam on her emotions.

'It was just a friendly kiss,' she said to herself, as she slid under the duvet. 'No need to get all worked up about it. Even if he was trying it on, you can handle that because you don't want it to be anything more. No more men for a long time. Men mean complications and you've got enough of those without adding to them.'

She plumped her pillows and tossed and turned. She counted enough sheep to populate the entirety of the Isle of Wight. She switched on the lamp and started a new book. She crossed her legs, sat up as straight as possible and tried to meditate, but started to think about Mark and Paloma's baby and the baby she had wanted. She returned to the sheep. She would have to move on to Welsh sheep. There were bound to be more of them or New Zealand sheep; about twenty-five million of those, her brother had said, five sheep to every person. She wondered how long it would take her to count to twenty-five million – days, weeks, months? The sheep turned into Labradors, hurtling over hedges and then mountains or distressingly off cliffs. Nothing worked. Sleep wouldn't come. In the end she just lay there waiting for her spinning mind to wear itself out, which eventually it did, not long before dawn.

She slept in late and had breakfast in the kitchen, a bowl of porridge with some blueberries and a selection of seeds.

Tomorrow she would have to go shopping. She couldn't believe how much food she had got through and that was with Rita dropping the odd thing around. She'd expected Guy at around eleven o'clock so made sure that she was dressed and showered. It was nice having the extra time to look after herself, to leave her hair conditioner in for a little longer and moisturise all of her body instead of just the bits which felt dry and scratchy. By twelve o'clock he hadn't arrived, and Carrie couldn't settle to anything. She wandered through the cottage, studying the paintings and slightly rearranging the ornaments. Some of the flowers were starting to wilt so she refreshed the water and primped the ones that had a few more days of blooming left. The church clock struck quarter past twelve. He wasn't coming. Why should he? He had better things to do on a Sunday than check up on her although he seemed like a man of his word. He'd probably just forgotten, and she didn't blame him. In a week she would be gone, and he would forget all about her and she would forget all about him. In time. Maybe she would keep in touch with Cressie and hear what he was doing through her. Maybe that was all some fantasy and as soon as she got back to real life everything would go back to how it was before, except she would be looking for a new job and taking up all sorts of weird and wonderful hobbies to take her mind off things on the date of Mark and Paloma's wedding and then the birth of their baby. They were going to be hard days to get through.

'Carrie!'

She jumped and looked behind her. A very frazzled looking Guy was standing in the doorway.

'I knocked but you obviously didn't hear so I came around the back.'

'Oh, sorry. I was just thinking about leaving here and going back to Manchester and...' She pulled a face.

'But you've still got nearly a week left.'

She nodded. 'I know but it doesn't feel enough.'

Was it her imagination or did he look slightly relieved?

'What have you done with Wilbur?' she asked, when the dog didn't edge past him and come to sit at her side.

'I've left him with my gran who, against all advice, has discharged herself. That's why I'm late. I got a call from the nursing home saying that she was on her phone booking a taxi, so I went to try and persuade her to stay for a few days longer but fat chance of that. She was waiting in the foyer with her case packed and a "don't mess with me" expression on her face. All I could do was drive her home and settle her in.'

He leaned against the door frame, as if needing the support.

'I've made her a sandwich and then she's going to have a rest, so I wondered if you fancied lunch? There's a really good pub just down the road. It gets busy at the weekends, but I know the chap who works behind the bar and he owes me a few favours. He'll squeeze us in somewhere.'

Us, that sounded good. She missed being part of an 'us'.

'I'm not the best company. I didn't sleep that well and the thought of going home and facing up to everything has made me feel pathetically sorry for myself all over again.'

'Is that a no then?'

Carrie pursed her lips. 'It's a warning. I won't be offended if you want to withdraw the offer.'

Please don't. I really don't want to be left with just my own company today but it's not fair to inflict it on anyone else either.

He grinned and threw up his hands and he looked boyishly attractive as the change in his expression dissolved the strain from his face.

'Hey, I'm a sucker for punishment and I could do with a bit of distraction, too.'

'You could seriously regret this.'

'I'm willing to take the risk.'

She smiled. *He had that ability,* she thought, *to make her smile even when she didn't really want to. And smiling made you feel better. All of the surveys said that: if you're feeling down just smile. It does something to your endorphins.* Already her endorphins were stretching upwards ready to balance on their toes and do a little twirl.

'On your head be it,' she called over her shoulder, as she went to fetch her bag and coat.

Guy turned the Land Rover carefully into the gravel carpark. The pub had diamond-paned windows with the occasional inset of green coloured glass. He jumped out and skirted around the front of the car to open the passenger door. He looked as if he was about to extend his hand to help her down but then thought better of it.

'Can you manage? It's a bit steep.'

'I'm fine, thanks,' she said, making a little leap to the ground.

'When it's warmer you can get a table outside and watch the sky constantly change over the sea,' he said, 'but it's still a bit chilly for that today. Only another few weeks, though, and the weather will be a bit more settled. With any luck Wilbur and I will be sitting over there sharing a pint of beer after work and pondering the meaning of life.'

'Sounds idyllic,' she said. 'I've no idea what I'll be doing in another few weeks. Probably waiting on tables from dawn until dusk in order to try and make some money to pay the rent.'

Inside the pub was dark but cosy with low beams and wooden pews strewn with brightly coloured cushions. It was busy but not overly so. At the far end of the long room a log fire glowed in the grate.

Guy turned to the man behind the bar and exchanged a few words of banter before asking Carrie what she'd like to drink.

'Dry rosé, please,' she replied.

'And a pint of the usual for me, Jay.'

'You here on holiday?' Jay asked, reaching below the counter for a wine glass.

'Yes,' Carrie replied, wondering how he could tell she wasn't local. Maybe it was a sixth sense or maybe she was dressed in a touristy way. She resisted the temptation to examine her dark jeans and suede jacket for any signs of Isle of Wight non-conformity, not that she thought she'd have been able to spot it anyway.

'Visited the island before?'

'Mmm, when I was eighteen months old apparently with my grandparents, so I don't remember anything about it. It's beautiful, though. Can't believe what I've been missing.'

He placed a glass of blush pink rosé in front of her and began to pull Guy's pint of local ale.

'Where are you staying?'

'In the next village.'

'Ah, Hideaway Cottage, I presume,' he said, raising his eyebrows slightly.

'Yes, I'm surprised you didn't know. Everyone else seems to!'

'They're nosier than I am,' Jay said.

'Or just more on the ball,' Guy joshed, leaning over the bar and punching Jay lightly on the arm. 'You're not so busy today.'

'School holidays have just finished and the tourist season's not fully under way. You just can't tell at this time of year. Sometimes we're so busy we don't know what to do with ourselves but at other times it can be just steady.'

He rang up the till and Carrie reached for her purse.

'First round is mine,' Guy said, picking up the tray where Jay had placed both drinks together with a small bowl of black and green olives and leading the way towards the fire. 'Mind the step.'

With his free hand he caught hold of her elbow and Carrie's heart did a little flip. Ridiculous but amazing. Life affirming even. It had been so long since she'd felt any attraction for anyone. Except she wasn't attracted to him. He really wasn't her type. Far too earthy. If she'd been unattached for the last few years she'd definitely have gone for the clean-cut types like Mark. It must be the sea air, or just pure sexual frustration! Guy gestured her to a seat on one of the deep leather sofas. She was partly relieved and partly disappointed when he didn't sit next to her but skirted the table and lowered himself on to the opposite seat before placing his phone on the table.

'Sorry about that,' he said. 'Normally I hate people who have their phone next to them while holding a conversation but...'

'You don't have to apologise. I'm just surprised you can get a signal. My network won't seem to work in many places here.'

'I've got Gran using WhatsApp. It's been the best thing and there's a Wi-Fi signal here so if she needs me, I'll know.'

'You're obviously very close.'

'I'd probably be completely off the rails without her.'

'I can't believe that.'

He took a sip of his beer and leaned back. 'I'd have thought you'd know all about my past from Heather.'

Carrie felt herself blushing the same colour as the rose. 'I wasn't...'

'It's okay,' he said. 'You don't have to apologise. Heather can't resist giving a running commentary on other people's lives.'

'All I know is that your father died and you were sent to boarding school.'

'Dad was in the RAF and died in a flying accident when I was five. Mum remarried less than a year later, and I didn't take to Colin from the start. It was mutual so I was packed off to boarding school just before I was seven. I admit to not being an easy child and it got worse after Mum and Colin had children of their own. I love my half-sisters, but my stepfather made it crystal clear where I came in the pecking order, so I stayed with Gran in the holidays more and more. Then, when I was eleven, they decided to move to Spain. I knew that Colin would resent paying the plane fares, so I was happy to stay with Gran most of the time. Mum didn't exactly put up a fight. I think she was just relieved to have a less stressful life.'

'Do you remember your father?'

'Not much and I'm not sure whether those memories are true or collaged from things people have told me. Gran's got loads of photos and of course she's talked about him a lot, so she's done her best to keep him a part of our lives. I do feel as if I know him a little.'

'And what about your grandfather?'

'Gran's husband left when she was pregnant with my dad so she brought him up singlehandedly. Mum's parents lived in Tenerife, which meant I never got to know them that well.'

'I had six grandparents when I was born,' Carrie said, 'two great-grandmas and two sets of grandparents. I was lucky but there's always one you're closer to than the others.'

He frowned and stared into his glass. 'I just can't imagine her not being around.'

Carrie leaned forwards. 'Is she that ill?'

He looked up. 'No, no. It's not cancer or anything awful like that. She picked up a virus after Christmas and just couldn't shake it off. It turned into pneumonia. She'd always seemed so strong and capable but at that age you can go downhill really quickly. She's been in hospital three times. The hospital called me in once and I thought...'

He took a gulp of his beer.

'Anyway, she's a fighter and now she definitely seems to be on the mend. In one way it's a good sign that she's discharged herself, but I'll need to try and take a bit more time off next week so that I can keep a close eye on her. My other worry is that she'll try to drive again before she's ready. I might have to hide the car keys, or she'll be off causing havoc on the island's roads.'

'Can you get someone in to look after her?'

'Ha! I wouldn't even dare suggest it. I know exactly what reaction I'd get. If the worst comes to the worst, I can pop back at lunchtime and surreptitiously check on her.'

'Well, I'm around and at a loose end,' Carrie said.

He looked at her appreciatively. 'You're meant to be on holiday. You've already helped me out in the gardens. I'm not going to steal any more of your time. Besides, knowing Gran, she'd get completely the wrong idea, put two and two together and make five.'

'Oh!'

'I'd have to make it abundantly clear that you were just a friend. She's desperate to marry me off.' He smiled at her. 'And I'm sure the last thing you want at the moment is to be match-made.'

'Oh, absolutely,' Carrie managed to say. 'No offence but I'm off men for the foreseeable future.'

'No offence taken. When my ex left me, I felt exactly the same about women.' He raised his glass in her direction. 'Here's to friendship. It's much less complicated. On the whole good friends don't let you down.'

Carrie clinked her glass against his. He was right, of course. Friendship was what she needed more than anything else. At least she knew where she stood. He obviously didn't want anything more, not that she'd ever really thought that he had. It was just that kiss which had played on her mind and the thought that if she'd moved her face slightly it wouldn't have been her cheek he'd made contact with. And then there were the daisies. In all the time they'd been together Mark had never floated daisies in a mug for her. He'd not even got around to buying her a ring when they got engaged. She settled back into the sofa and looked around at the other tables; people laughing and chatting, eating and drinking together, sharing moments from their lives. It made her feel a part of something bigger. Something good.

'This is so nice. Thank you. I'm sorry I was a bit grumpy when you arrived.'

'Everyone feels like that from time to time.'

'I've been like it too much over the last few months.'

'Sounds as if you've had good reason.'

He leaned back and gazed at her. She sipped at her wine. It was fruity and delicious, the glow from the flames enriching its colour.

'On top of everything my ex has just got engaged.'

'Ah!'

He sounded genuinely surprised, and she felt profoundly grateful to Cressie for not indulging in any pillow talk.

'I should hate him enough not to mind, but I do. He's taken the job which should have been mine, found romantic bliss with Perfect Paloma, made me feel like a complete failure and...' She bit her lip and looked over his shoulder through the window to where the trees were bursting into leaf. '...and they're having a baby.'

He was quiet. She threw him an apologetic smile.

'Sorry.'

'No need to apologise. That's an awful lot of stuff to have to deal with. No wonder you needed to get away.'

Guy pushed the bowl of olives towards her and she took one, savouring its saltiness.

'He swears that nothing happened between him and Paloma before we separated but I'm not sure he's telling the truth. I just keep going over and over things, whether I could have done anything differently, whether I'm to blame for everything.'

'A few months is no time at all to get over someone, especially not if you've loved them for a long time.'

'We'd been together since uni. We were barely grown-ups. I think the trouble is Mark still hasn't grown up.'

'Some people never do.'

'Jack?'

He placed a hand to his mouth and massaged his bottom lip. He had perfect lips, she thought, just the right depth and width. She could imagine kissing them which was totally inappropriate, and Cressie had obviously got there first. Not that it should matter but somehow it did.

'It can take a long time to fall out of love with someone,' he mused, totally ignoring her effort to change the conversation.

A log fell forwards in the grate and they both turned to watch the skittering of sparks on the hearth.

'I suppose that's what I'm afraid of,' she said, 'that a little bit of me will always be in love with Mark and because of that I won't be able to move on.' She leaned forwards and reached for another olive. 'How strange that I've only just realised that.'

'If you don't mind my saying, he doesn't sound the sort of person that's worthy of staying in love with.'

If Jules or her mother had said that, she'd have leapt to Mark's defence but not this time.

'You're right!' She laughed. 'Oh, my goodness! I'm actually annoyed with myself for still being a little bit in love with him, for hoping that his whole relationship with Paloma will implode and he'll come running back to me. It makes me sound like some desperate Victorian spinster, not a modern, independent, twenty-first-century woman.'

'Except she wouldn't have been annoyed with herself,' he said with a grin. 'Annoyance is good!'

'Denial, anger... What are the five stages of grief?'

'Denial, anger, bargaining, depression and acceptance but I don't think everyone necessarily experiences them in that order.'

'I'd like to get to acceptance. It sounds so freeing. What

about you?' she asked, looking up at him from beneath her eyelashes. 'Have you reached acceptance?'

'There's still a bit of anger there, too.' He threw her a rueful smile. 'I never have quite fitted the mould.'

'Me neither,' Carrie said. 'I've tried for the sake of my parents really. But I don't know how much longer I can follow their dreams rather than my own. To be honest, I don't even know what mine are.'

'I joined the RAF because of my dad. Wanted to follow in his footsteps, to do something that would have made him really proud, but it didn't take long to realise it wasn't for me. Then I went to work for a commercial airline but that was mainly because I refused to accept that all those years of training were for nothing. I spent quite a long time going in the wrong direction.'

'But now you have your plants,' Carrie said.

His eyes shone. 'Gran says I love plants more than most people.'

'So there's never been a Mrs... do you know, I don't even know your surname.'

'Simmonds, and no, there's never been one. I was close at one point but now, looking back, I realise I had a lucky escape.'

And as he picked up a menu from the table and handed it to her Carrie sensed that the subject was firmly closed.

'Will I see you tomorrow?' Guy asked, as he dropped Carrie off outside the cottage.

'Probably not,' she replied and wondered for a second if he looked a bit disappointed. 'Cressie's asked me to go to the Pottery Barn with her. Apparently, the coffee and cake is good there and Jack's heading off first thing in the morning so she wanted some distraction. Then I need to do a bit of food shopping, but I can come on Tuesday if that's okay?'

'It's voluntary, remember. You can come when you like.'

'Tuesday then,' she said. 'It will give my back time to recover.'

'Not if you're lifting those twins.'

'True. Especially Freddie. He's a solid lump of a baby.'

'Gorgeous, though,' Guy said, and she instantly knew how good he would be with children.

'Yes, absolutely gorgeous.'

'You've got plenty of time, you know.'

She turned to look at him.

'For children.'

She smiled gratefully. 'Thank you. I hope so.'

They sat for a moment and Carrie didn't want to get out of the Land Rover. She felt safe in here as if the outside world couldn't intrude with all of its pressures and problems. But he had better things to do than sit here with her.

'Thank you for taking me out for lunch,' she said. 'I had a really nice time.'

'Me too.'

There was so much more she felt she wanted to say but it was all jumbled up inside her and she didn't know exactly what it was.

'Tuesday then,' he said, and all of a sudden, she wanted to kiss him.

He leaned over to open the door.

'The handle's a bit dodgy,' he explained.

He was so close. If she leaned forwards slightly, she could kiss him on the cheek and then he would turn his head towards her and...

A blast of sea air brought her to her senses as the door was flung open and he was already sitting upright again in his own seat, leaning slightly away from her and towards the driver's window.

'Tuesday,' she confirmed, before hopping down onto the road and slamming the door shut again.

He waved as he pulled away and she stood, watching him drive up the narrow lane until he was out of sight. Opening the gate to the garden she smiled. She hadn't wanted to kiss anyone for ages, expect for Mark. Jules would definitely say that she was making progress. And progress felt liberating.

FOURTEEN

Carrie left the Pottery Barn feeling completely churned up. Cressie was right about the coffee and cake, and the pottery was beautifully tactile. They'd found a picnic table in a sheltered corner outside and Cressie had parked the double buggy while Carrie went inside to place their order. They'd sat for quite a while chatting while the twins both slept. *It was amazing,* Carrie thought, *how sometimes you met people and just hit it off straight away, felt completely on the same wavelength and at ease.* Normally she wouldn't pick up someone else's baby without asking but she knew Cressie wouldn't mind. As soon as Olivia woke and looked as if she was going to demand immediate attention, Carrie lifted her out of the buggy and sat her on her knee, delighting in her squeals as she was bounced up and down. *What if I'm never able to do this with my own children?* she thought. *What if it never happens? How will I make my peace with that?*

'She loves you,' Cressie said.

'It's like you said, it's because I'm someone different.'

'And you're a natural,' Cressie said. 'She senses that. I wish I was.'

'But you are,' Carrie said, leaning forwards. 'You're doing a fantastic job.'

Cressie pulled her sunglasses down from the top of her head even though the sun wasn't in her eyes. She let her hair fall partly across her face.

'I need to tell someone this, and I don't know who else to confide in because they'll think so badly of me. You'll think so badly of me.'

Carrie was silent. She stopped bouncing Olivia and the baby's mouth formed a rounded shape of imminent protest. She stood her up so that Olivia could look over her shoulder at the hanging basket full of orange pansies. *Don't tell me*, she willed Cressie. *I don't need to know for sure about you and Guy.* She tried to control her face so that it wouldn't register shock or disapproval or even disappointment. She was going to fail but at least she could try.

'The thing is...' Cressie began.

She swallowed hard and bit her lip so hard that Carrie thought she might draw blood.

'The thing is...'

Cressie's voice had dropped to barely a whisper. Her following words could so easily be lost on the breeze. Carrie hoped they would be, that she could pretend not to hear them.

'...I don't love Olivia.'

Cressie let out a large sob.

'There, I've said it out loud,' she said in a strangled voice. 'It's the most terrible thing but I don't love my baby.'

Carrie sat very still as Olivia played with her hair. She could feel the warmth of chubby, little hands against her neck, feel the baby's heart beating against her chest. Instinctively, she reached her free hand up to cradle Olivia's crown as if to protect her from the impact. So it wasn't about Guy after all, not yet anyway. Maybe that confession would come later.

'I'm a wicked person, aren't I?' Cressie said. 'There must be something wrong with me.'

'No, no, you're not wicked at all,' Carrie said. 'And there's nothing wrong with you. My friend Jules is a midwife, and she says that some mothers take a while to bond with their babies.'

'But not months.'

'Longer than that sometimes.'

'She knows,' Cressie said, looking at Olivia. 'She knows that I'm just going through the motions with her, that sometimes I wish she wasn't here, that I'd just got Freddie. It's as if all the love I've got goes to him and there's nothing left over for her.'

Tears slid down from beneath Cressie's sunglasses.

'What am I doing to her, Carrie? What damage am I inflicting on her, maybe for life?'

'Feeling guilty isn't going to help either of you. Does Jack know how you feel?'

She shook her head. 'Not really. He just says I need to be more patient with her. She's a daddy's girl. Whenever he's around she seems much calmer. He doesn't see the worst of it. Guy knows I'm not coping very well. He thinks I should get some help but that feels like admitting failure and all our money is tied up in the house so I can't afford to indulge myself.'

'Cressie, it isn't indulging yourself. You need to talk to someone, your doctor, your health visitor.'

'I'm scared, Carrie. What if they think I'm a bad mother? What if they take Olivia away? What if they take both of the twins away? Jack would never forgive me. I would never forgive myself.'

'Would you like to talk to Jules? That might help.'

Cressie's lower lip trembled. 'Do you think she could find the time?'

'Jules is the sort of person who finds the time for everyone.'

'Then yes, yes please. I feel so guilty. It's not normal. I'm not normal.'

Carrie reached out and clasped Cressie's shoulder. 'The first thing you need to do is stop putting so much pressure on yourself. We'll sort this out. I promise. I'll send her a message right now.'

Carrie leaned over to pat the carefully wrapped jug which was on the passenger seat beside her. The greeny-blue colour would remind her of the sea around the Isle of Wight and the exquisite glaze would lift her on the bleakest of Manchester days. She had felt guilty leaving Cressie to go home alone but she'd promised to call in later when she heard back from Jules. Manchester seemed such a long way away and her job at Winterson's already felt like a different life, as if she had been living a dream.

She remembered her granny talking about the family having to move out of their rented house when she was sixteen and thinking it was the worst thing in the world. But Granny had said it turned out to be one of the best things that happened to her. Carrie smiled. If Granny were here now, she'd be telling Carrie that story and focusing on all the positives. Granny had been quite an accomplished watercolour artist, and she'd always encouraged Carrie and Charlie to be creative. *Perhaps I'll book myself into a class when I get back*, Carrie thought. Perhaps she could even come back here and try her hand at pottery. She could enrol in one of the workshops at the Pottery Barn and check in on Cressie at the same time. Perhaps she wouldn't even stay in Manchester long term. There was a whole world of possibilities out there.

In the village shop she was just reaching for a truss of enticingly red-ripe, locally grown tomatoes and wondering whether to retrain as a nutritionist or a dietician or a yoga teacher, when her phone pinged. Only a matter of days ago she'd have put the fruit on hold, unable to resist the urge to check the message. In fact, thinking about it she'd have put virtually everything on hold. She straightened, focused on the firmness of the tiles beneath her feet, the little hairs on the tomato stems prickling her skin, the breeze coming through the open door and caressing the back of her neck. *It's probably Jules and she'll still be there in a couple of minutes. The world won't fall apart if you don't respond this instant.*

All the same, it was harder than it should have been to pluck a brown paper bag from its hook and place the tomatoes carefully inside before depositing her purchase in the wire basket at her feet. But the small act of resistance gave her a surge of pride. Until she came here, she'd never truly realised how addicted to her phone she was, how it sapped her time and her energy, each ping sending her brain into high alert in case it was an emergency.

Gently she touched her fingers against the back pocket of her jeans and carried on browsing the aisles unhurriedly before waiting patiently in the small queue. It felt good to unfold notes from her purse and sort out the change. That was something else she had resolved to do while she was here – to use cash – to be totally in control of what she spent instead of just swiping a card, sometimes barely looking at the total to confirm that it was correct. She couldn't afford to be blasé with money now, not that she ever really had been able to, but a coffee here, a magazine there, a sandwich for lunch from the swanky deli down the road from the office – it all added up to an eye-wateringly wasteful amount at the end of the month and that was even before she considered the larger items she put on her credit card. If she was honest, some weeks she had no idea how much she was spending, just a vague unease that it must be too much. If she wasn't going to have a job when she first went back to Manchester, she'd have to be more frugal. In a strange way it was almost appealing, the paring back, the simplifying, the taking away of pressure to have things.

'We've just had these in this morning,' the lady behind the counter said, as she weighed the tomatoes.

'They look delicious.'

'I can confirm that.' She chuckled. 'I had one with a bit of cheese for my lunch and one of those bread rolls over there. All local. We've got to support each other especially when times are hard, haven't we?'

'It's a wonderful shop,' Carrie said.

The woman beamed.

'Thank you. It's been a real labour of love, and you never quite know when you move into an area how things are going to go, but everyone has been amazing.'

'So, you're not from the island?'

'Goodness no, can't you tell from the accent?'

Carrie shook her head. 'I'm rubbish with accents. Sorry.'

'From the Midlands. Came here on holiday a couple of years ago and that was that. Completely fell in love with the place and here we are.'

'Did you have family here?'

'No, didn't know a soul.'

'That's a big move.'

The woman straightened a small stack of brandy snap boxes to the right of the till. 'They say that it's the things you don't do which you regret, don't they? And sometimes you have to be brave and make the leap? Something or someone can give you a nudge that you're not living your best life and we're only here once, aren't we?'

'I suppose so,' Carrie said, picking up her canvas bag.

'And apart from death and taxes, nothing's a certainty, is it? Can't remember who actually said that...' She paused, looking up at the ceiling as if for inspiration.

'Benjamin Franklin,' Carrie offered.

'That's him. Thank you. Well, as I said to my youngest daughter when she was playing up about coming here, nothing's certain. It might work out. It might not. But we've at least got to give it a try.' The woman shrugged. 'She's still not happy, though. Talking about returning to the mainland and living with her sisters as soon as she can.'

'How old is she?'

'Fourteen. She's left all her friends behind and it's not always easy to make new ones. At least, she's never found it easy.'

'Hopefully she'll settle.'

'Maybe. Her younger brother's fine about the move. Loves it over here. The older two were happy for us to come, too. "Go for it, Mum," they said, but they're in their twenties and they've got their own lives now. Sometimes you have to put yourself first, don't you? At fourteen you don't understand that us oldies have dreams, too. Not that I'm bracketing you with me,' she said, laughing apologetically, 'you're nowhere near an oldie. I'm past fifty and my husband's a bit older. If we hadn't made the change now, it would have been too late, and he would probably have had a heart attack from stress and all the travelling he had to do. Look at him now, bless him.' She cast her gaze outside where a portly man was whistling under his breath as he rearranged some trays of pansies. 'Happy as Larry, he is.'

She leaned towards Carrie.

'I had to make a choice, you see, my daughter's happiness or my husband's health.'

'That can't have been easy.'

The woman's eyes widened. 'I don't doubt that I made the right decision. I still have a husband, and Summer might come around but if she doesn't – well, it's a small world these days. We can still visit wherever she is. It's about priorities, isn't it? Trouble with me is I spent too long just muddling through.'

Carrie's phone rang this time and suddenly she felt on edge. What if something was wrong? She gazed apologetically at the woman.

'I'm so sorry but I ought to get that. It might be urgent.'

The woman smiled. 'It's been nice chatting. That's something we have time for here, having a chat. Hope to see you again. Next time you can tell me all about you.'

'You might need to close the shop for that,' Carrie said with a laugh, her free hand already reaching into her back pocket.

Carrie's heart jumped as she saw the name lit up on the screen. Mark. What did he want? Her hand was actually shaking as she waved a thank you to the woman and walked out into the sunshine. Should she answer? Yes. No. What harm could it do?

'Hello.'

'Carrie?'

'Yes. Mark, can you give me a minute? I just need to open the car.'

'Do you want to call me back?'

'No, no. It'll only take a second or two.'

She placed the bag of shopping on the passenger seat before sliding behind the wheel and checking her reflection in the rear-view mirror. Stupid. It wasn't as if he could see what she looked like, more's the pity. Her skin was clear, almost luminous from the good food, the rest and being outside, her hair for once in her life was behaving and she looked... how did she look exactly? Despite the churning emotions, she looked put-together, as if she could handle anything. Carrie leaned her full weight back against the car seat and licked her lips.

'Okay. I can talk now.'

There was a pause.

'Mark? Are you still there?'

'Yes.'

She had a sudden sense of foreboding.

'Is everything okay? Is there a problem at work? Apart from me, I mean. I realise I'm a *major* problem.'

'No, everything's fine.'

'Oh, good.'

'Do you mean that?

'Yes.'

'I wouldn't if I were in your shoes considering everything.'

'I'm wearing some new pink plimsoles,' she said, flexing her toes, 'and they're making me feel very benevolent towards the world.'

'They sound nice.'

'They are.'

'You're a good person, Carrie.'

She felt a little glow deep inside her. *So why didn't you come back to me? Why did you go off with Paloma?*

She took a deep breath. 'Is your back okay?'

'Fine.'

She felt her shoulders drop and closed her eyes briefly.

'Thank goodness. I really didn't mean to chuck that champagne glass. It just flew out of my fingers.'

'I know that.'

'But Paloma thinks I did it deliberately.'

'She doesn't know you as well as I do.' He paused again. 'I wanted to check that you're all right.'

After more than a week! On the very first day here I could have walked into the sea, my pockets weighted with stones like poor Virgina Woolf. Actually, I could have thrown myself under a tram back in Manchester and you're checking up NOW?!

'I was, until you called. Now I'm not so sure. Have you called to tell me I'm losing my job?'

Unconsciously she had started chewing on her nails again. Slowly, deliberately, she removed her left hand from between her teeth and placed it under her buttock.

'No.'

'Oh! Okay. Well, that's a surprise. I was convinced I would be.'

'Can I come and see you?'

He blurted the words out so quickly she almost wondered if she'd misheard.

'I'm not at home, Mark.'

'I know. I've got an appointment in Southampton tomorrow. I thought I could get the ferry over and we could meet up.'

She let the words sink in.

'You know where I am?'

'Yes.'

Carrie moved the phone away from her ear and stared down the winding main street, at the chocolate box cottages with their pretty front gardens, seagulls meandering in the sky above. This island had become her sanctuary. Did she really want him here potentially spoiling everything?

'Carrie, Carrie, are you still there?'

'Did Beth tell you? Did you twist her arm? That's really unfair. Just because you're a partner now...'

'Hang on a minute. You obviously have a pretty low opinion of me, and perhaps that's justified...'

'Perhaps? Did you really say perhaps?'

He sighed at the end of the line. 'I didn't coerce her at all. I saw the landline number on her pad and tracked the area code down. I guessed it must be for you. Then this appointment came up and I thought it would be a good opportunity to clear the air away from everyone and everything.'

'I gave that number to her for emergencies because my phone doesn't work where I'm staying. I didn't think it would be used so you could stalk me.'

'I'm not stalking you. I just want to chat, to check you're managing.'

'You're lucky to get hold of me. There's barely any signal here.'

'Bet that's frustrating for you.'

She bristled at his tone. As if he knew her inside and out. Well, not anymore.

'Actually, no.'

'If I hadn't got through, I'd have tried the landline later.'

'That definitely sounds stalkerish.'

He sighed, a long, deep exhale. She'd forgotten how good he was at sighing. Could have auditioned for the RSC on his sighs alone.

'Look, if you don't want to see me that's fine,' he said, sounding hurt. 'I understand but there's something important I need to talk to you about.'

'What?'

'It would be better face to face.'

'Why?'

'Because some things are.'

'Difficult things, you mean. Things I won't want to hear.'

She frowned. That wasn't like Mark. If it was a difficult conversation, he was much more likely to avoid it altogether let alone meet up to chew things over.

'Because I still care about you, Carrie, and I really want to see you.'

He said it with tenderness, as if he really did mean it, and she felt herself softening. Just the two of them, on their own, talking. It could be cathartic.

'Okay.'

'Really? Are you sure?' He sounded gratifyingly pleased.

'No, so don't push it.'

'Where do you want to meet? Shall I come to where you're staying?'

'Definitely not. I'll meet you somewhere near the ferry port. I'll have to ask around and then I'll message you.'

'I should be able to get over by early afternoon. Message me in the morning if that's okay.'

'So Paloma doesn't find out?'

'Better if she doesn't. I don't want to upset her.'

'Or she might not let you come.'

'She wouldn't be happy, and you can't blame her.'

Actually, Mark, Carrie thought, *I can blame her in a heart-beat. I can blame her for the total mess my life is in right now.* But she bit her lip because instinctively she knew that this had to happen. If she was to move on, then they had to meet and better here than back in Manchester where it had all gone so horribly wrong.

Rita had recommended the cafe in Bembridge, and it was homely. Just what Carrie needed. She hadn't wanted any of those stark or echoey places which Mark favoured. She'd taken ages to get ready: washing her hair, bracing herself for a final ice-cold rinse to make it shine followed by subtle but carefully applied make-up. Finally, she selected her dark jeans, the ones which Mark had always complimented her on and said made her bum look really pert, together with a white t-shirt spotted with little blue hearts. But then she'd thought he might miscon-strue the hearts, so she'd changed it for one with little pink and caramel coloured ice creams on an ivory background. The ivory was more flattering for her skin, which had caught the sun.

It isn't about him, she said to herself. It was about her although it wouldn't do any harm to remind him of what he was missing – her at her best. Looking in the full-length mirror Carrie knew she looked good. And if she looked good, she felt good. Or at least as good as she could under the circumstances.

She was determined to get there early to compose herself. Only a couple of days ago in the *Island Life* magazine she'd read that one of the best ways to eliminate stress was to get every-where early. She'd planned to do that on the fateful Thursday. Today she was going to allow for total mayhem; roadworks, several flocks of sheep or a boat on a broken-down trailer blocking her route, or maybe all three. She had plenty of time. She was in control so there was no reason for her shoulders to be up near her ear lobes or for her ribs to be locked. She stretched, shook herself a little to release from the automatic brace posture which had become part of her previous life. That was better. Now she looked taller, and she was almost ready for whatever Mark had to say.

The clock had a scornful tick. This meeting was a huge mistake, she could see that now. The nerves which had woken her in the night and done their best to stop her eating what Jules would call 'a proper breakfast' were back in a big way. If she wasn't losing her job, what *did* he want to tell her? Perhaps he'd spoken to Ian and suggested that she was made a partner as well, if not now in a few months' time, or perhaps he was standing aside, overcome with guilt because he knew the job should have been hers in the first place.

'You're such a romantic, Carrie, always thinking there's a happy ever after,' she scoffed under her breath. 'Not with Mark. No way. And surely not with the job. But what if...? Could she be that shallow to allow herself to be treated so badly and just forget about it in the interests of advancement? Was being a partner at Winterson's really that important? Wouldn't she despise herself for ever if she caved? Catching sight of herself in the glass frontage, she looked so much less sure of herself than barely an hour ago. She definitely wasn't in the right frame of mind to talk things over with Mark. *Get up and leave. But he's come all this way. He's on the ferry and it's on time. He'll be here any minute. You owe it to him to stay and see it through.* Except she didn't owe him anything. She picked up her bag from the neighbouring chair. But it was too late. There he was walking past the window and pushing open the door, his eyes skimming the tables before spotting her.

'Carrie!'

The cinnamon and cream patterned shirt was obviously Paloma's choice, but it suited him, perfectly matching his pale suede brogues with tan laces. The chinos and navy jacket were obviously new, too, and he'd had his hair cut, changing his parting which emphasised his eyes. There was no sign of the bad back that she'd envisaged. Slowly Carrie uncurled her fingers from the handles of her bag and half stood up. She'd thought it all through, how she would behave and how she would look, glowingly independent obviously, as if what he said didn't matter one way or the other. All she had to do was put her mental rehearsals into practice and remember that there were other jobs out there and other men.

Good thing Jules didn't know about this meeting. She hadn't dared tell her when they'd finally spoken last night. The reaction would have been apoplectic. Fortunately, Jules was going out to a newly opened sushi restaurant, so the conversation was pretty brief, ending with a promise to call Cressie the following morning. *Jules would have been right to tell her not to go ahead*, Carrie thought. Seeing Mark here, in what should be her territory, had completely thrown her but she mustn't let him know that.

'Hello, Mark.'

All the breath felt as if it had left her body as he leaned slowly forward with the intention of kissing her. He never, ever kissed her anymore. There wasn't even any bodily contact if it could be avoided, unless they were pressed too close together in a lift or brushed arms when going through a door. Taken by surprise, she allowed his lips to brush her cheek and despised herself. Instantly she felt her skin flare. He smelt good. It was a different aftershave to his usual one but citrussy and very appealing. *Please don't let it be obvious that I'm blushing. Smile. Lower your head. Sit down.* She wriggled on the chair. *Another failure. No wriggling. Sit calmly and securely.* The chair creaked ominously. *What if it collapses?* She had a vision of herself squirming on the floor beneath the table as he helped her up, but maybe that would be a good thing; maybe he'd think she was injured this time and realise how he still felt about her...

No, she didn't want that. She was beyond that. That was just her ego talking but hang on, he was saying something, and she had to pay attention.

'This is nice,' he said, looking around, 'in a retro sort of way.'

She sensed him quickly assessing how he would 'improve' it before turning his attention back to her.

'And you look...' He studied her face which she was sure was an unattractive puce colour. '...well. Really well.'

Ha, she thought. What did you expect? That I'd run away with my tail between my legs, and you'd find me a satisfyingly threadbare version of my previous self? She unclenched her hands and lifted them from her lap, placing them palms down on the tabletop. Between the glass and the blue liberty print cloth beneath was an arrangement of black and white photographs; people at the beach, driving tractors, in uniform. She glanced at the face of a woman with a strong chin, her hair in a 1940s' roll, her tea dress blowing in the sea breeze as she leaned back against some railings, a smile completing her beauty. *I wonder what you went through, Carrie wondered. I wonder what life threw at you and how you coped.*

'Do what you can, with what you have, where you are,' she murmured.

'Theodore Roosevelt,' Mark replied.

'Oh, sorry, I wasn't aware I'd spoken out loud.' She frowned. 'Are you sure it wasn't Franklin D.?'

'Positive.'

'I must have been getting mixed up. I was actually thinking of Eleanor Roosevelt and all those strong wartime women.'

'You're strong, Carrie.'

She glanced up at him fully and suddenly saw the tautness of his jaw, the apprehension beneath his skin. What was he here for?

'You look as if you've lost weight. Not that you needed to.'

She raised an eyebrow.

'Not that you look gaunt or anything.' He shook his head and half grinned. She used to love that grin. 'Digging myself a hole here, aren't I?'

'Yes, but I'll take it as a compliment.'

'It's meant to be. Have you been working out?'

Carrie felt her self-esteem rise a little. She sat up a little straighter.

'I've started running again. Just a little.'

'Good. I'm pleased.'

'And I've done a bit of work at the local gardens, so I've been outside a lot.'

'You always did want a nice garden,' he said, smiling affectionately, 'and the sun has brought your freckles out.'

He seemed so much more like his old self here, she thought, *away from the office, away from Paloma*. It was almost like old times.

'Shall we order some lunch?' she said. There was a nauseating pit in her stomach, and she needed to fill it with something. Maybe then she would feel better. 'Then you can tell me what it was that was so urgent you had to interrupt my holiday.'

FIFTEEN

Carrie sipped her elderflower presse and waited. She hoped what he was about to say wasn't going to make her feel even more nauseous. Mark shook his head. His hair didn't move. *Too much gel*, Carrie thought.

'I don't quite know where to start.' He looked up, his eyes full of remorse. 'I'm so, so sorry that everything has been handled so badly.'

Carrie felt a lump rise in her throat.

'I should have told you about the partnership. You were right.'

'Yes,' she whispered. 'I was. The old Mark would have told me.'

'He would. At least, I hope so.'

He picked up his large gin and tonic and fished out the lime, placing it on his side plate where it shimmered in the patch of sunlight coming through the window.

'Ian wanted to speak to you himself that day...'

'So why didn't you wait just a little longer? I'm hardly ever late. You know that. I missed the bus and...'

He reached over and took hold of her hand. Carrie froze,

stared at his fingers wrapped around hers as the blood raced around her body.

'I should have,' Mark replied. 'But Paloma had insisted on coming with me and she was excited to hear it actually announced. She had to get right across town to a meeting at ten, some big new office contract which she's pitching for, so...' He shrugged. 'This means so much to her. Almost more than it does to me, to be honest. Although I was very flattered to be offered the partnership.'

'And so you should be.'

He stretched out his arms. 'As you can see, Paloma's given me another makeover in honour of my elevation.'

'I'd noticed. Two in three months – that's dedication. I'm surprised she went for you in the first place if you were so "unmade". Or perhaps that was the attraction, like one of those houses that need completely doing up, faulty to flawless in a few short weeks.'

He winced. 'You have every right to feel bitter. I've behaved badly.'

'Are we talking personally or professionally?'

'Both. I want you to know that your job is safe.'

Carrie was silent. He had obviously put a word in for her. She should feel this whoosh of relief, an outpouring of gratitude. So where was the sense of elation? Maybe it would come later.

'I do feel guilty, you know. By rights, the partnership should have been yours.'

She swirled her glass and watched the bubbles rising to the surface and popping. *Don't allow your emotions to get the better of you, Carrie.* Holding back the tears, she looked directly at him.

'I didn't play the game, though, did I? I didn't do all of that going to the pub or the wine bar after work and schmoozing. Instead, I stayed at the office and actually worked. Jules says that's why I wasn't chosen, not because I wasn't good enough.'

'It'll be your turn next time, Carrie. I'm sure of it. I'll make sure of it, if I can.'

She dabbed at the corners of her eyes with her napkin. Did she really want to be beholden to him like that?

'You're assuming I'm coming back.'

She hadn't intended to say it but *goodness* it felt good. Until that very moment she'd felt trapped by the feeling that she'd spent so much time working at this job; she couldn't possibly throw all of that away, or could she? And Jules said that no experience was wasted, that everything had value somewhere along the line. The sense of freedom was heady. Maybe it was the carbon dioxide or the sugar in the drink. Whatever it was, it was amazing. She felt like laughing at Mark's shocked expression.

'You can't possibly mean that?' he said.

'Why not? Anyway, I'd have thought you'd be pleased that I was going to find something else.'

'Of course not. I like working with you. I-I like having you around.'

'Picking my brains for ideas,' she said, keeping her tone light.

At least he had the grace to look shamefaced. 'I just like knowing you're there. I mean that. I can't imagine working at Winterson's without you.'

What did that mean exactly? Was it just because he needed her there to give him business advice or was she reading more into it?

She leant to one side as the waitress slid her plate of lemon sole and shrimp butter in front of her. Someone else placed a dish of vegetables between them and a selection of mustards to go with Mark's steak.

'I thought you'd gone vegan?'

He flushed.

'Not exactly. I'm meant to be teetotal as well.'

'Ah, I see. Just when Paloma's around.'

He concentrated on spooning the Dijon mustard on to the side of his plate.

'I bet she doesn't like the fact that you could still be working with me. Does she know?'

'Not yet.'

Interesting, Carrie thought. *He always told Paloma everything*. She speared a shrimp and placed it on the tip of her tongue. It was deliciously buttery and salty.

'The engagement ring's quite something,' she said. 'Must have cost several months' salary. Got around to buying it quickly too.'

'I didn't buy it. It was her grandmother's.'

She was sure a piece of the purple sprouting broccoli had just got stuck between her teeth. It was incredibly uncharitable to feel so thrilled that he'd not shelled out for that knuckle-duster, but she just couldn't help herself. He offered her a chip from his little wire basket. She took a couple with her fingers and bit into them.

'That was one of the things I wanted to talk to you about,' he said, lowering his voice as if Paloma might be just around the corner, listening in. 'I wanted you to know that I didn't actually propose.'

Carrie frowned as her knife and fork hovered in mid-air.

'So, it's all some misunderstanding and she's just started wearing the ring. You're not really engaged at all?'

Amazingly, her heart was still beating steadily.

'Not exactly.'

She studied her fish. It was extremely good and now the nauseous feeling had dissipated it would be tragic to let the meal go cold, but it seemed heartless to keep on eating when he was being so earnest. His steak was barely touched.

'It was Paloma who proposed to me.'

She stared at the tablecloth. There was a small speck of parsley at the side of her plate, and she dabbed at it with her finger.

'I wanted you to know that.'

She shifted, and under the table her foot made contact with his. He didn't move it away.

'I thought it was a bit fast for you.'

She paused, waiting for him to address the elephant in the room. Nothing, just the sound of him sawing into his steak.

'After all, we were together for well over a decade before you suggested we got engaged. It's almost as if that was the next step on the ladder of life and you always put off choosing a ring. Why was that?'

He frowned. 'I just never thought that we needed that statement.'

'Perhaps if I'd fallen pregnant,' she said, very quietly.

He put his knife and fork down on his plate. 'That wasn't planned.'

'I should hope not, unless, of course, you've been seeing her a lot longer than you said.'

She willed him to look at her, but he wouldn't. Who knew that a piece of lettuce could be so fascinating?

'Ah!'

'Not much longer,' he said, the words spluttering across the table straight at her.

'How much longer?'

'A few months. It started when—'

She held up her hand. 'I don't need to know when it started.'

'Even with the baby,' he said, 'I wasn't thinking of marriage.'

'But you still said yes. Didn't try to persuade her to wait a little longer.'

Mark rubbed his forehead. 'She's not the sort of person you say no to.'

'No,' Carrie murmured, trying not to let bitterness spill out across the table. 'Paloma sees what she wants and goes for it. I suppose that's admirable in a perverse sort of way – if you're not part of the fall-out.'

'I did worry about how it would affect you, Carrie. I mean, I know you talked about starting a family and we tried a bit but...'

He slumped in his chair suddenly looking totally defeated and Carrie's eyes widened. She knew what he was going to say before he uttered the words. Only a few weeks ago, this was the sentence that she had played over and over in her dreams, the one she had prayed for but never quite believed would happen. And here it was, now, filtering through her disbelief.

'The thing is, Carrie,' he said, 'you're the only person I can tell this to but I'm really not sure that I'm doing the right thing.'

Carrie needed something stronger than elderflower presse; some of Rita's whisky should be on prescription for situations like this. *Stay calm, Carrie. Deep breaths. Don't get carried away with visions of a perfect future which you might not even want anymore.*

'Say something,' he pleaded.

What could she say that was rational? Because he obviously needed rational right now. Suddenly the façade had fallen, and he was on the brink. She should have seen it before. Once she would have picked up on it straight away.

'Mark, you're going to be a father. Paloma is the mother of your baby. You should be talking to her, not me. I'm hardly unbiased.'

'But you're the only person I trust enough to give me the right advice. I still think of you as my best friend, Carrie. God knows, I don't deserve for you to think of me in the same way or even care what happens to me at all.'

She stretched out her fingers and studied her nails. Only

twenty-four hours ago they'd looked so much better. She must make an effort to stop biting them again. Paloma had her nails done every three weeks, a different colour each time. Carrie thought that maybe she would start doing the same. A fresh turquoise blue, perhaps, or green like the lanes around Hideaway Cottage – a colour that she wouldn't normally choose. A colour for the new her. What should the new her say to him? *No, you definitely shouldn't marry her, Mark. She'll force feed you spirulina smoothies, never allow you to slump on the sofa with a ready meal and leave the baby with you at every opportunity while she goes off and does her own thing.* Or should she say what Jules would advise? *Yes, you should marry her because she'll force feed you spirulina smoothies, never allow you to slump on the sofa and eventually make you miserable because you won't be allowed a life of your own and serve you right, too.* Obviously, she wouldn't utter the last bit out loud. But did she want him to be miserable? If you loved someone, you wouldn't inflict that on them, would you? And she did still love him, sort of. Would he have gone off with Paloma, even with her powers of persuasion, if he'd been totally happy in the first place?

'Carrie...?'

'Perhaps,' she said, slowly, 'perhaps if you have a long engagement that will give you the time you need.'

He gave a wry smile. 'No chance. Paloma's already looking at venues for June so that she isn't looking too big in the photographs.'

'Well, I can see she wouldn't want that. I mean, photographs are so important.'

He ignored her sarcasm or perhaps he just missed it altogether.

'Paloma says there's no point in waiting when we'll end up getting married anyway.'

'How romantic.'

'I don't want to disappoint her.'

But you were prepared to totally crush me.

'She's not a child, Mark. This isn't some toy she wants. It's your life. It's your child's life.'

He didn't reply.

'I presume she wants a big wedding?'

'Mega.'

'Will she get a venue? The good ones can be booked up to a year in advance.'

'She's ringing around for cancellations. I'm hoping there won't be any.'

'You really need to talk to Paloma about this, Mark. Not me.'

'I know,' he groaned. 'But I've tried and then she gets upset and then she sulks and... can I come and stay with you for a few days, Carrie?'

'What? No! Besides all sorts of other considerations, Jules is all loved up with her new man so you really wouldn't want to be there. It would be too upsetting for you.'

'I didn't mean back in Manchester. I meant here. You're staying for another few days, aren't you?'

'You've just been made a partner, Mark. You can't walk out after little more than a week.'

'Ian's fine about it. Says I can take time to sort myself out.'

'You've already asked?'

'I might have mentioned that I was thinking of staying down here.'

'With me?'

'No, no, of course not.'

'Well, that's something, I suppose.'

'I know it's a bit presumptuous, but I really don't want to stay in a hotel.'

'Not even on a partner's salary when you could afford a super deluxe room,' Carrie shot back.

'I just don't want to be on my own.'

'And where does Paloma think you are?'

'She thinks I'm away on business. In Kent. I know what you're thinking. That I'm lying to her like I lied to you.'

'Not quite like you lied to me, Mark. You *were* seeing Paloma when we broke up, weren't you?'

'I never meant for that to happen.'

'Well, it did. *I* would never have cheated on you.'

'You might.'

Carrie shook her head. 'I wouldn't.'

'You're a better person than I am, Carrie.'

'Yes,' she said, sitting up straighter. 'Yes, I am.'

'Please can I stay? Just for a couple of days. Just to give me some breathing space. I wouldn't ask if I wasn't desperate.'

She sighed. 'No, I know that.'

He looked at her hopefully.

'Two nights, that's all, and then you'll go and leave me in peace?'

'I promise.'

The trouble was, Carrie thought dubiously, *Mark's promises didn't really mean very much.*

The journey back from Bembridge was a blur. She couldn't believe she had agreed to this. Several times she wanted to stop the car, get out and tell Mark it was all a mistake, that he had to go back to the mainland. But she didn't. She wound the window down to clear her thoughts. It was just two nights and one day. He'd be asleep for most of it. How difficult could it be?

Carrie groaned and briefly rested her head on the steering wheel as she pulled up in front of Hideaway Cottage. Wilbur was lying by the front gate as if he was waiting for her. Mark's car swept in next to hers and he leapt out. He looked a lot less dejected than he had half an hour ago.

'This is amazing,' Mark said, looking around. 'What a beautiful spot.'

Yes, Carrie thought, *and just for these two weeks it was meant to be all mine.*

'Who does the dog belong to?'

'Guy. He looks after the garden.'

'Cool,' he said, heading for the back to unload his holdall.

Carrie wound up the window, got out, and crouched down to fondle the dog's ears.

'No offence,' she whispered to Wilbur, 'but you're not really who I wanted to see right now, especially as I take it you're not alone.'

Wilbur thumped his tail and picked up his ball from near the gate.

'This way,' Carrie said to Mark, as they walked around the side of the cottage to the rear garden where Guy, sleeves rolled up, was deep in concentration clipping the edges of the border.

'Oh, you can see the sea!'

Mark stopped to admire the view and Carrie paused by the back door, Wilbur leaning against her leg as if to offer comfort, tongue lolling out of his mouth.

'Yes.'

Now she was here, everything seemed calmer. This was a choice she had made. She could have said no. But she didn't and she was proud of herself for handling it so well. Mark may not have done the same for her in a similar situation but that didn't mean she shouldn't help him out. Guy straightened up and wiped his forehead with the back of his hand before half-turning as if sensing that he was being watched. He threw her a broad smile.

'Wilbur's been waiting for you,' he said. 'He missed you this morning.'

'I left a message with Heather to say I couldn't make it until later.'

'I know. I hope you don't mind my doing this while you're out. Just wanted to finish it off. The garden always looks so much better once the edges are trimmed and...' He looked down at his feet. 'I just wanted to check that you were okay, that nothing else had happened to upset you.'

She shook her head, suddenly unable to speak. It felt so good to come back and find someone there even if he wasn't exactly waiting for her.

'Something has happened, hasn't it?' he said, starting to move towards her.

'You could say that,' she replied, as Mark entered his field of vision, 'but it's nothing to do with the cottage.'

She watched Guy's expression change and she stepped forwards a little as if standing closer to him would make the situation seem better. She wanted to explain that this wasn't what it looked like.

'Guy,' she said, 'this is Mark.'

There was the briefest of pauses.

'Oh, right,' he said, before striding forwards, wiping his hand on his jacket and stretching it out. 'Welcome to the island.'

'Thank you,' Mark replied. 'It's good to be here.'

There was such a contrast between them; Mark, still crisp in his jacket and chinos, even though he had loosened his tie, and Guy, his boots speckled with grass cuttings, the knees of his trousers soil-stained from where he had obviously been doing some weeding. There was even a ladybird crawling in his hair which he was totally oblivious to. Carrie wanted to lift it away with her finger, but it would look too familiar, so she folded her arms in front of her, tucking her hands tightly around her ribs.

'I'll come back and finish this another time,' he said. His tone was pleasant enough but suddenly more formal.

'No, no, it's fine,' Carrie replied. 'Please stay. I'm going to make tea.'

'Don't go on my account,' Mark added. 'Have you looked after this garden for long?'

'A while, on and off,' Guy replied.

'Good to have the work, I suppose,' Mark said. 'Can't imagine that it's easy to make a living from gardening.'

Carrie cringed. He was making assumptions. She'd forgotten how he used to do that. She noted the slight flicker of Guy's eyelids and wondered where Wilbur had suddenly bounded off to. She felt vulnerable without the warmth of his doggy body next to her.

'I get by,' Guy replied, an unmistakably dry tone crisping his words.

'Guy is in charge of the gardens at The Manor,' Carrie said, trying to salvage the situation and feeling that she was failing. 'They're beautiful. You should take a look at them while you're here.'

'I will. We could go around together,' Mark said, extending his arm around Carrie's shoulder. 'Do you get a house thrown in with the job?'

Guy half smiled. 'No.'

'Shame. I expect that would help a lot.'

'The wolf's not quite at the door yet.'

'That's good to hear.'

'Mark,' Carrie said, shrugging herself out of his reach, 'Guy's not just a gardener.'

'I'm sure he isn't,' Mark said, throwing her a condescending smile. 'We're all more than the sum of our parts. Especially Carrie. She's amazing.'

'Isn't she just?' Guy replied.

What did he mean by that? Better not to overthink it.

'Guy used to be a pilot,' she said quickly. 'This is his second career.'

'Oh! I see. So why did you stop flying and...'

He cast his eyes around the garden and Carrie just knew he

was taking in the unraked leaves under the magnolia, the nettles left deliberately for the small tortoiseshell butterflies near the hedge and the daisies which were already springing up again in the lawn.

'...do this?'

'It's a long story,' Guy replied, 'but this job suits me.'

'Perhaps if I come over to the gardens you can tell me all about it.'

'You're staying a while then?' Guy asked, leaning lightly on the long-handled shears.

'A couple of nights at least.'

At least!

Carrie glared at him, but he was oblivious. There was an unmistakable testosterone sparring match between the two men. Why did Mark do this? It wasn't as if Guy was a threat. It wasn't as if Mark was still interested in her.

'I know it's meant to be just me, staying here,' she said to Guy, unable to look him full in the face, the words coming out in what sounded like a garbled mess. 'If the owner wouldn't be happy with another person turning up, if it affects the insurance...'

Please, please say no, that you think he or she won't be and then I can send Mark to a hotel.

'He doesn't even need to know, does he?' Mark butted in. And Carrie couldn't believe her eyes as he winked at Guy. 'I don't smoke. I don't do drugs and I'm very tidy so I can't see that it would be a problem,' he continued.

Guy was studying him impassively, but Carrie knew that he was weighing Mark up and the results were far from favourable. Why did she feel it reflected so badly on her? How Mark behaved wasn't her responsibility. He shouldn't still have the power to embarrass her.

'I'm sure it will be fine,' Guy said at last.

They all stood there for a moment in silence. *Please, some-*

thing rescue us from this moment, Carrie thought. And as if on cue, Wilbur lolloped across the lawn and dropped something rotten and putrid right on top of one of Mark's new shoes.

'Oh my God!' he shrieked, jumping backwards and almost falling over a terracotta pot filled with apricot pansies. 'What the hell is that?'

'Wilbur! What have you done?' Guy scolded. He picked up the offending article. 'It looks like half a beetroot. Sorry, he must have got it from the compost heap. He does love to rummage in there.'

'That's disgusting!' Mark replied, staring at his foot, a pink stain splodged on the café-au-lait-coloured suede. 'Have you any idea how much these shoes cost?'

'They look expensive,' Guy said.

'And now they're ruined,' Mark shouted, causing Wilbur to cower behind Carrie, 'thanks to that filthy dog.'

'Mark!' Carrie said, tugging at his sleeve. 'Don't shout. You're frightening him. Wilbur is not a filthy dog. He's a normal dog.'

'Which is why I've never wanted one,' Mark replied.

'Usually, he's very well behaved with strangers,' Guy added.

'So you're saying I should be flattered?' Mark snapped. 'That the beast doesn't consider me a stranger?'

'Perhaps he brought it for you as a present,' Carrie offered, trying to calm him. 'He's left a couple of rotten apples outside the back door for me.'

Mark just looked at her open-mouthed.

'It's not the sort of present that I want.'

'We'll try and clean them up,' Carrie soothed. 'Stain Devils – aren't they the answer to everything? If that doesn't work, we could always dye them pink. I've got my pink plimsolls. They're very uplifting.'

'You think this is funny? You'll be suggesting that they look like a modern art interpretation of a beetroot latte next.' While

Mark dabbed at the shoe with a handkerchief, Guy rummaged in his pocket and scribbled a note on a piece of paper.

'This is my email address. Send me the link when you get back and I'll buy you a new pair,' he said.

'You don't have to do that,' Carrie protested.

'It's no big deal and Wilbur is my responsibility. I'm going to take him away before he creates any more mischief. Besides, you two want some time alone together. Sorry if we've ruined your reunion.'

'Oh no,' Carrie began, but before she had the time to explain, he was striding around the corner of the house, Wilbur following, head down, as if he knew he was in disgrace.

WAITING

Eliza had walked up to the woods. How she loved that track along the bosky pathways, up and up, the trees as protective as old friends until the wide-open sky revealed itself right at the top. She always paid homage to the Longstone, marvelling at its endurance, thankful for the hope and comfort it brought. Future generations would come here, making the same pilgrimage and she hoped they would gain something positive from the journey. Of all the walks she'd undertaken in her long life and still took now, this was the one which never failed to give her the most sustenance.

Returning home she loitered in the churchyard to watch a brimstone butterfly, admire the primroses and, above all, to remember the past or at least some of it. There were still parts which were blank, panic-stricken voids but Isaac told her not to worry, that one day if it was deemed to be for the best, her memory would return.

Sauntering across the sheep field she saw Guy and another man almost squaring up to one another with Carrie looking on anxiously. Isaac was standing half hidden next to the old holly tree. She skirted the edge of the garden just in case anyone glanced across and noticed her, not that it was likely; they were too preoccupied. Only Wilbur looked in her direction and wagged his tail.

'Who's that man?' she whispered to Isaac.

'That's Mark,' Isaac replied, 'our guest's previous beau.'

They shrank back, pressing together as Guy strode past them and around the corner of the house. Wilbur paused, lifted his head and sniffed. Eliza waved her hand to shoo him away at the same time as Guy called him to heel.

'What's he doing here?' Eliza asked, detaching some fallen holly leaves from the hem of her dress. That would look strange, floating holly leaves on a day without an ounce of breeze in the garden. 'Carrie only consented to a brief meeting in Bembridge and to be honest, if she'd asked my advice I would have counselled against it.'

'How can she ask your advice when she does not know we are here, Eliza?'

'That is beside the point, Isaac! This was not part of the plan.'

Isaac kissed Eliza on the top of the head.

'Not another of your plans,' he teased.

'He is not right for her, Isaac. I feel it. She came here to get away from him. Why has he followed her? It worries me.'

'Perhaps because he still loves her?' Isaac suggested, tentatively.

'Pah!' Eliza snorted.

'Or,' Isaac ventured, this time taking one of Eliza's hands, 'perhaps he, too, has lost his way in life. There are many who have through no fault of their own. We must not be judgmental, my love.'

'But you heard how he behaved,' Eliza retorted. 'I am wondering now whether I should have acted to prevent this meeting.'

'Acted in what way?'

'Oh, I don't know, a punctured tyre, a burst pipe, a disturbed night so that she overslept.'

'No, Eliza! We agreed, no meddling.'

Eliza sighed.

'But everything has been going so well and now our dear guest who was throwing off her past cares, beginning to gain some perspective, getting on reasonably well with Guy, seems quite out of sorts. And that Mark person is behaving very strangely? Why has he removed his shoe and is hopping about like a one-legged bird?'

'Possibly because Wilbur dropped a rotten beetroot on one of his new shoes. I gather they were very expensive.'

Eliza threw back her head and pealed with laughter. 'I do adore that dog.'

By the back door Carrie turned to look towards them and Isaac pulled Eliza down low behind the trunk of the tree.

'Shh!' he said. 'I think she heard you.'

They stayed very still, locked together, as Carrie hesitated, Mark's hand on her shoulder.

'What are you waiting for?' he said.

'I thought I heard something. Over there, by the tree.'

Mark, too, looked in their direction and Isaac pulled Eliza back even further.

'Oh, Isaac,' she said affectionately, 'you don't need to worry about him. He won't see us.'

'You're imagining things again, Carrie,' Mark said tersely. 'Now are you going to sort this shoe out or not?'

'Did you hear that?' Eliza asked Isaac, standing up and brushing her dress down once more as Carrie and Mark disappeared inside. 'Did you see and hear how proprietorially he behaved?'

'Indeed I did, and I do not condone it but perhaps he is stressed. Perhaps he is here in an attempt to make things right.

We must give him a chance, my love, and not jump to conclusions.'

Eliza looked doubtful but a little abashed.

'You are so much better than I, Isaac,' she murmured. 'Sometimes I feel that I do not deserve you.'

'Nonsense, my love. It is I who do not deserve you.' Isaac gathered her in his arms and held her close.

'I think you were sent to save me,' she whispered.

'I would not be the person I am without you, Eliza. I knew from the moment we met that you would make me better than I could possibly hope to be, that you were irreplaceable.'

'We were so lucky to meet when we did.'

'Just in time, I recall.'

She smiled up at him. 'My life would have been so different.' She shuddered. 'I cannot bear to think of it. And I cannot bear to think of Carrie making a mistake and falling into this man's arms again.'

'If that is what he desires. If that is what she desires. We do not know all the facts yet.'

'We must watch carefully and find out,' Eliza said, tiptoeing towards the kitchen window.

'We must wait,' Isaac said, catching hold of her hand and attempting to pull her back.

Eliza smiled at him over her shoulder. 'I am not good at waiting,' she murmured.

'I am well aware of that,' Isaac replied, 'but in the meantime, no meddling.'

'Of course not, my love,' she replied with a sweet smile. And as she turned to peer around the window frame, she whispered to herself, 'Not unless it's really necessary.'

SIXTEEN

Carrie showed Mark to his room.

'It's only small, I'm afraid. Not quite what you're aspiring to with Paloma.'

She knew it was a cheap shot, but she couldn't resist it. She was so angry with him. Why couldn't she have been stronger and said no? Then she wouldn't feel so disgusted with herself, so weak.

'It's charming. This place is an advertiser's dream. It's got everything.'

'Except the internet, but that must suit you at the moment.'

He had the grace to look slightly ashamed.

'I just need a bit of space, Carrie. You used to give me that.'

'Obviously a bit too much, the way things turned out.'

'Do you think I don't regret what happened? That I hurt you?'

Carrie gazed out of the window to where the scarlet tulips were nodding in the breeze. A bee banged against the glass and made her jump.

'I can't talk about this now, Mark,' she said. 'Not now. Not here. You're welcome to stay for a couple of days but I came here to find some perspective, some balance. I was just beginning to do that when...'

'When I turned up. I'm sorry.'

'Will you stop saying you're sorry?' she said. 'What good does sorry do now?'

'I thought it might make you feel better to know that...'

'No, saying it makes you feel better. I don't think I factor in this at all. It's all about you.'

'That's not true, Carrie. You're acting hysterical.'

Carrie sucked in her breath. If there was one word guaranteed to make her hysterical it was that one.

'I am not hysterical,' she said, through gritted teeth. 'A bit put out, yes, but hysterical, no.'

She moved towards the landing.

'I'm going to make a nice cup of tea, and I have cake if you would like some. Rita, the housekeeper, has dropped in a coffee and walnut cake.'

'Decaf coffee?'

Carrie glanced at him.

'In a cake? Really? I doubt it.'

'Paloma doesn't like me having too much caffeine. She says it makes me edgy.'

It's more likely that Paloma herself makes you edgy, Carrie thought. *She makes me edgy and I'm not even in a relationship with her. Except I am, aren't I? By default. An unwilling frayed thread of a relationship. We'll always have a connection even if it's one that neither of us want.*

'Well, Paloma won't know, will she?' Carrie replied, returning to the safer ground of cake. 'Unless you tell her. I'm not going to snitch.'

'I suppose one slice won't do any harm. She doesn't like me having too much sugar either.'

Carrie turned on her heel. It was going to be a long couple of days.

. . .

It was strange having Mark there. It should have felt like old times, but it didn't. He seemed irritatingly relaxed, lounging on the sofa, flicking through the TV channels or picking up the various magazines. She cooked a vegetarian pasta dish for supper, not because Paloma would have approved, but because that was what she'd planned and she could bulk it out with extra vegetables. If she'd known he was going to turn up like this, she'd have purchased the ingredients for a full fry up. That would have sent Paloma into a complete meltdown once she found out. Carrie smiled to herself at the thought.

'What are you grinning about?' Mark asked, standing in the doorway as she served the pasta into two copious bowls. How long had he been standing there, watching her?

'Nothing!'

'Is it that gardener?'

'No! Why?'

Mark shrugged. 'I saw the way he looked at you.'

Carrie felt the heat begin to rise in her body. It was just the cooking. She concentrated on spooning the roasted vegetables through the pasta, giving herself extra roast garlic just in case he tried anything on later.

'I have no idea what you mean.'

'He fancies you.'

'You're imagining things. Can you get the parmesan out of the fridge?'

'Paloma says that dairy doesn't suit me.'

'Okay,' Carrie said, slowly, 'but it does suit me so could you get it out anyway? Please.'

He opened the fridge, extracted the blue and white bowl into which she'd already grated the cheese and handed it to her.

'We'll take our food through on trays if you don't mind.'

The last thing she wanted was to have an in-depth conversation with him over dinner. God forbid he might even be tempted to light the candles on the table. Sitting in front of the TV was a much safer option.

'Paloma says it's not good for my digestion to eat on my knee.'

Carrie placed one of the pure white pasta bowls very firmly on the small island unit in front of her.

'I thought you wanted to get away from Paloma! You used to like nothing better than slobbing out on the sofa. I tell you what, so that you don't feel that I'm undoing all of Paloma's good work on your digestive tract in the space of a few short hours, you eat in here and I'll take mine into the sitting room. Then I can pick exactly what I want to watch, and you can sit up straight and chew everything forty times or whatever it is you're meant to do.'

He looked slightly surprised. 'I thought you'd want to eat with me. You never used to like eating on your own.'

Ha! she thought. *You might have changed, Mark, but so have I.* At that precise moment the thought of eating on her own was pure bliss.

Carrie settled herself on the sofa and scanned the channels. She didn't want anything about love or romance. Actually, she did, but not with Mark here, so she settled for a wildlife series on Africa and hoped that it wouldn't be too gory. Within a couple of minutes, Mark had sidled through and sat down on the other sofa.

'This is good,' he said, tucking into the pasta.

'Thank you.'

'Especially with a bit of parmesan.' He grinned sheepishly. 'Sorry. I'm being a bit of a pain, aren't I?'

She leaned back and looked at him. 'Nothing I can't handle.'

And she realised that she could handle it, whatever the outcome. If he went back to Paloma she would survive. There would come a time when the urge to cry at the thought of the life they might have had would fade away to nothingness. And if he decided that he'd made a mistake, that he wanted them to get back together with the prospect of their child coming to stay at weekends and in the holidays – she wasn't going to dwell on that now. But somehow, she would handle that, too. She would even cope with the job situation. For once she was going to go with the flow and not plan anything. Everything will turn out for the best, Granny used to say, and Carrie had a strange, deep-seated feeling that she might be right.

The following morning Mark slept in. Carrie grabbed a quick cup of tea and piece of toast and, leaving a note on the kitchen table, she headed off to the gardens.

The sun was shining, the birds were singing. She couldn't wait to get there. It was a day which encouraged you to think kindly of everything and everyone. Guy was talking to Heather as she entered through the shop.

'Morning,' Carrie said with a broad smile.

Guy turned, a frown clouding his face. 'I wasn't expecting you today.'

Carrie tried not to show how taken aback she felt.

'Thought I'd make up for my absence over the last couple of days. There must be loads to do.'

He stared at her, and it wasn't friendly. 'Yes, but I thought you'd be otherwise engaged.'

There really wasn't any need for him to be so hostile. It wasn't as if he had any claim on her. Coming here today had obviously been a huge mistake.

'If you don't need me...'

She heard the quaver in her voice. He must have heard it, too, but his face was impassive.

Heather came over and put her arm around Carrie's shoulders.

'Of course we need you, dear.' Carrie was aware of Heather sending Guy a stern glare. 'The more help, the better. Isn't that what you've always said, Guy?'

He made some sort of ungracious noise which Carrie took to be reluctant agreement.

'Someone needs to move those plants down from the greenhouse,' Heather carried on. 'I've got big spaces in my display and you're creative, Carrie, just the person to help me arrange them prettily and attract the customers. We make good money on the plants. We don't buy them in like lots of places. Most of them are grown here and people like that. They can get something a little bit different.'

She grabbed her gilet from behind the counter.

'Right,' she said, 'if you wouldn't mind staying here, Guy, until Jenny arrives, I'll go and show Carrie what I want.'

And without waiting for him to reply she steered Carrie out of the shop and out into the open air.

'I'm very sorry,' she said, when they were well out of earshot. 'I don't know what's come over him. He can be a bit taciturn sometimes but he's never normally rude like that.'

'Perhaps I'm more of a hindrance than a help,' Carrie said.

She glanced at the border she had weeded a couple of days previously and at the cosmos she'd planted out, already showing signs of extra frondy, feathery growth.

'But I've really enjoyed being here. It's been a great help.'

'Gardening's like that,' Heather said. 'I reckon if everyone could have a garden and grow something, the world would be a much kinder and happier place. I can see how much you benefit from being here.'

'Can you?'

'Definitely. Even the Major has taken a shine to you. Was

even asking where you were yesterday. I've never known that before.'

Carrie smiled and relaxed a little. Heather was like Rita, one of those people who just made you feel better about the world and about yourself.

'Here we are,' she said. 'All of these plants here need to be put in the wheelbarrow and arranged on the wooden staging outside the shop. I'll probably have some of those Erigeron, too, if Guy can spare them. They're always popular. It'll be a few loads. Can you manage?'

Carrie flexed her muscles in Popeye style. 'No problem.'

'Well, I'd better get back to old misery guts then and free him from minding the shop, not that anyone's likely to come in before we open but I'm expecting a delivery of stationery, and I don't trust Guy to check that they've sent the right thing.'

'I'll be fine here,' Carrie said, already heading towards the wheelbarrow propped up against the potting shed. 'And Heather... thank you.'

Heather just smiled and headed off down the path in her heavy-footed, solid as a rock way.

Carrie spent a good hour transporting and arranging the plants.

'Very pretty,' a voice said, as she placed the final clematis in place, pink flowers to the front.

Rita had an oval dish in her hands covered with a tea towel.

'Looks good, doesn't it?' Heather said, emerging from the shop. 'Carrie's a natural. Much better than I am at displays. Look at the way she's placed those metal chickens in amongst the plants.'

'It looks just as if they're foraging for food,' Rita said with a chuckle.

'If Guy can spare you, I'd love you to cast an eye over the inside space later,' Heather said to Carrie.

'I'm sure he'll be delighted to spare me,' she replied.

Rita raised an eyebrow, and Heather shook her head slightly. It was almost imperceptible, but Carrie didn't miss it.

'That smells delicious,' Heather said. 'Is it for the Major?'

'Lamb and mint pie,' Rita replied. 'I'll leave it in the porch as usual.'

'He's not been around today,' Heather said. 'Hopefully he'll find it later.'

'Unless it's one of those days he just doesn't venture out,' Rita replied.

'It's in the lap of the gods,' Heather said. 'You're a saint to keep on trying, Rita.'

'It's what Honoria would want, for us to look after him. Can't let him waste away, can we?'

'Sometimes I think that's what he wants, so that he can go and join her,' Heather murmured.

'Don't you knock on the door or ring the bell to let him know it's there?' Carrie asked.

'We've tried that,' Heather said. 'Doesn't make an ounce of difference. In fact, I think it just makes him crosser.'

Carrie looked towards the house. 'But the front door's ajar. Why don't you take the pie in and put it in the fridge?'

'Oh no, no, no, no, no,' Heather said, shaking her head emphatically. 'No one goes in uninvited. Even Guy is only allowed in the office at the front and that's when the Major arranges a specific time.'

'How long have you been cooking these meals which often get uneaten?' Carrie asked Rita.

'Ever since he was on his own. I try to pop something around a couple of times a week.'

'Sometimes it just ends up being thrown away,' Heather added.

'That's ridiculous!' Carrie said. 'And extremely ungrateful.' She took the pie from Rita. 'I'm going to take this lovely pie and put it in the fridge. I can't bear to see things going to waste. It's my Methodist roots.'

'Oh no! You can't do that,' Heather gasped, hands flying together as if in prayer.

'Just watch me!' Carrie said, and she walked out of the shop and purposefully across the gravel towards the front porch.

Inside, the house smelled musty, and the oak panelling made the hall dark and more than a little forbidding. Carrie found herself tiptoeing. She stopped by a portrait of a stern-looking man in a wing collar.

'It's all right,' she said. 'I'm not a burglar.'

Taking a few steps forwards, she peered through a doorway to the right. It was obviously the office, dominated by a large oak twin pedestal desk with impressive brass handles and several occasional tables groaning beneath piles of books, paperwork and copies of *Country Life* magazine. She was surprised. The Major was so precise in his appearance and yet this room looked a complete muddle. She couldn't imagine him finding anything he wanted in here.

'Hello?' she called, venturing further down the hall. 'Major, are you there? It's me, Carrie, your favourite interloper.'

She paused to listen for a reply but all she could hear was the muffled sound of the mower from the top lawn. The air was thick as if the windows hadn't been opened for ages and she had the unpleasant feeling of being hermetically sealed in a mausoleum. Opening a few more doors leading to several unused rooms she finally found a quarry-tiled corridor which she guessed led to the kitchen. A single plate, knife and fork were precisely arranged on the stainless-steel drainer, a single placemat on the kitchen table. The room was brim-full of loneliness. Carrie shivered. If this was what getting old meant, she didn't want it. The despair felt as if it could be catching. She needed to deposit the pie and get out of here as quickly as possible. The fridge was ancient and made a loud rattling noise as if it, too, was on the verge of giving up. Apart from a mouse-like piece of cheese, three small tomatoes, half a sausage roll, a jar of Rita's homemade chutney and some very suspect-looking milk, it was empty. Carrie placed the lamb and mint pie on the top shelf and closed the door firmly as the seal didn't look too reliable.

She hurried back down the corridor desperate for some fresh air but was waylaid by another door, three-quarters open, and a glimpse into a beautiful, panelled living room. The view through the gap in the partially drawn green velvet curtains overlooked the terrace and the herbaceous border. Two deep sofas covered in floral Sanderson fabric flanked the carved marble fireplace. Against the walls stood oak bookcases filled with leatherbound volumes and pieces of Meissen china. Covering most of the parquet floor was a Chinese rug decorated with pink and peach lotus flowers and edged in pale blue. Instinctively Carrie walked towards the window and drew back the drapes a little, allowing extra light to flood into the room.

'What...?'

He startled her and she spun unsteadily, her rubber soles squeaking on the polished floor.

Andrew struggled to his feet from the wingback chair, blinking furiously.

'I'm so sorry,' Carrie said. 'I didn't see you there.'

'Clearly.' He reached for his stick. 'What are you doing here? I suppose I should have known. If you're going to turn up in someone's garden uninvited, you're likely to do it in the house, too.'

'I'm sorry,' Carrie said again. 'Actually, not wishing to be pedantic but I wasn't uninvited into the garden that day.' She paused. 'And I think you know that very well.'

He stared at her.

'I've bought a pie from Rita...'

'Blessed woman.'

Carrie bit her lip. It really wasn't her place to say this, but she had to. 'Don't you think that's ungrateful?'

He was silent.

'Rita is an extremely caring person...'

'Well, I don't need her caring for me.'

Carrie perched on the arm of the nearest sofa despite his disapproving look.

'Why not? I can't imagine she's the sort of person who's going to say, "I've done this for you so you ought to do this for me".'

'No.'

Carrie glanced at the portrait above the fireplace. It was of a beautiful woman wearing a midnight blue lace evening gown and a single string of long, lustrous pearls.

'Is that Honoria?'

'Yes.'

'How old was she there?'

'Twenty-one. We'd just got engaged.'

'It's a beautiful painting.'

'I think so.'

'Don't you think that she'd want you to look after yourself better?'

He started to open his mouth and Carrie held up her hand.

'Don't you think she'd be pleased that you have people around you who care? People who give up their own precious time to try and make sure you're eating properly, people who are helping you to run this garden so that you can hold on to the house for future generations?'

'You're an extremely forward young lady and I didn't ask you in to lecture me.'

'Actually,' Carrie said, with a sympathetic smile, 'you didn't ask me in at all. From what I understand, you don't ask anyone in these days.'

'Honoria was the sociable one.'

Carrie looked again at the portrait.

'I can see that but I'm not talking about hordes of people. Just the odd one, from time to time. It might help with the loneliness.'

'What do you know about loneliness? You're only a slip of a thing.'

'I don't think it has anything to do with age, although obviously when you're older it must be harder in some ways. But younger people can be lonely, too.'

He twisted his hands on the top of his stick.

'I can't pretend to begin to comprehend the depth of your grief,' Carrie continued, 'but I do know how lonely I felt before I came here. I clutched on to things which I thought would make it better, like my promotion.'

'And that didn't work?' he asked at last, when the space she had given him obviously proved too much.

'Well, I didn't get the job so I'll never know if it would have worked. I suspect not.'

'Is that why you're here?'

'Now there's a question you might wish you'd never asked,' she replied with a wry laugh. 'Life is so much more complicated than one disappointment throwing us off course, isn't it?'

He stared at her gravely.

'I'd rather you didn't perch on the arm like that. It's not good for the furniture.'

She stood up ready to leave but he extended his arm, gesturing to the deep cushion on the sofa.

'But I've got plenty of time if you want to talk,' he said.

She smiled. It felt like a small breakthrough.

'Likewise,' she replied. 'Shall I make some tea or coffee?'

He nodded.

'It'll have to be black,' she said. 'Your milk smells decidedly iffy.'

'Honoria used to take black tea with a slice of lemon,' he said, wistfully.

'That's just how I like mine,' she said. 'I saw a lemon in the fruit bowl.'

'I like to keep one there for her still.'

Carrie placed a hand on his shoulder as she passed. 'Do you mind if I use it?'

He looked up at her, eyes watering, face pinched with pain. 'No,' he said. 'In fact, I think that would be a very good idea.

'Goodness, is that really the time?' Carrie said, as the single chime of the church clock drifted in through the open window. 'I'll be in trouble for skiving.'

'And I was meant to be having a twelve thirty meeting with Guy in the potting shed,' Andrew added.

'We'll both be in trouble,' Carrie said, with a grin.

She jumped up and collected the cups and saucers on to the tray.

'Leave those, my dear. I can wash them up later.'

'Will you think over what I said about the socialising?'

'I really wouldn't know where to start. Sometimes things can just go on for too long to be rectified.'

'Stuff o' nonsense, as my granny would say,' Carrie replied, taking his arm.

They strolled down the hall towards the front door, Andrew picking up his Panama hat from the Pietra dura side table as they passed.

'You're never too old to change.'

'Is that what Granny would say, too?'

'No,' Carrie said, 'that's what I say. I've learned that just from being here for a few days.'

As she opened the heavy oak door fully to allow the

sunlight to flood in Guy was striding down the path towards them.

'There you are,' he said, and Carrie wasn't sure who he was talking to.

'Sorry,' she and the Major said at exactly the same time, before bursting out laughing.

'The interloper and I have been taking tea together,' Andrew explained to a surprised-looking Guy. 'We were unaware of the time.'

'Mark has been looking for you,' Guy said, avoiding eye contact with her.

'Here? He came here?'

'I think he's still around.'

How embarrassing. It was as if he was chasing after her.

'I suppose I'd better go and find him then.' She turned to the Major. 'Thank you for listening.'

He took her hand and raised it to his lips. 'Thank you for pointing out the error of my ways.'

She smiled. 'You're welcome. And you will eat that pie, won't you?'

'Scout's honour,' he replied.

And with a brief glance at Guy's disapproving face, she walked back to the main garden to look for Mark.

After Carrie left, the Major rearranged his meeting with Guy and headed for the kitchen. He opened the fridge and lifted out the offending milk. He removed the lid and sniffed. The interloper was right. It was on the turn. Tipping it down the sink, he rinsed out the plastic bottle and placed it on the worksurface ready to be taken out to the recycling bin. She was an interesting girl, Carrie, direct but in a gentle way. She reminded him a little of Honoria. More fidgety but she'd had a lot of stress, poor girl. And then that cad of hers turning up here. What a cheek! If he'd been younger, he'd have given him a piece of his mind. These days he tried not to get involved in other people's problems. Better not to even think about them. He had enough of his own. The weight of extra ones would sink him. But wasn't that what he wanted? Wasn't he just ticking off the days until he could join his beloved again? After she'd died, he'd got his shotgun out of the cupboard and lain it on the carpet next to the bed. In the small hours of the morning, he'd been tempted to use it. But then that infernal blackbird would start to sing right outside his window – such a joyous sound even to someone who felt he had nothing to be joyful about. He couldn't shoot himself when the blackbird was singing or when the church clock was striking, or when there was an r in the month.

'What a lily-livered apology for a man you are, Andrew,' he would mutter to himself. 'Too afraid to live and too afraid to die.'

The only thing he could do was to pray, although he didn't really believe in that anymore. How many times had he sat in that front pew in the little church over the road, where his ancestors had worshipped for generations, and begged, pleaded, bargained with God for Honoria to live? All to no avail. You'd think that would have turned him away from Faith for good. He'd done his very best to shake it off, to send God packing, but He just wouldn't seem to let Andrew go. Even though He never answered his subsequent prayers – that he would go to sleep and never wake up, or that he would find the courage to use that gun. In the end he'd put the gun back in its cupboard and locked it away. He hadn't even got it out since to shoot rabbits. He wandered back to the sitting room and sat in an old leather chair directly opposite Honoria's portrait.

'Why were you taken from me?' he murmured. 'You'd have coped much better on your own. It should have been the other way around.'

Tears prickled behind his eyes. He took out a handkerchief

and blew his nose. Ridiculous tears! What good would they do? He'd been brought up not to blubber.

'Every day,' he said to Honoria, 'every single day I wonder why I'm still here and you aren't.'

Sometimes when he stared at the painting for long enough, he could imagine her expression changing, her eyes softening, her lips parting as if to speak to him. He had made so many promises to her as she lay dying; that he would look after himself, that he would continue to care for the house and garden, that he would be more patient with Sebastian, that he wouldn't cut himself off from the world. He had let her down with every single one of them. What if, when they finally met again, she was waiting at the Pearly Gates and instead of welcoming him she was poised to berate him? What if she was awash with disappointment in him? What if she said that he had failed her? What if, as a result of that, she didn't want to be with him for eternity? Would the pain of that be worse than the pain he felt now? Although there wasn't meant to be pain on the other side, just love.

He sat quietly for a few moments. Outside he could hear children laughing as they ran around the grass labyrinth. With trepidation he leaned over and picked up his leather address book from the side table, flipped a few pages and before he could talk himself out of it, picked up the phone.

SEVENTEEN

Mark was sitting on a bench, head thrown back, eyes closed, drinking in the sun. Behind him, a double pink camellia bush was heavy with flowers.

'This is the life,' he said, as she approached over the grass. He hadn't even opened his eyes or not that she'd noticed. 'Where have you been? The gardener couldn't seem to find you.'

'I was talking to someone.'

'Long talk.'

'Yes.'

'Whereabouts? I looked for you everywhere.'

'Why?'

He gazed lazily up at her, squinting into the sun. 'Just thought it might be nice if we spent some time together.'

Just behind him, in one of the conifers, a red squirrel darted for cover. Carrie felt like doing the same.

'I could live here,' he murmured.

'No, you couldn't. You're a city person.'

'Well, maybe I could have a holiday home then.'

'You'd hardly ever use it. Besides, Paloma would hate it

here. And that's the last thing this island needs, more people buying holiday homes and leaving them empty.'

He opened one eye. 'You're sounding very passionate considering you've only been here a few days.'

She shrugged. 'I care about it.'

'Just the island?'

'No, not just the island. I care about the people who've made me feel very welcome.'

'It's obviously not rubbed off.'

'I don't know what you mean.'

'You've not made me feel very welcome.'

'I've let you stay. I cooked you a meal. What more do you want?'

'The old Carrie. We were good together, weren't we?'

She didn't want this. Not now. Not here in this beautiful place which had given her so much, which had helped her to begin to restore her self-belief.

'Don't,' she said.

He stood up and came towards her.

Carrie wanted to back away, but her legs wouldn't seem to move.

He took her face in his hands.

'Mark, please don't...'

But he wasn't listening.

'I miss us, Carrie.'

'You made a choice.'

He stroked along the underside of her jaw. She froze.

'I still love you.'

'You're having a baby, Mark, with somebody else.'

It was as if he hadn't heard her. His face was getting closer and years of kisses flowed through her mind. She had thought that he'd kissed her for the last time but now, unless he was repelled by last night's garlic, unless she moved her face away... For some reason every ounce of strength seemed to have left her body. It wasn't that she wanted him to kiss her – or did she? What would it feel like? Would it be the same? She'd have to try and block out the images of him kissing Paloma but, once she was lost in the moment, that should happen naturally. Perhaps it would make him realise what a fool he'd been. He'd always said she was a good kisser. She was a bit out of practice, of course. They hadn't kissed much in those last few months before he left. That alone should have told her something – the fact that he stopped kissing, said he was too tired for sex. *Were good kissers born or made?* she wondered. *Born kissers wouldn't have lost the knack over a few short weeks.* There was only one way to find out. She placed her hands lightly against his chest. He'd obviously been working out more. His breath washed warmly across her face, and she parted her lips as his came down to meet hers. She waited for the fireworks, those little sparks travelling deliciously through her body. But there was nothing. No surge of adrenaline or desire or tenderness. Just a fast-growing feeling that this was wrong, terribly wrong. She pushed him away and ducked underneath his arms which still encircled her. She had an overwhelming urge to wipe her mouth with the back of her hand.

'I'm so sorry, Mark. That was wrong.'

'Don't be sorry. I'm not.'

His arms were stretching out for her.

Carrie stayed just out of reach.

'You should be. You have other responsibilities now.'

'But I want to be with you. Not seeing you at the office made me realise how much I missed you.'

Carrie could have laughed. Is that all it would have taken to get him back? Just to go away for a week right at the beginning and he'd have come running? He meant it. At least in this moment. She could see that. She believed him but she didn't believe it would last. For one thing, Paloma wouldn't let him go that easily and for another...

'You see,' he said, 'you feel it, too. I can see it on your face.'

And Carrie realised that she was smiling, more and more broadly, and that he had totally misinterpreted it.

'No, Mark. I'm afraid I don't,' she said, as gently as she could. 'What you can see on my face is the relief that I'm totally over you.'

He frowned and in a couple of strides had clutched her to him.

'If I begged for your forgiveness. If I promised to tell you every day for the rest of my life how sorry I am for what I did to you,' he whispered into her hair.

'You did it to us, Mark,' she replied, her voice muffled by his shoulder.

'I would do anything to turn back the clock. I just want things to be as they were.'

She lifted her head a little as he loosened his grip slightly.

'No, you wouldn't. Because obviously you weren't totally happy with the way things were, or you wouldn't have been susceptible to Paloma.'

'It was a moment of weakness,' he said, 'and then I just couldn't seem to stop seeing her.'

Carrie unclasped his hands from behind her back. 'But I don't want a man who is going to succumb to a moment of weakness, Mark.'

'You've always said that people deserve a second chance.'

'You had plenty of chances but in the end, you decided that you wanted her more than me. I need someone who I can rely on, someone who will love me through thick and thin, someone who puts my happiness above their own. That's the way I loved you, but you and I are in the past and so is my time at Winterson's. I'll write a formal letter of resignation.'

He dropped dramatically to one knee and grabbed her hand.

'Carrie, please no! You don't need to do that.'

'No, I don't *need* to and thank you for putting a word in for me to smooth things over, but I need a fresh start.'

'What will I do? How will I manage without you?'

'You'll find a way, Mark. You always do.'

'But we can meet for a drink from time to time? Have a catch up?'

Carrie shook her head. 'I doubt it. I don't think I'll stay in Manchester.'

'Where will you go?'

'I don't know yet. I might come here, to the Isle of Wight.'

'Really? Why?'

She laughed. 'You really don't know me at all, do you? But then I can't blame you for that because I'd actually lost touch with myself until a few days ago. This is my sort of place, Mark. It's small, it's green, it's peaceful, it's where I feel that I belong. It's where I feel that I can flourish.'

She tugged at his hand.

'Please get up,' she said. 'You look as if you're proposing!'

'I will if that's what it takes to get you back.'

'You're about to be a father. You need to concentrate on that.'

'I'm not ready, Carrie. I don't know whether I'll ever be ready. To be honest, I was relieved when you didn't get pregnant.'

She took a step back and rubbed her temples. 'So you didn't want to take a break from us because I couldn't conceive and all of those times you comforted me were just a sham?'

'I was disappointed for you, obviously.'

'That's something, I suppose. But not for yourself.'

He swallowed. 'No. Sorry.'

'Except it's not all about you any longer, Mark.' She pulled him to his feet and held on to both of his hands. 'You owe it to this baby to go back home and face up to your responsibilities.'

'I don't know if I can. It's so daunting.'

'You have to, and the sooner the better.'

'I'd rather hide away here with you.'

She laughed. 'Is that what you think I'm doing? You couldn't be more wrong. When you've packed up your stuff you can leave the key under one of the pots by the front door.'

'You're chucking me out?'

She nodded. 'It's for your own good and for mine, too.'

'Aren't you at least coming back to the cottage with me to see me off?'

'No. We've said all there is to say. I'm going to don my pink gloves and head for the potting shed. I shall sift some compost and talk to the seedlings as I prick them out and tell them what beautiful flowers they are going to be, how much pleasure they will bring to people, how they will brighten lives, and that brightness will remain for longer than a visit to these gardens. That's one of the things that I love about working here. It's about so much more than gardening – it's about spreading joy, or at least that's how it feels to me.'

She leaned forwards and kissed him gently on the cheek.

'I presume you'd prefer me not to work my notice, so I'll get Beth to clear my desk. Good luck, Mark. Make good choices.'

And with that she turned to walk away. Glancing up towards the softly mown grass path that snaked up the hill and overlooked the whole garden she saw Guy, standing, watching, Wilbur seated at his side. How long had he been there? How much had he seen? As if in answer to her unspoken thoughts he turned abruptly, snapping his fingers for the dog to follow, and strode at pace up towards the woods, presumably as far away as possible.

Carrie didn't see Guy for the rest of the day. His absence felt like a gaping hole in the garden. The liberation, euphoria she had felt when she had realised that she really didn't love Mark anymore, at least not in the way she used to, had been replaced by a sense of utter loss.

'You look done in, lovey,' Rita said, as they passed on the road to Hideaway Cottage. 'You're meant to be having a rest, you know. No point working yourself into the ground here or you won't feel the benefits of a break.'

'I'm okay. Just a bit tired.'

'Your guest's gone. Saw him speeding away just as I was putting some eggs on the table by the front gate.'

'Oh, good. His visit was slightly unexpected.'

'Well, the cottage is all yours again now.'

Carrie smiled. 'I'm pleased about that.'

'Thought you would be.' Rita checked her watch. 'Oh, Lordy! I'd better put my skates on or I'll be late.'

'You look very nice,' Carrie said, noticing for the first time Rita's smart double-fronted navy shirtdress and the small sweep of blue eyeshadow and hint of pink lipstick.

Rita leaned closer and lowered her voice as if there might be someone listening behind the hedge. 'I've had a touch of the unexpected myself.'

'Oh?'

'Yes, a telephone call from Andrew,' Rita continued conspiratorially, 'thanking me for the pie and asking me if I'd like to share it with him. I always make double the quantity, so it lasts him a couple of days. There'll be plenty for the two of us.'

'That sounds lovely.'

'I don't do it for the thanks, though.'

'I know you don't but it's still good to feel appreciated, isn't it?'

Rita nodded. 'And you'll never guess what else? He's asked me around for a drink first. Don't know what's come over him. He sounded like a different person on the phone. It's like a miracle but as the Good Book says, "With God all things are possible." Lucky it's not my WI night. Mind you, I'd have missed it to go to The Manor and it'll do me good to get away from the farm for a while. Besides, the Major might be back to his old self tomorrow so strike while the iron's hot, I say.'

And with a cheery wave of her plump hand, she bustled away, leaving Carrie to quicken her step at the thought of a calm Hideaway Cottage waiting for her return.

Carrie stood for a few minutes in the back garden, looking out towards the sea, listening to the sparrows in the hedge and the occasional bleat of a lamb. Inside, all was serene. It was as if Mark had never been there, except for a Miffy keyring which lay in the centre of the kitchen table.

He'd bought it for her on one of their first trips to Paris. They'd laughed so much together in those days. She didn't imagine he and Paloma laughed much at all. She picked it up and ran her fingers over the smooth enamel. It represented so much. She'd used it for the keys to every home they'd ever had together. When she'd left the flat that day just over six months ago to move in with Jules, she'd left the keys and Miffy behind. Why had she done that? Had she possessed some sixth sense that she'd never live there again? Had Mark been carrying Miffy around with him all this time or had he just brought her with him to the Isle of Wight? She'd probably never know but leaving the key ring here was definitely his way of saying that he accepted what she'd said. She could throw it in the bin but that would feel like a betrayal of all those years together so for now she would put it in her suitcase and wait. The time would come when she would know what to do with it.

She'd just made a cup of tea and set light to the kindling in the fireplace when the phone rang.

'Aren't you at work?' Carrie asked Jules.

'Yes. I'm on a break. I just had to call you and tell you my news. Gavin's proposed.'

Next to Carrie the wood started to crackle and glow.

'What?! Jules, you hardly know each other.'

'I know. Ridiculous, isn't it, but incredibly romantic.'

'You haven't accepted, have you?'

'I love him, Carrie. It's the real deal this time. I've waited my whole life for someone like him. Please don't burst my bubble. He's the best thing that's ever happened to me.'

Like all the others, Carrie thought, but bit her tongue.

'I'm not bursting your bubble, Jules, but...'

'I want you to be happy for me.'

'If he's the one, of course I'm happy for you. I don't want to see you get hurt, that's all.'

'You've always said that I'm the hurter because I'm the one who ends it.'

'Not in so many words. I wouldn't be that harsh.'

'But I knew that's what you meant.'

'You've had a lot of disappointments. I don't want that to happen again.'

She could hear Jules running a tap and presumably rinsing out her mug.

'It's not going to. No more disappointments for either of us, you or me.'

Carrie thought about Guy and how disappointed she'd felt at not having the chance to explain things to him.

'That would be nice, even if it's not very realistic. You have been right about one thing, though.'

'What's that?' Jules asked, obviously biting into a biscuit.

'Being here has given me a fresh perspective on things. I'm handing in my notice when I get back. In fact, I've done it unofficially already.'

'So, you're finally getting away from Mark. That's wonderful.'

Carrie smiled down the phone. 'You'll be doubly pleased with me because I'm not just getting away from him physically, I'm completely over him emotionally.'

When she told Jules about Mark's visit it was crowned with a 'hip, hip, hooray' down the phone.

'I think I just couldn't let go of the idea of loving him.'

'Perhaps it wasn't loving him,' Jules said soberly, 'but someone. It feels good to love someone special.'

'Jules, I'm thrilled for you. Really, I am.'

'But...?'

Carrie took a deep breath and wriggled her shoulders to loosen them. 'No more buts. I'm going to pour myself some wine and raise a glass to you both.'

She slept fitfully and woke early with the light barely filtering through the curtains. There was no point trying to get back to sleep so she got up, put on her jogging bottoms and a zip-up top, grabbed her shoes from beside the back door and headed out into the awakening day. The air was moist and the dew heavy as she brushed against the plants lining the front path before setting off at a gentle pace up the lane towards the village. She hadn't intended to turn left and take the route past Cressie's house, but she couldn't help herself. She had to see if he was there. It was ridiculous but all she could think about was Guy, his face, his hands, his hair, the way he smiled and his look of disapproval when he'd seen her with Mark. She needed to explain things to him, as a friend, nothing more, but before that she needed to compose herself, to think about what she was going to say, to sort out her feelings.

Approaching Cressie's barn, she felt the breath catch in her throat. *Please don't let him be there. Maybe the previous time was just a one-off.* She could forgive him that, especially if they were both lonely. The house was in darkness. She stood by the gate and after a moment lifted the heavy metal bar that kept it closed and stepped into the garden. To one side of the gravel driveway was a ribbon of turf and then a flower border. If she crept along there, she definitely wouldn't be heard but she could be seen, whereas if she kept low and skirted the walls of the house she was less likely to be seen but could be heard. *Leave it, Carrie. Go back out of the gate and carry on with your run. He's not going to be here. He's got his gran to look after. Besides, he's nothing to you. Only yesterday you thought you might still be in love with Mark. You're turning into one of those women who can't bear to be on their own, who dive from one relationship to another. How many times have you scolded Jules for that? Guy's not interested in you anyway. Nobody's going to be interested in you if you turn into some sort of a psychopathic stalker.*

She hadn't even heard the window open.

'Carrie? Is that you?'

Instinctively, she flattened herself against the cob wall, as much as she could with all of its lumps and bumps. He leaned out further and looked down at her.

'What are you doing here? Is there a problem?'

Yes! Yes, there's a big problem.

'I thought I saw a chicken in the road,' she spluttered. 'I thought I'd better come in and check if it managed to squeeze under the gate.'

He frowned. She hadn't sounded at all convincing. 'And did you find it?'

'No, no, must have been imagining things.'

'That's good.'

'Yes, it is.'

'Will I see you later?' he asked.

'No, I don't think so.'

She was already fumbling with the gate latch, desperate to make her getaway.

'I see.'

No, you don't! And I don't see either. This place has cast a sort of spell on me, made me want to believe in rediscovery and reclamation and happy ever after. It's done its best to make me feel loved and protected but it's just an illusion. How can you know people after such a short time? They're just strangers, incomprehensible, untrustworthy strangers.

Suddenly she wanted to leave as soon as possible. Why wait until the end of the week? Why not go back now? Head back to Hideaway Cottage and pack her things and get the next ferry out of here. If Jules and Gavin were all loved up back in Manchester, so be it. She could cope with that better than she could staying here where she had felt that she belonged for the first time in her life and now realised that she was fooling herself.

'Stupid, stupid woman,' she said to herself. 'Just because you wanted to feel that you fitted in here you made yourself think something that isn't true. You made yourself think that this could be your soul home, somewhere you could be happy and relaxed and involved in the community. That's what happens when you try to think the best of people. Much better to expect the worst and then you stand at least a chance of being pleasantly surprised.'

Without another word she turned and ran as fast as she could back to Hideaway Cottage, aware of him staring bemusedly after her.

HOPE

Eliza searched the garden.

'Isaac, Isaac, where are you?' she called, her voice unavoidably louder and more urgent by the second.

Isaac emerged from the sea mist and strode towards her across the field.

'What is it, my dear? Is something wrong?'

'Yes, yes,' she gasped. 'Terribly wrong. Our guest is leaving.'

'Leaving?' Isaac replied. 'But it isn't time yet.'

'Something has happened to upset her, Isaac. She left the cottage in her rather strange clothes, the ones she wears for running.' She rippled with distaste. 'I have no understanding of this desire to run and run and get out of breath and perspire. It was my expectation that she would be out for some time but no! She was back before I even got the chance to cleanse the spare bedroom from the effects of that... that... gentleman, although I struggle to call him by that name.'

'And what was the cause of her sudden return, my love?'

'I don't know, Isaac. If only I had followed her. Running wouldn't have been as terrible as this!'

Isaac took hold of her trembling hands.

'Calm yourself, my love. Getting into this state will do no good at all.'

'But the cottage hasn't had time to fully do its work, and I feel such a sense of loss, Isaac...' She paused and dropped her head. 'But I always feel such a sense of loss. Why is that, do you think? What is it that I'm missing?'

As she looked up, a tremor passed across his face and she felt real fear. Then he gripped her hands and the steadiness, the stillness of him, pacified her a little.

'Your hopes aren't to be abandoned yet, Eliza. We shall try to think of something but if it's meant to be that Carrie leaves us sooner, then we must accept that. There are some things that are beyond our control.'

'But...'

Isaac placed a finger to her lips.

'I know you want to rescue the world, Eliza, but we're here to help, to encourage, to support, not to control.'

She nodded, her face still anxious.

'But we can make an effort to persuade, can't we? If we feel with our whole being that something is right?'

'That depends,' he said, his eyes dark with concern, 'upon the method of persuasion.'

'Perhaps a punctured tyre, a sprained ankle, a storm which prevents the ferries from sailing.'

Isaac smiled and looked up at the benign sky.

'And you think that you're capable of whisking up a gale in an instant?'

'Well, maybe that last one was a little ambitious,' she conceded.

'And we don't really want to cause our guest an injury, do we?'

Eliza shook her head. 'It will have to be the car then. I will go and look for a sharp implement.'

Isaac caught hold of her hand just in time.

'Eliza,' he said, reeling her back in towards him and holding her close. 'Wait for a moment. Let's take a little time to consider this.'

'But we haven't got time, Isaac,' she said, as he led her across the garden and parted the waterfall fronds of the weeping willow tree.

'A few minutes, Eliza, that's all I ask. We need to be sure that any action we take is for the right reasons.'

Eliza acquiesced. But she wouldn't allow Isaac to delay her for too long. One way or the other, she was determined to stop Carrie leaving.

EIGHTEEN

Carrie had gathered her toiletries from the bathroom and placed them on the dressing table ready to pack in her little vanity case. She took off Granny's eternity ring and put it next to them, then headed through to the bathroom to clean the basin. Over the sound of running water, she was sure she heard the sound of a car engine getting closer. Surely, it wouldn't be coming here. Hardly any traffic passed by apart from the odd tractor. Turning off the tap so she could hear better, the sound of spraying gravel was unmistakable as was something coming to an abrupt halt at the front of the cottage. She peered out of the landing window and watched as an elderly woman slammed the door to a little purple Honda, before taking a few paces and patting the front. Determinedly she made her way up the front path towards the door, large navy handbag in one hand and a small bunch of lemon-yellow flowers tightly clasped in the other.

'Bother!' Carrie said, ducking back out of sight. Although the woman's footsteps were slow, the movement of her head was brisk and Carrie suspected that she'd been spotted. *Bother!*

Bother! Bother! She'd been hoping to have a final visit to the Longstone before catching the eleven thirty ferry and was already cutting it fine. Apart from one last lingering look at the landscape, she wanted to leave Jo's amethyst in one of the little hollows. It hadn't done her much good so far; she might as well leave it for someone else.

The rat-a-tat-tat on the front door was surprisingly loud. *She'd obviously got the wrong address,* Carrie thought, heading down the stairs and pulling open the door. *She must be patient. God willing, she'd be old herself one day and maybe get things mixed up.*

'You must be Carrie,' the woman said, with a smile that lit up her whole face.

Definitely not the wrong house. So, it was either going to have to be the Longstone or the ferry but not both, unless she could get rid of this woman quickly.

'I have been so longing to meet you.'

An elegantly manicured hand extended and took hold of Carrie's yellow rubber-gloved fingers.

'I do hope you don't mind my dropping in unannounced like this, but I've been in hospital and I'm not quite sure how I'm going to feel from one day to the next so it's difficult to arrange anything in advance. Having said that, I've always been a spur of the moment sort of person. These are for you.'

She thrust the posy of artfully arranged flowers and herbs towards her.

'The primroses won't last long but they're lovely to have in the house. Yellow is such a cheering colour, isn't it? And if you pinch the rosemary from time to time, it releases its aroma which is just heavenly.'

'Thank you.'

'How rude of me, I haven't even introduced myself. I'm Irene, Rita's cousin and Guy's grandmother,' the woman added, her eyelids fluttering.

'Oh!'

Carrie stood stock still for a moment as she processed this information. A bee landed on one of the primroses. She had the distinct impression that Irene was weighing her up.

'I had no idea that Guy and Rita were related.'

'Well, Guy wouldn't tell you, would he?' Irene said, with a chuckle. 'Always been reluctant to share information, even when he was a little boy.'

She cast Carrie a quizzical look.

'He has talked about you, though. In fact, you're the talk of the village at the moment.'

Carrie felt a slight flutter beneath her breastbone, a sense of foreboding. 'Really?'

Irene swayed slightly.

'Would you mind if I came in for a moment, dear? My legs aren't up to full strength yet and I find standing a little tiring.'

Carrie resisted the temptation to look at her watch. 'I'm so sorry. Yes, please do come in.'

She ushered Irene into the hall.

'I can see that I've called at a bad time,' the older woman said, her glance falling on the suitcase at the bottom of the stairs. 'Are you leaving us already?'

'Yes, I really need to get back to Manchester.'

'Oh, that's such a shame, and we haven't had the chance to get to know each other. I was at Manchester Art College, you know, back in the previous century. I loved it there. I was hoping we could chat about the city. Then there's this other business.'

Irene put a hand up to the door frame and leaned against it.

'Do you think I could have a glass of water? Perhaps Guy was right when he told me to stay put. Leaving the house has taken it out of me more than I thought it would.'

'Oh, my goodness,' Carrie said, taking her arm. 'Are you all right? You have gone a bit pale. Come in and sit down.'

She plumped up a couple of the cushions on the sofa and placed Irene's soft leather bag on the floor beside her as she settled back.

'I feel such a nuisance and with you being in a rush to get off as well. What time's your ferry?'

'I haven't actually booked it. Didn't think there was any need at this time of year.'

She could see beads of perspiration breaking out on Irene's forehead.

'Let me get you that water and then perhaps I'd better call Guy and he could come and fetch you.'

'Oh no, dear, there's no need for that. I'd rather he didn't know I was here. He doesn't want me going out, let alone driving. He actually hid the car keys, would you believe? Didn't take me long to find them, though!'

Carrie watched her closely as she took a sip of water from the tall glass.

'Don't worry. I'll be fine in a few minutes. It's amazing how quickly the body weakens when you're not exercising, not that I go to the gym or anything. Can't see the point of marching away on one of those machines when there's so much to see outside. I know we're lucky here with beautiful countryside but even in the city I'd rather get out and walk.'

'Me too,' Carrie said, surreptitiously checking the time. What difference would another hour make?

'Would you like a coffee? And I have some biscuits somewhere. I kept them out for the journey.'

'That would be lovely. The coffee in the hospital was terrible, worse than the food. If it hadn't been for Rita and Guy bringing me delicious things to eat, I think I'd have just faded away. He's a good cook, you know.'

'No, I didn't,' Carrie said, heading through to the kitchen and putting together a tray with cups and saucers before fishing out a couple of pods for the coffee machine.

'And he's done wonders with this place,' Irene said, following her and perching on one of the pine chairs. 'I haven't seen it since all the finishing touches were put together. It's just so homely but I expected it would be. Home has always been very important to Guy.'

Carrie turned to look at her visitor as the coffee machine hissed and gurgled.

'Did he do everything then? I thought he just did a bit of the building work.'

'Oh no. This was a very special project. He wasn't going to pass it on to anyone else. This cottage has been in the family for a hundred and fifty years.'

Carrie frowned.

'I thought he might move into it himself, but he said he had this feeling that it was important to share it. That there were people out there who needed somewhere like this for a short time just to recalibrate. Old romantic that he is, he wants this place to nourish you from the moment you walk in. He wants it to be a place for people going through hard times to find strength and realise that things will be fine and that life is good. I hope you have found that, Carrie?'

Carrie placed a cup of coffee on the table in front of Irene, aware of her every move being monitored as she tried to take in what was being said.

'So, Guy owns this cottage?'

She fished the packet of Rich Tea biscuits which she'd bought for the journey home out of her basket and tipped a few into one of the beautiful small bowls which she'd dried carefully earlier that morning and placed back on the windowsill.

'I thought you knew. Oh dear, I've got the feeling I shouldn't have said anything.'

Carrie sat down opposite her.

'He never mentioned it and neither did Rita.'

'Thick as thieves, those two,' Irene murmured. 'Rita and her husband George helped me to look after Guy when he was younger. I always had to go out to work because my husband left when Guy's father was a baby, so Rita would step in. I was worried that she might be a bit jealous when Aunty left Hideaway Cottage to Guy instead of her sons, but if she did feel a bit peeved, she's never let on. Not quite the same story with that daughter-in-law of hers, I'm afraid. But then she's one of those people who if they won a million on the lottery, she'd want two million. Poor Rita, she does her best to keep everything on an even keel but one day she won't be here to hold the family together. And one day I won't be here for Guy.'

She snapped a biscuit in two and looked eagerly at Carrie.

'He liked you. I could tell from the way he talked.'

Carrie glanced up, wondering if the use of the past tense was a slip of the tongue, but Irene didn't look like that sort of woman.

'He's been extremely kind. Working at the gardens was very therapeutic for me. I don't think I mistook anything precious for a weed.'

'I'm sure you didn't. And you got on well with the Major, I hear.'

'His bark is worse than his bite,' Carrie replied.

'Normally, that's true,' Irene said.

The sudden tautness around the older woman's jaw made Carrie's heart flutter. This was obviously not just a social call.

'Has something happened?'

'Yes, dear, I'm afraid it has. The Major has sacked Guy.'

'Why would he do that?'

Irene had a disconcerting gaze, just like her grandson. 'Because of you.'

'Me? Why would he sack him because of me? I'm sorry, I don't understand.'

Irene leaned back a little and the chair rocked on the uneven floor. She didn't appear to notice. 'No, I can see that.'

It was ridiculous but Carrie felt as if she had passed some sort of test.

'Andrew has got it into his head that Guy employed you in an undercover capacity to gather information as to how the gardens could be made more "marketable", I think is the expression. And when you went into the house that day, Guy had put you up to it because everyone knows that the house is out of bounds. But Andrew, silly old fool, thinks that you were taking a good look with a view to opening The Manor itself to the public on certain days.'

Carrie's mouth had dropped open, and she couldn't seem to close it properly.

'But that's absurd. Guy wouldn't do that. I wouldn't do that. Where did this all come from? The Major knew I worked in PR from the beginning. We discussed it when he first showed me around the gardens so it's not as if that was a secret. If I was working undercover, as you put it, I'd have said I was a teacher or a nurse, anything but a PR person.'

'Guy did point that out to him. I think the idea arose from a combination of things; firstly, from a comment your young man made?'

'My young man? Oh, you mean Mark. He's not mine, at least not anymore. I didn't even know he'd met the Major. He left the gardens yesterday and was meant to be heading straight for Cowes to catch the ferry.'

'I gather he loitered in the carpark until everyone else had gone home and slipped into the gardens through the woods at the back. Andrew was having his usual late afternoon stroll of the perimeter when Mark accosted him, so to speak.'

Carrie dipped her head into her hands for a moment.

'What did he say?' she asked, looking up at Irene.

'Was full of praise for your creative capacity, I believe. Said how talented you were and how your firm could turn the house and gardens into a real money-making venture.'

Carrie groaned.

'That sounds like Mark – at least the last bit does.'

'And then about an hour ago the Major found the business card in the potting shed on top of a pile of paperwork. Guy says he has no idea how it got there. Mark never went near the potting shed, to his knowledge. Anyway, I suppose you can see that the Major has put two and two together.'

'And reached totally the wrong conclusion,' Carrie said. 'How can he think that of Guy? He loves those gardens. He's totally committed to retaining their authenticity, to staying true to Honoria's memory while trying to make enough money for the Major to remain in his home.'

Irene's cup rattled a little in its saucer before she lifted it to her trembling lips. She took the smallest of sips and put the whole thing down on the table in front of her.

'I can't tell you how pleased I am to hear you say that, to know that you understand.'

Carrie studied Irene's hands, now neatly folded on her lap, their skin as delicate and textured as once-used tissue paper, the pearly pink of her painted nails gleaming in the sun coming through the side window. Her right hand covered her left, but Carrie could still see the bruise, nauseatingly multi-coloured in its intensity from where a canula had been inserted. This woman really didn't need any more stress in her life.

'I'm so sorry. I will do my very best to put this right. Where's Guy now?'

'He's gone for one of his walks with Wilbur. He does that when there's a problem. The bigger the problem, the longer the walk. I don't expect to see him for several hours.'

Carrie stood up, all thoughts of her ferry pushed to one side.

'I'll go and find the Major now. Can I give you a lift home?'

Irene drained her cup and used the edge of the table to lift herself from the chair.

'No, thank you, dear. I'll be all right to drive now. The caffeine has done its trick and I can take my time.'

She linked her arm through Carrie's as they walked to the front door.

'I'm glad to have met you, Carrie. I knew, at least I hoped, that Guy wouldn't have misjudged you.'

Carrie went cold, as if something had passed over her grave.

'Does Guy think I was here with an ulterior motive as well?'

'I don't believe so, dear, but you know Guy. He can be a bit of a closed book, even to me.'

'When you see him, will you tell him I'm sorry?' She raked her hands through her hair. 'I seem to be making a mess of everything at the moment.'

She gazed around the hall. Was it really only thirteen days ago that she had walked in here?

'This place is so special. What you said earlier, about Guy wanting it to restore people's faith in the world, it was starting to do that. I've been writing a journal and I've read several books and just sat in the garden and listened to the birds in the evening. And I've had time to think about who I really am and what I want, as opposed to who other people think I am and what they want for me. I've never dared to do that before.'

Irene squeezed Carrie's forearm.

'If you stayed a little longer, you could tell Guy that yourself. I'm sure it would mean more to hear it from you rather than from me.'

Carrie felt a lump in her throat. 'I would if I could but...'

'You have to get back,' Irene added. 'I understand.'

No, Carrie thought. *You don't understand. You don't understand that, in spite of all my efforts to resist, I'm falling in love with your grandson. And I can't even begin to tell you how I feel because he's already besotted with another woman.*

As soon as Irene had left Carrie grabbed her coat and the

letter she had written for Rita, and headed for the gardens. Heather was just about to close the gate as she rounded the bend.

'What are you doing?' she asked.

'The Major's sent us home,' Heather replied, her voice quavery, her eyes red-ringed.

'Haven't you got any visitors?'

'He's sent them away, too,' Heather said, a tear trickling out of the corner of her eye.

'That's going to look good on Tripadvisor,' Carrie said, with a groan.

Heather shot her a wary glance.

'I'm not the enemy, Heather. I had no ulterior motive coming here, I promise you. Guy offered me a temporary job, and I took it. I love it here. It's perfect. It doesn't need changing in any way.'

She moved towards the gate.

'Where are you going?'

'To see the Major.'

'I can't let you in. I'll lose my job as well and my husband's out of work. We need my wage, not that it's much, but it helps us to get by.'

She started to weep more copiously and fished about in her pocket. Carrie handed her a clean tissue.

'I have a stack of them,' she explained. 'I've been keeping Kleenex in business these last few months what with one thing and another.'

Heather gave a wan smile and blew her nose loudly. 'Thanks.'

'I'm going to sort this out, Heather. Don't you worry. And don't worry about letting me in through the gate, I'll just go and climb over the wall. It's not very high. I wouldn't dream of getting you into trouble as well as Guy.'

'He took to you,' Heather said. 'I could tell.'

'Everyone has been very kind to me. I shall always remember my time here very fondly.'

'You're leaving then?'

'When I've sorted this mess out.'

'The Major can be stubborn.'

'That makes two of us. I promise I'll do my best to change his mind, Heather.'

'I know you will,' Heather said. She stood aside from the gate and turned away. 'Go on, slip through while I'm not looking and I can pretend I never saw you! Don't want to think of you scrambling over that wall and doing yourself an injury.'

'Or even worse, damaging some of the plants in the border on the other side,' Carrie said, with a grin. 'Thanks, Heather.'

'You're welcome. And Carrie, don't be a stranger.'

Carrie hugged her before slipping through the gap and under the archway. She paused for a moment as Heather locked the gate behind her. *Just gather your thoughts, Carrie. This could be the most important thing you've ever done. All of those contracts you gained in the past were nothing compared to this.*

The gravel crunched loudly as she walked across it, as if announcing her. Without any of the staff or visitors, the whole place felt different, sorrowful despite the efforts of the daffodils and the verdant greenery of spring. The wrought-iron gate creaked as she pushed it open and walked up the path to the front of the house. Everything seemed magnified in the stillness, the knock on the door, her breath, quick and ragged despite her efforts to calm herself. She didn't expect an answer and there wasn't one, so after a couple of minutes she scouted around the perimeter, peering through windows, but there was no sign of Andrew. He could be upstairs, of course, could have taken to his bed, but he didn't strike her as that type. Where would he retreat to after an upset such as this?

She took the route she had on that very first visit with

Wilbur. How she wished he was by her side now. The Major was sitting on the bench, head down, hand on his stick.

'You've got a nerve,' he growled as soon as he saw her.

'We need to talk,' she said.

'Nothing to say,' he retorted.

Carrie pressed her lips together and went to sit next to him. He shifted to one side, leaving the maximum gap possible between them.

'It is good manners,' he said, 'to wait until you are invited to take a seat.'

'Thought I'd be waiting quite a long time,' Carrie replied, 'and I have a ferry to catch.'

Out of the corner of her eye she detected a slightly raised eyebrow.

'Running away, are you?'

'Not for the reason you think.'

'And what is that?'

'That I came here as part of some undercover plan to promote, develop, upgrade or whatever term you like to use, and that Guy was a party to this subterfuge.'

He turned slightly, his eyes blazing.

'I have proof.'

He reached inside his tweed jacket and waved a business card in front of her.

'This was in the potting shed on top of Guy's basket of seed brochures. This is your company, is it not?'

'It is. At least, it was. I've handed in my notice.'

He didn't even blink.

'May I?'

She took the card from him and turned it over, pointing out the name on the back.

'This is Mark's card, not mine.'

'I'm well aware of that. My eyesight isn't so poor that I can't read. However, it's obvious that you're in cahoots. He's your boss, I understand, as well as the two of you having had a previous dalliance.'

Carrie leapt up from the bench and rounded on him.

'Dalliance! Is that what he said or is that your surmising of the situation? I think over a decade together constitutes more than a dalliance, don't you? Perhaps we should go inside and get a dictionary definition as to how long a dalliance actually lasts.'

He looked slightly taken aback.

'I appear to have touched a nerve,' he murmured.

'You have touched several. If I was going to be in cahoots with someone, it would certainly not be Mark, the man who dumped me for a woman who wheedled her way into his life through bending over wallpaper samples in a low-cut top when he'd never shown the slightest interest in interior décor or bountiful bosoms before. It was only the promise of Swedish meatballs that enabled me to get him to IKEA for a few things to brighten up our home but then Paloma swans into our office with her swatches and samples and her decolletage to die for and suddenly he's as knowledgeable as David Hicks or Philippe Starck.'

She took a large gulp of air and put a hand up to stop him interrupting her.

'And as for him being my boss, that isn't exactly accurate. He's in a senior position to me but that's because he took the job which should have been mine. He schmoozed his way around the partners, used me for ideas because between you and me he's not great at coming up with his own, and he's a man and whatever people say women are still viewed with suspicion in some companies because we're "emotional at certain times of the month" or "difficult to work with" or "might go off and have babies". If I was going to be so crass as to make a pitch for a contract to market this garden, I wouldn't do it by befriending you or Guy or pretending to come on holiday and being in need of something to take my mind off life stuff.'

She paused and looked around. The energy had completely drained out of her. She flumped back down. Next to her the Major was silent and still apart from his thumb gently massaging the top of the stick. All around them nature was at work, the roses throwing out new shoots, leaves unfurling from the hedges, the wind getting up and rustling in the trees beyond.

'So how would you do it?' he asked at last.

'I wouldn't,' she replied. 'To me this is perfect just as it is.'

'Then why is Guy always saying that we need to change this and alter that and open for another day here and there?'

'Because,' Carrie said softly, 'he loves this place almost as much as you do. Can't you see that? He wants Honoria's garden to be a fitting legacy and those things take not just time but money. I don't have to tell you that a place like this needs constant care and those visitors who you so resent pay for that every time they put their hands in their pockets for the entrance fee or to buy a piece of cake or a plant. But I think somewhere like this is about more than that. I don't think you realise how much pleasure people get from coming to your garden, how they are able to carry a piece of it with them when they go back to their ordinary, probably challenging lives. Isn't that something to celebrate? That you have the opportunity to share this with others and make their existence a little more bearable in some small way, which means they are better able to cope with any difficulties because of the peace and sustenance they have found here.'

Still he was quiet.

'Guy doesn't want to promote this place more, Andrew,' Carrie said. 'He just wants you to be able to carry on living here and he wants to preserve its soul.'

Carrie stared at him, willing a response.

'I knew you'd be trouble from the first time I saw you,' he said at last.

'I could say the same about you,' she replied.

'If you want my opinion and I doubt you do, but I think you've had rather a lucky escape with that Mark person. Struck me as being rather superficial. Also, he's lacking in manners.'

'I'm sorry. Irene told me he ambushed you. He can be quite... persistent.'

'Hmph! Might have known she'd stick her oar in. I presume she's sent you to plead Guy's case or has Guy himself asked you to argue his corner?'

'Do you really know that little about him?'

The Major's lips twitched slightly.

'Neither of those are true. I haven't seen Guy and if I had he certainly wouldn't ask me or anyone else for that matter to come and beg for his job back.'

'Is that what you're doing?'

'Not begging, no. I don't do that. It rarely works in the long term.'

'He won't accept it anyway. Once Guy's made up his mind, that's it.'

'A bit like someone else I could mention by the sound of things,' Carrie replied. 'With all due respect, I think you're wrong. I think if you both swallow your pride, beginning with an apology from you, Andrew, and an admission that you made a big mistake, Guy will come back. If you do that, chances are that he'll turn up tomorrow morning as if nothing had happened.'

She stood up, turned to face him and held out her hand.

'Do we have a deal?'

The Major placed his other hand on the stick and twisted them both around.

'I'll think about it.'

'Well, that's something, I suppose,' Carrie said. 'But I wouldn't think for too long. People like Guy are rare. There are other big houses on the island, or even just over the water, which would benefit from his talents. You wouldn't want him to go and find another job while you were still cogitating. Take care of yourself, Major Andrew Fox-Patterson. Remember to eat Rita's food and thank her for her kindness and don't forget to check the date on your milk.'

With a brief wave, she walked away, wondering whether she'd managed to achieve anything at all.

NINETEEN

Instead of heading straight back to the cottage, Carrie took the path up towards the Longstone. She wasn't in a fit state to drive to the ferry just yet. Perhaps a walk through the woods would help with the frustration and despair she felt. Trees were meant to be healing. She thought it amazing how they all supported each other through their root systems – if only humans could do the same. Would the Major get in touch with Guy? She really couldn't tell. It was perfectly possible he would leave things as they were. She felt in her pocket for her phone. She had Guy's number. She could call him. There was signal at the top of the hill, but what could she say, and would he really want to hear from her?

Carrie emerged into the clearing and took a deep breath. What a shambles, as one of her primary school teachers frequently used to say. It had been the right thing for her to come to the island but now she'd messed up someone else's life and she couldn't bear that. She was so fond of this place, these people, but she would never come back. It would be too painful.

'You're leaving?'

Carrie jumped at the sound of Jo's voice as she emerged from behind the Longstone.

'Oh, Jo, you gave me a fright! Yes, I'm heading back to Manchester. News does travel fast.'

Jo shrugged.

'No one told me, but you're dressed as if you're leaving.'

Carrie looked down at her jeans and t-shirt. 'I dress like this all the time when I'm not working.'

Jo smiled. 'Plus, you have the air of someone who is on their way to somewhere else.'

'Oh, I see. At least, I think I do. The trouble is I don't know where I'm going. Well, obviously, physically I do. I'm heading back to Manchester for now but metaphorically...' Carrie put a hand out and touched the Longstone. She had the sudden urge to cry. '...I have absolutely no idea,' she whispered.

Jo walked over and took her hand. Carrie realised how cold she felt. Jo's warmth was like being wrapped in a comfort blanket.

'We don't always need to know everything,' Jo said, applying a little more pressure with her fingers. 'Sometimes we just have to trust that everything is working out for the best.'

'I just can't see that at the moment,' Carrie said, shaking her head. 'In some ways I feel worse than when I arrived.'

'Ah! That's all part of the process.'

Carrie was quiet.

'The process of recovery isn't a straight line, Carrie. It has twists and loops. Sometimes it feels as if we're going back on ourselves before we shoot forwards. Rediscovery can lead us to what might seem like dead ends, but everything is valuable, everything is progress, if we yield to the power of time and nature to heal.'

'But what if by trying to help we cause havoc? What if by coming to a place to help ourselves we cause pain for others? How can that be healing?'

'Something has happened to upset you, and I'm sorry about that, but maybe the situation hasn't fully played out yet. Perhaps you need to give it more time.'

'I can't. I have to go. There isn't anything more for me here. In fact, I think I'm doing harm by staying.'

'And you're resolved not to come back.'

Carrie stared at the older woman looking at her so intently.

'I don't believe I will.'

She felt in her jacket pocket and held out the amethyst.

'Thank you for this. It did bring me deeper understanding of some things, or something did.'

'I would like you to keep it but if you would rather leave it here, as you intended, that's a kind gesture. Everyone who comes here leaves a little of themselves at this place and takes something away with them.'

She squeezed Carrie's hand again.

'Give yourself time, Carrie. Take good care of yourself and everything will sort itself out. I am sure of it.'

'I hope that you can reconnect with your daughters one day.'

Jo smiled. 'It's that hope which keeps me going, that and being here for my son. I won't give up.'

After she had left Carrie circled the Longstone, caressing the amethyst between her thumb and forefinger before she found the perfect crevice in which to place it. And there she left it, nestling from the wind and rain and with the wish that it would begin to heal all who came across it.

She really didn't want to be spotted by Rita and have to explain herself, so she almost tiptoed down the drive to Orchard Farm, wincing in anticipation of the old letterbox's grating protest. Except someone had obviously oiled it and the letter dropping on to the tiled floor made more of a clunk than the hinges.

Inside the house Hercules barked and guiltily Carrie made a brisk retreat.

Wandering through every room of the cottage, Carrie pretended to be checking that she hadn't left anything behind, but she wasn't fooling herself. She plumped up cushions which didn't need plumping, straightened a pile of magazines which were already perfectly aligned and gave the tiniest amount of extra water to the peace lily in the living room window.

'Goodbye, peace lily,' she said. 'Thank you for your company.'

In the bedroom she had left Granny's ring and a few toiletries on the dressing table. Before putting on the ring and packing the bottles away, she couldn't resist throwing open the window and perching on the little seat for one last time. Looking across the garden she half-hoped that Wilbur would appear around the corner, closely followed by Guy. But there were only sparrows diving in and out of the hedge and the sheep concentrating hard on munching the grass in the field. Carrie sighed. Who would have thought less than two weeks ago that she would have come here thinking she was in love with one person and leave thinking she was in love with someone else? She thought about the walk back from Cressie's barbecue, the way Guy had draped his jacket around her shoulders, the gentlest of kisses under the starlit sky. *This is why people have holiday romances*, she thought. *It's so easy to think you're falling in love when there aren't any of life's other pressures to get in the way.* Once she was back in Manchester, she would forget all about him in a few days and if she didn't? Well, it was immaterial because he would certainly have forgotten all about her. Good riddance would be what he was thinking.

'But I am still grateful to you,' she murmured into the soft scented air of the cottage. 'I have learned a lot from being here. I've learned about who I really am and what I really need, so thank you for that. Thank you for giving me the space and comfort to come back to myself.'

As she lifted her arm to pull the window closed an unexpectedly strong breeze gusted into the room, the curtains billowing around her, and a couple of the half-empty bottles rocked on their bases. Carrie reached out to stop her favourite perfume toppling to the floor and accidentally swept Granny's ring on to the carpet. She got down on her hands and knees and scrabbled about, looking beneath the dressing table, under the bed, lifting the edge of the rug, even checking it wasn't caught in the turned-up cuff of her shirt. She knelt back on her heels and tried to quell the feeling of panic. *Be logical*, Carrie. *It was here a couple of minutes ago so it must still be here now. But where?*

She checked her watch. At this rate she'd be lucky to make the two o'clock ferry and then she had the long drive north, but she couldn't leave without the ring. Why hadn't she put it straight back on after Irene left? In a couple of places there was a slight gap where the skirting board met the old sloping floor. Fetching a torch from the cupboard under the sink in the kitchen Carrie squinted and shone it into the spaces. Nothing. The only other place it could have disappeared into was a narrow divide where two of the oak boards met. It would have had to roll across the rug and meet that opening at just the right angle. What were the odds on that? All the same, she lay on her front, put her face to the floor and angled the beam from the torch into the darkness. Was she imagining it or had something glinted?

The radiator was on the other side of the room and this particular board didn't look as if it had been moved for years. She opened all of the cupboards and drawers looking for a screwdriver and finally ran into the garden to try the shed. It was padlocked, of course. She could call Guy or go and find him at the gardens. No, there was no way she was doing that. She could go to the shop and buy a screwdriver and pair of pliers to wrench up the floorboard, but she might make a horrible mess. She'd have to contact Rita. There was no alternative that she could think of.

Rita would have heard the letter drop on to the floor even if Hercules hadn't barked. There was nothing wrong with her hearing even though Christabel had tried to make out there was. But then Christabel was always trying to make out that she was on her last legs and 'wouldn't she be more comfortable in the nice little bungalow on the other side of the farmyard?'

Actually, she probably would have been perfectly all right in the bungalow in spite of having been brought up in this rambling old Victorian farmhouse, but she wasn't going to be pushed out. Yes, the plan had been for her and George to move into the bungalow and Alastair and family to move in here, and they'd have done that willingly if Christabel hadn't been so blatant in her desire to get her hands on the big house and 'bring it up to date'. If Christabel had taken the time to get to know her better, she would have realised that, when pushed, Rita always dug her heels in. Had been like that ever since she was a toddler. She knew it was unreasonable, petty even, and she prayed for forgiveness constantly but still she couldn't acquiesce, not just yet.

Hercules waited impatiently as she took two freshly baked wholemeal loaves out of the range and turned them out on to a rack. Finally, when he thought he would burst from her slowness, she opened the kitchen door a fraction and gave him his instructions, not that he needed them.

'Post, Hercules,' she said. 'Fetch!'

And off he scooted, reappearing a few seconds later to drop a lilac-coloured envelope into her floury palms. She sat at the kitchen table and he jumped on to her lap as if to read the missive himself.

Dear Rita,

For various reasons I'm leaving a little sooner than expected and I wanted to thank you for all you have done while I've been here. Your island, the people I've met and the kindnesses I've been shown will always hold a special place in my heart. Please will you say goodbye to the Major for me when you next call in with a pie! We didn't exactly part on good terms. I will drop him a line and thank him for letting me work in his beautiful garden. Like-wise, Cressie. Please tell her that I will be in touch in due course. I will leave the key to the cottage under the flowerpot as it was when I arrived. This place has been such a sanctuary, and you look after it with such love and attention that I'm sure it will prove to be a great success and a comfort to many people going forwards. Thank you again, Rita. Take care.

With love, Carrie Xx

'Oh!' Rita said out loud. 'Oh dear, Hercules, I wonder what's happened.'

She lifted him to the floor and scuttled to the front door, yanked it open on its creaky old hinges because everyone used the back entrance these days, and stared up the drive but there was no sign of her. She must have made a quick getaway. Rita felt a sudden sadness wash over her. It was a nice letter, warm, thankful, but there was much not said, so much suppressed. She headed back to the kitchen and sat down on one of the old pine chairs, the one with the wobbly leg which she must get Alastair to look at when he had a moment. Not that he ever did, the farm and Christabel saw to that. Or Guy, she could mention it to him. Rita frowned. She wondered if Carrie's quick departure had anything to do with Guy. She hoped not.

'I liked her, Hercules,' she said, giving him a biscuit. 'I liked her a lot.'

'Who did you like?' Christabel asked, stepping into the kitchen in what looked like another pair of brand new impossibly white trainers.

'Carrie, the girl staying at Hideaway Cottage.'

'Oh, her,' Christabel said. 'I didn't get around to talking to her at Cressie's party. Has she left early?'

'Yes.'

Rita eyed up the blazer casually draped over Christabel's arm.

'Maybe it was too quiet for her. This island isn't for everyone.'

'No,' Rita said, leaning down to rub Hercules' throat so he wouldn't growl. He'd never liked Christabel.

Rita watched as her daughter-in-law dropped languorously into the chair opposite her.

'Is there another guest booked in?' she asked, in what Rita had come to know as her faux casual voice.

'Not at the moment.'

'That's good. You won't have to rush around there and clean for a quick turnaround.'

Rita pressed her lips together. She knew exactly what was coming.

'And I was wondering,' Christabel continued with her sweetest smile, 'if you have a few moments to spare, that is, which I expect you do now, if you wouldn't mind mending William's blazer.'

She pushed it across the table towards Rita.

'The lining in the pocket has gone and everything he puts in there just falls through to the bottom of the jacket, which is very irritating for him and means that it looks all out of shape. I could do it myself, of course, but you're so much better at this sort of thing than I am, Rita.'

Rita made a show of examining the pocket. She could say no but if she did that it would never get done. Besides, she was constantly demurring about the house move. She suspected the fact Christabel couldn't get her own way with that was something of a novelty. Pick your battles, her mother used to say, and she was right. Sometimes it was better to bite her tongue for everyone's sake and just give in to the small demands, even if they were put in such a sycophantic way that it made her want to reach for George's whisky decanter alongside sending up a prayer to the Good Lord for extra strength and grace. She tried to remind herself that she wasn't the only person who had a difficult daughter-in-law. Now Carrie, she would make a lovely daughter-in-law for someone. She was going to miss her, whereas – and God forgive her for thinking this – if Christabel sailed away from the island this very day and never came back, Rita didn't think she would miss her one jot. In fact, she thought that she and maybe the whole family would breathe out in a way they hadn't for years. She folded the blazer carefully and placed it to one side of the table.

'I'll do it this evening,' she said.

And sure enough, as soon as she'd got what she wanted, Christabel had stood up to leave. Rita hauled herself up, too, not for the first time astounded by the amount of energy resentment could sap from your muscles. She didn't expect a thank you. Those could be counted on one hand, not that she should be counting. What was it Luke said – to love your enemies. It felt so wicked to think of Christabel as an enemy and yet... She gave herself a shake. What she needed was some fresh air.

She looked down at Hercules who was virtually bristling with repressed emotions.

'What we both need,' she said, grabbing his lead from the back of the door, 'is a bit of a stress relieving walk.'

TWENTY

Carrie had tried to call both the farmhouse number and Rita's phone. There was no answer from either and now she couldn't find her car keys. She was sure that she'd left them on the kitchen table. This was ridiculous. It was almost as if someone or something was conspiring to stop her leaving. At this rate there wouldn't be any point getting a ferry today. She might as well wait until tomorrow morning rather than drive all the way up to Manchester in the dark.

She was walking as briskly as was humanly possible without breaking into a run when she spotted Rita coming down the lane towards her. She could hardly remember being more pleased to see anyone in her entire life.

'I was just coming to find you,' she gasped.

'Goodness me, lovey,' Rita said, placing a hand on Carrie's arm. 'What on earth's the matter? I thought you'd already gone.'

'I-I should have done but...'

Stupid tears started to trickle down her cheeks.

'Now, now, don't you upset yourself. Whatever it is, we can sort it out.'

Carrie dabbed at the tears with her fingers.

'Sorry,' she said, sniffing, 'ridiculous to cry. I was all ready to leave and that felt harder than I anticipated and then I dropped my ring. At least, this gust of wind knocked something over which swept it on to the floor and now I can't find it and it was my granny's and she gave it to me just before she died and we were really close and—'

'Shh, shh,' Rita said, wrapping both arms around her and holding her close.

'I can't leave without it,' Carrie mumbled into Rita's cardigan, which smelt of a mixture of freshly baked bread and lightly scented soap.

'Of course you can't,' Rita said. 'These things are precious. My earrings belonged to my great-grandma and whenever I wear them, I feel that she is close to me.'

Reluctantly, Carrie disentangled herself from Rita's strong embrace and looked at the little drop sapphires glinting in the sunshine.

'They're beautiful,' she said.

'I used to save them for best but one difficult day I said to myself, "Rita, why are you leaving these in a drawer to be hardly ever worn? You don't know how many more days the Good Lord is going to grant you in this wonderful world. He would want you to wear these earrings, as would your great-grandma." So now, at least once a week, I get them out of their little velvet lined box and pop them on and I swear that they give me a sort of strength.'

'Sapphires are meant to be good for mental wellbeing,' Carrie said. 'They can help promote wisdom and peace of mind.'

'Well, fancy that!' Rita exclaimed, her whole face radiating with wonder. 'It may be a bit late for the wisdom, but I won't say no to a bit of peace of mind. And what about your ring? What's that made from?'

'Diamonds.'

'And what do they represent?'

'Strength,' Carrie replied. 'Resilience, courage.'

Rita grasped her hand.

'I may not know much but I do know that courage comes from the French word *coeur* for heart, so let's take heart and be confident that we can find this ring of yours.'

'I think it might have fallen through a gap in the floorboards. I've looked everywhere else and it's the only explanation, but I can't get the floorboard up because I haven't any tools and I don't want to do any damage and...'

'I'll call Guy,' Rita said.

'No!'

Hercules jumped at her legs and she bent to stroke him.

'I mean, I'd rather you didn't.'

Rita made a pretence of scolding Hercules and reeling in the lead a little.

'He's not around.'

'Not at the gardens?' Rita asked, with a disconcertingly direct gaze.

'No, at least, I don't think so.'

'Well,' Rita said, after Carrie had given her a brief precis of the morning's events, 'a lot has been going on while I've been baking my bread.'

She fished her phone out of her cardigan pocket and linked her arm through Carrie's.

'Oh, look, I've got a missed call from you,' she said. 'I didn't even hear it ring.'

'Perhaps you've got it on silent,' Carrie suggested. 'My mum often does that.'

Rita looked bemusedly at the phone.

'Have I? Oh well, no harm done. Let's head to the top of the lane and see if we can get a signal. If he's not too far away, Alastair will come and see if your ring has fallen beneath the floor.'

They paused by the village green, and Carrie took hold of Hercules' lead while Rita tilted her head to one side and pressed the phone to her ear.

'We're in luck,' she said, gleefully. 'It's ringing.'

Carrie followed Hercules in his quest for an exciting scent and tried to avoid looking at The Manor over the road. She wondered where Guy was now, perhaps being comforted by Cressie or perhaps the Major had already spoken to him and he was back at work in the garden.

'Oh!' she heard Rita exclaim. 'You didn't mention it to me. Why isn't he coming to the farm as usual?'

There was a long pause and Carrie watched as Rita turned away, her posture unusually closed in.

'Is everything all right?' she asked, when Rita finally came off the phone.

'I'm sure it is,' Rita said, with an unconvincing smile. 'Alastair's meeting with the farm consultant in Cowes so I'm afraid he's a bit tied up for the next couple of hours.'

She gave herself a little shake.

'Never mind. We're independent women, aren't we, and I've got a shed full of George's old tools at home. I'm sure we can shift this floorboard between us.'

Carrie shivered as Rita dug the pliers into the old oak. The room had gone very cold.

'I don't want you to damage the floor,' she said. 'Guy won't be very pleased.'

Beads of perspiration bubbled up on Rita's brow.

'Don't you worry about him,' Rita said.

But I do, Carrie thought. *I do worry about him, and I can't stop myself.*

'It's certainly not been moved for a while,' Rita huffed.

'Here, let me have a go,' Carrie said.

She felt something flutter against her neck. Suddenly the air seemed to be stirred up as if there was a storm coming yet the day outside was bright and calm.

Rita straightened up and rubbed her back.

'You can try,' she said.

As Carrie stepped forwards, she felt something in her way. There was the sensation of palms jamming against her shoulders, a face inches from hers and suddenly she was being shoved backwards with force. She staggered, almost overbalanced and put a hand out behind her to reach for the edge of the bed.

Rita's mouth was open in surprise.

'What on earth was that?' she asked. 'You looked as if you were flying.'

Carrie sat on the bed and put one hand across her chest.

'It felt as if someone pushed me.'

They were silent for a moment. Rita came and sat on the bed next to her.

'You've turned as white as a sheet.'

'I'm all right. Really, I am, but perhaps we should leave this for Guy,' Carrie said. 'I feel...'

She looked around the room.

'I feel as if by doing this we might be upsetting someone.'

'Well, there's certainly a lot of history with this cottage, so I suppose that's possible,' Rita said, 'but Guy's never mentioned any trouble.'

'Things did move, though. He told me.'

'But there was never anything malevolent,' Rita said.

'I don't think this was malevolent,' Carrie replied, 'more fearful.'

'Of what we might find?'

'Maybe.'

'For nothing is hidden that will not be made manifest, nor is anything secret that will not be known and come to light,' Rita said. 'The gospel according to Luke, if I remember correctly, and although I believe that some secrets are better to remain just that, I also believe that some secrets need to be brought into the light. Perhaps your ring slipping down beneath the floor was the catalyst needed. Listen to me,' she carried on with a tinkling laugh, 'I'm getting all philosophical and my George would tell me to stop talking and start doing.'

She reached for a crowbar lying on the floor behind her.

'I think it's time for the big guns.'

'Oh, Rita, I'm really not sure about this.'

'I can see something glinting and you're not going home without that ring. If there's anyone in this room, they can come and give me a shove instead of you.'

Carrie doubted that any entity would dare to give Rita a shove, even her beloved George.

Rita positioned the crowbar into the gap and gently began to exert pressure. There was a sound of splintering wood and gradually the whole board began to lift. Carrie tiptoed over from the bed, switched on the torch and shone it into the hole.

'Can you see it?' Rita asked.

'Yes, and there's something else down here, too. A box, I think.'

Carrie tried not to think about creepy crawlies as she reached for her ring.

'That's very pretty,' Rita said, as Carrie slipped the ring on her finger, 'and back where it belongs.'

She gazed at the little circle of diamonds sparkling in the afternoon light.

'Thank you. Now I can go home without leaving anything behind.'

Rita smiled.

'Oh, I think we leave something of ourselves behind wherever we go, don't you? And some places just draw us back, however much we might try to resist. I do hope you'll keep in touch.'

Carrie hugged her.

'I will. I promise.'

'Now what about this box? Do you think it's buried treasure? Guy could do with some good fortune one way or another.'

'I hope it's not a dead cat,' Carrie said. 'Didn't people place those in the walls of houses for good luck a few hundred years ago?'

'They were meant to ward off evil spirits,' Rita said, 'but in spite of what's just happened, I don't believe there are any of those here. Protective, maybe, not evil.'

'Perhaps they aren't here because there's a dead cat in a box under the floor,' Carrie countered.

Rita laughed and shone the torch into the hole.

'A very small cat, looking at the size of that box, and there's only one way to find out.'

'Perhaps we should leave it where it is,' Carrie replied, but Rita was already on her hands and knees, one arm outstretched.

'It's wooden,' she said, sitting back on her heels, 'and it's got little feet. In fact, I think it's a tea caddy.'

Carrie grabbed a tissue from the windowsill and wiped the box clean, revealing rippling mahogany and small brass ball feet.

'Why would anyone put a tea caddy under the floor?'

Again, that feeling of something or someone passing too close, almost restraining her.

'I think we should put it back, Rita. I've got this feeling that it's not right to pry.'

'We'll put it back,' Rita said, 'but don't you want to know what's inside?'

Carrie was sure there must be some biblical quote about curiosity but if there was, Rita was ignoring it.

'It could be a time capsule. It could be nothing.'

'It's not nothing,' Carrie said.

'But it's not Pandora's box either, is it, lovey?' Rita said soothingly.

'I suppose not.'

The feeling of pressure suddenly released, and a swoosh of air swept through the room. A few seconds later, downstairs a door banged. Carrie flinched but Rita seemed unfazed as she placed the caddy between them and turned the small key. Inside were two compartments, each with their own little lids.

'You lift one and I'll lift the other,' she instructed. 'One, two, three.'

Carrie's fingers were trembling as she took hold of the little ivory knob. This felt wrong, very wrong. Intrusive. Something in Rita's hand jangled softly.

'Look, Carrie,' she gasped. 'Look at this. Isn't that the prettiest thing?'

In Rita's palm was a slender piece of coral, about three inches long with delicate silver bells attached at one end.

'It's a teething ring,' Carrie said, a lump forming in her throat, 'and in my side is a bonnet.'

The apricot-coloured silk was carefully folded and had two slightly frayed satin ribbons. The crown was embroidered with daisies and a little frill had been added at the base of the neck together with a silk flower where one of the ribbons was joined. Carrie placed her fingers inside and twirled the bonnet around. She had the distinct feeling that they were being watched.

'We should put them back,' she said.

Rita nodded.

'Except there's something else in here. An envelope.'

The copperplate writing was faded but still legible –

'Philly'. Tentatively, Carrie lifted the back flap. Inside was a perfect auburn curl.

'Oh, Rita,' she said. 'For some inexplicable reason I feel as if my heart might break.'

Rita nodded and without speaking they placed the items back in the caddy and returned it to its home beneath the floorboards.

MEMORIES

'Isaac! Isaac! Where are you?'

Eliza ran around the garden, across the field and up into the woods. Her hair, which had been piled on top of her head and tied in a loose knot, now tumbled down her back.

'Eliza, come away,' he had urged, as she stood in the doorway watching Carrie and Rita try to loosen the floorboard.

She nearly always obeyed him. After all, it had been part of her wedding vows, but not this time. She just couldn't. She was compelled to stay there, a creeping feeling of dread rising from her feet up towards her head. And then Isaac had pushed past her and pushed Carrie. Her lovely, gentle, courteous Isaac had actually put his hands against their precious guest's shoulders and shoved. Carrie had staggered backwards, and Eliza had wanted to reach out to her, to catch her, to beg forgiveness, but none of those things were possible. Isaac, his face an agony of exasperation, had come to her side and grasped her hand.

'We need to go,' he whispered.

But she had resisted. She felt safe in the limbo of the door frame, neither moving backwards or forwards.

'Eliza, we need to leave now,' he persisted. 'Our work here is done.'

She had torn her gaze away from Carrie and Rita lifting that box from its hiding place and looked at her husband.

'Go where?'

'To the other side. I have indulged you. We have remained here for too long.'

His grasp on her tightened.

'But, Isaac, you know that if we pass over it isn't possible to easily come back. We can watch from afar, but we don't have the same power.'

'Power can be misused,' he said.

Eliza felt a flare of anger ripple through her.

'I was doing what I thought was best. I was trying to help.'

'And now you need to help me, Eliza. I need you to come with me now.'

He had tugged at her arm.

'Isaac, you're hurting me.' She twisted away. 'I'm not ready to leave.'

'It's for your own good, Eliza.'

She had stared at him for a moment and shook her head. 'Maybe this time you're wrong, Isaac. Maybe, my love, this time I know what is for my own good, better than you, and maybe that's staying here just a little longer.'

He took an abrupt step back.

'Then I will go without you,' he said, and without so much as a departing kiss he flurried down the stairs and away from her.

When Eliza turned her attention back to the room, Carrie and Rita were sitting on the bed. She recognised the tea caddy resting between them but couldn't remember where from. Isaac had stirred up her senses even more and confusion was crashing through her. The rattle was the first to emerge and the tinkling of those bells was like a balm. Feelings of wonder and contentment threaded their way through the frustration. She wanted to capture them, hold them close, rock them like a baby. Whose rattle was that? Had it been hers? Had she brought it with her when she had made her escape, a memento of a time when she had felt truly loved by her family? Was the pocket of emptiness at her core due to her alienation from them? She had always thought they'd come around to her marriage to Isaac, but her father was an intransigent man and her mother in thrall to him. She should have known better. And that bonnet, its ribbons drifting through the air as Carrie twirled it around on her fingers – was that hers, too? Were these objects preserved from her own childhood? A childhood that had seemed at one time to be gilded. How lucky she had felt to be the youngest child of such doting parents.

But devotion, it turned out, had its price. And that price was pain. The curl lay in Carrie's palm now. It was definitely her colour or at least the colour Eliza's hair had once been. But who was Philly and why was the box secreted beneath the floor? Isaac knew the answers to these questions. She was sure of it, and she needed him to explain.

She didn't wait to see what Rita and Carrie did with the box. With an indiscreet flurry she found the strength to flee: down the stairs, through the hall, into the living room, out through the kitchen and the partially open back door. She had gone straight to the willow tree, their place. But he wasn't there so she had gathered up her skirt around her knees, which was most unbecoming and still, after all of these years, brought her mother's remonstrations to her ears as if she was a teenager again.

'You'll never find a good husband, Eliza,' she had repeatedly said, 'if you persist in such unladylike behaviour.'

But she had found a good husband, the best of husbands, if only her parents had possessed the grace to acknowledge it. And now she ran as fast as she could, so fast she was almost flying. It was as if she was a girl again, haring across that beach at Bamburgh where she and Isaac had first met. She ran across the field, startling the sheep, and up into the woods, the harshness and disappointment of Isaac's last words ringing through her.

'You have meddled, Eliza,' he had hissed in her ear, 'and I told you not to. Nothing good will come of it. Why did you not listen to me?'

She had only been trying to buy time, to make things right so that Carrie wouldn't leave before Guy returned from his long, solitary walk. But it wasn't just the meddling that had upset Isaac so much. It was the taking up of the floorboard, the little wooden tea caddy. He hadn't even waited to see what it contained. She had rarely seen him so distressed and angry. He had flounced off, not caring that he might draw even more attention to himself. It had seemed, in that moment, that nothing mattered apart from his prising her away from that room.

Eliza sat on a fallen tree trunk, surrounded by the unfurling leaves of the beech trees and the sweet scent of bluebells. She knew that he always had her best interests at heart, and she had defied him. Would he ever forgive her? Had he really left her alone here? No, that was unthinkable. Isaac would never leave her. He was just sulking. He would be back soon and she should be waiting with an apology and a kiss.

TWENTY-ONE

Carrie stood on the top deck and watched the Isle of Wight recede from view. It had been hard enough saying goodbye to Rita and to the cottage, but now leaving the island she felt heart-broken all over again. She had stayed an extra night, and Rita had been on the doorstep at seven thirty with a small basket of food for the journey.

'I hope it's not too early,' she said apologetically, 'but I didn't want to miss you and thought you'd be eager to make tracks.'

Carrie was up and dressed even though she didn't feel eager to make tracks at all.

'That's so thoughtful. Thank you.'

'It's a long way up to Manchester and that motorway service food can be very hit and miss. Don't want you fading away before you get home. Will that friend of yours be waiting? I don't like to think of you going back to an empty house.'

'I think she'll be working but it doesn't matter. I'll be fine.'

'And that boyfriend of yours, he won't be lurking around?'

'No,' Carrie said, with a tremulous laugh. 'I don't think so.'

'Good,' Rita said. 'You deserve better.'

Carrie nodded. 'You're right. I do.'

'And your job?'

'I've already decided to move on from that.'

Rita nodded.

'But it's a positive decision. I haven't done it because I feel forced out.'

'That's the spirit. Maybe coming here has done you some good, after all, in spite of the few problems you've had.'

Carrie had leaned forwards and hugged her.

'It's a magical place. It has done me more good than you could possibly know. You have done me good, Rita.'

'I'll miss you,' Rita said, her eyes watering. 'Sometimes you just connect with people, don't you?'

Carrie tightened her grip.

'I think *you* connect with everyone.'

The older woman extricated herself and fanned her face.

'Goodness me, you're sending me all hot,' she said, blushing profusely, 'and I don't know about that. I can think of one or two who aren't quite on my wavelength.'

'I will stay in touch,' Carrie said.

'And you're welcome back, any time,' Rita said.

'Guy might not want me staying here,' Carrie replied, glancing up at the low eaves and reaching up to stroke the rough ends of the thatch. 'I feel awful about what happened. I do hope the Major comes around. I've left a message on Guy's phone, but he hasn't replied.'

'He can be stubborn, that one.'

'The Major or Guy?'

'Both of them.'

'Not much hope then?' Carrie said, ruefully.

'Oh, I don't know. There is a bond there. Let's hope that's stronger than their pride.'

'Will you let me know what happens?'

'You could try ringing him again. He might pick up his phone.'

Carrie shook her head. 'I don't think so.'

Rita gave her a penetrating look. 'I suppose you know best. Anyway, don't you worry about that. It wasn't your fault and if needs be I'll try to knock some sense into them both myself. Remember, you can have a bed at the farm any time. The spare room is always made up with the best linen.'

'Thank you. I can lock up if you need to get back there now.'

'Do you know, lovey, I think I might just stay here a while longer. I could do with the peace and quiet. There isn't anyone else booked in, but I can do a bit of cleaning – not that I'm sure you haven't left it spick and span – get the sheets in the machine and have a bit of time to myself.'

'You don't get much of that, do you?'

Rita blinked. 'It's good to be busy.'

'But sometimes it's good to pause,' Carrie said, stroking Rita's arm. 'You do so much for everyone else. Do something for yourself for a change.'

'I tend to think that doing things for other people *is* doing something for myself. That's how I was brought up. But perhaps you're right. Some people can take advantage when they think you'll always say yes.'

Carrie leaned forward and kissed Rita on the cheek.

'Sit down with a magazine and a cup of coffee for half an hour. No one will disturb you.' She glanced behind her into the cottage. 'Not even the ghosts.'

'You know what,' Rita said, 'I think I will.'

A few minutes later Carrie was driving away, tears blurring her eyes. Rita stood at the front door waving and as Carrie took a final look in her rear-view mirror, she had the uncanny impression of another more translucent figure also watching her leave.

Now she stood on the ferry deck and clung to the railings, watching the island recede into the distance.

'You should face the way you're going, Carrie,' she whispered, 'not where you've been.'

But it was too hard to tear herself away. Something thudded against her leg, and she dropped her gaze to see a brown Labrador looking up at her adoringly.

'Oh!' she gasped, instinctively dropping her hand to the top of the dog's head. 'You look just like someone I know.'

'He is someone you know,' a voice said behind her.

Carrie spun around. Guy was standing about three feet away, the wind whipping at his hair, eyes crinkled against the sun.

'You didn't think he'd just let you sneak away, did you? Without even a goodbye biscuit?'

'I'm not sneaking.'

'Looks like it to me. You didn't come and say goodbye to me either.'

'I left a message on your phone.'

'I heard it. It was quite curt.'

'That's not like you.'

'You don't really know what I'm like.'

He moved a little closer. 'Possibly not.'

What was he doing on the ferry? Was he going to Southampton to collect something? *Move downstairs, Carrie. Get yourself a coffee and sit somewhere as far away from him as possible.* Except Wilbur had just sat down on her feet, anchoring her to the spot.

Guy frowned.

'Have you been crying?'

She resisted the urge to wipe the back of her hand across her cheeks.

'No.'

'Must be the wind then. It can make your eyes water.'

He was quiet and still, apart from rocking gently with the movement of the boat. Wilbur was now not just sitting on her feet but leaning heavily against her, pinning her to the railings.

'Are you going back to him?'

Carrie twisted from the waist and looked past him towards Southampton.

'I don't think that's any of your business. What are you doing here anyway?'

Now he was standing very close, so close she could smell him over the salt spray, and she could hardly breathe. Why was he tormenting her like this? Except he wasn't doing it deliberately because he didn't know how she felt. She didn't know how she felt. Less than two weeks ago she had thought she was still in love with Mark and now... how could she trust herself to know what was true and what wasn't?

'I came to find you,' he said. 'I wanted to know why you were leaving so suddenly. Was it something to do with the cottage? I spoke to Rita. She said you'd lost your ring.'

So that was it. He thought she was going to put a bad review up of his cottage. Don't stay here, it might be haunted, and the owner's a liar and a cheat. Something along those lines.

'Your cottage is perfect, Guy. You don't need to worry on that score. I've left an assessment on the kitchen table and there really isn't anything that needs changing. I'll put up a good review and I'm sure you'll get loads of visitors.'

He winced and she felt a little guilty at the sharpness of her tone.

'I'm sorry I didn't tell you that I owned the cottage,' he said. 'I made that decision before I'd even met you. I just wanted an honest opinion, and I thought you might be influenced if you knew that it was mine, especially after we started to get to know one another better.'

She slid one foot from underneath Wilbur's hind legs and took a step to the side.

'It doesn't matter one way or the other.'

He was looking quizzical now, as if trying to fathom her out.

'Except it obviously does.'

'I don't like being lied to.'

'Neither do I.'

'Excuse me!' she said, raising her voice so that the couple of other people on the deck looked over. 'I did not lie to you.'

'I saw you in the gardens with Mark.'

'What did you see? Him kissing me? And you jumped to conclusions. It meant nothing, not to me anyway.'

He was searching her face, as if trying to work out whether she was telling the truth.

'So, you're not going back to him?'

'No! But I don't see what it's got to do with you. I'm not about to be lectured on relationships by someone who's having an affair with a married woman with children.'

He looked stunned, as if she had slapped him, and then perplexed before a dawning expression of realisation.

'Cressie! You think I'm having an affair with Cressie?'

'Well, aren't you?'

'Of course not! How can you think that?'

'Because I've seen you a couple of times leaving her house really, really early, creeping away before anyone would see you.'

Anger flared across his features.

'Now who's jumping to conclusions?'

'She was in her dressing gown!'

'Because she'd been in bed but not with me. She'd been sleeping while I took charge of the twins. Olivia has bad colic and it's worse at night. Jack often turns up later than he says and then swans off a couple of days earlier than planned. Cressie may look cool and composed and the epitome of the perfect mother, but underneath it all she's struggling and Jack doesn't want to face up to it. Cressie and I are friends, Carrie, good friends, and have been for years, but that's all. We have never ever slept together. I love her but not in a romantic way and I wouldn't have a relationship with someone who was married. For the record, I wouldn't get involved with someone who was still in a relationship or thought they were still in love with someone else. It may sound old-fashioned, but I try to be honourable.'

Disappointment swathed his features.

'I would have hoped you thought better of me than to...' He shrugged. 'Cressie's been there plenty of times for me in the past and I'm trying to do the same for her now.'

Carrie couldn't bring herself to look at him. Instead, she fondled the tip of Wilbur's ear, taking comfort from its softness. How could she have got everything so wrong?

'I'm sorry,' she said. 'I've made such a mess of things, including your job. I tried to tell the Major that he'd got it all wrong, that he was a fool to let you go but I'm not sure he was listening.'

'He was listening. Actually, he listens to you more than anyone I know. He called me yesterday evening.'

'So, you've got your job back?'

'If I want it.'

'Of course you want it!'

Guy grinned. *Please, please don't look like that,* Carrie thought. *It just makes me want to fall into your arms and I can't.*

'I know that,' he said, 'and you know that, but I'm letting the Major stew a little. It will do him good.'

'And the business card in the potting shed – that wasn't anything to do with me. I love the gardens just as they are.'

'I know that, too. Mark must have sneaked back there when I wasn't looking.'

'Oh, Mark could get an A* for sneaking,' she quipped, 'but I'm not so sure that even he would have done that.'

'Well, how did it get there then?'

'I'm not sure but ever since I've been here, I've felt that someone or something was trying to help me, to guide me.

Maybe, and I'm aware that this sounds far-fetched, the business card in the potting shed was something to do with that.'

'Trying to sever your ties with Mark for good?'

'Perhaps,' she replied. *Or delaying me*, she thought, *someone trying to stop me leaving.*

'Did Rita tell you about the tea caddy under the floorboards?'

He nodded.

'I would like to know who Philly was.'

He pushed some hair away from his forehead.

'So, apart from that mystery, we're all sorted? Misunderstandings resolved?'

'Yes,' she whispered. 'I think so.'

He clicked his fingers and called Wilbur to his side before turning and striding back towards the door. Was that it? Was he leaving just like that? Had she completely ruined everything?

'Don't,' she wanted to shout over the sound of the waves and the gulls. Please don't leave me. And then he turned and made his way back towards her.

'Right,' he said, standing very close, 'now that we've got all of that stuff out of the way, I think we ought to start again, don't you?'

She looked up into his face and for the very first time saw the trepidation in his eyes. And it gave her hope. Because she felt the same way. Afraid to open up. But one of them had to make the first move so she reached for his hand and felt his fingers curl around hers.

'Definitely.'

'Lucky I called Rita early,' he said, 'or I might have missed you and had to drive all the way up to Manchester.'

'You'd have done that?'

'Absolutely.'

'And you haven't got some plants to collect from the mainland?'

He laughed.

'No, for once plants are the last thing on my mind. I'm here for you, Carrie. Just you.'

'I thought you didn't care.'

'I tried not to. I don't want to complicate your life even more and I don't even know how you feel about me but from the very first time I saw you...' He shrugged. 'I don't know how to describe that feeling. I just knew that I had to tell you that I don't want you to go.'

'I don't want to go either,' she whispered.

'Then why are you on the ferry?' he teased.

'Because...' She swallowed. It was a risk. She might get hurt again but it was a risk worth taking. '...because I didn't think there was anything left for me on the island.'

He moved some loose strands of hair from across her face.

'There's finding out about Philly.'

'There is that,' she said softly.

'And there's finding out about us,' he said.

'Us?'

'You're not making this easy, are you?'

'I'm a bit out of practice.'

He half smiled. 'That's something else we have in common.'

He took both of her hands between his and held them close to his chest.

'Will you come back with me? Please. So that we can get to know each other better.'

Still she was afraid to believe what she hoped he was saying.

'I think there's everything for you on the island – if you want it.'

'What does that mean exactly?'

And he leaned forwards to kiss her.

'Does that explain it?' he asked eventually.

'I think so,' she replied.

'Perhaps at last,' he said, with a grin, 'we seem to be on the same page.'

'It feels like a perfect one to me,' Carrie replied. 'You are aware that you hardly know anything about me.'

'I know that my dog likes you.'

'He's a Labrador,' Carrie chuckled. 'He likes everybody.'

'Not entirely true and he likes you better than most. I trust his judgement.'

'I will have to go back to Manchester at some stage to sort a few things out,' she said, 'and I'll have to find a job on the island and somewhere to live and...'

He put a finger to her lips.

'Hideaway Cottage is yours for as long as you need it. I think I'm falling in love with you, Carrie.'

'And I began to fall in love with you when you floated those daisies in your mug,' she said shyly.

'If we have enough love for each other, it will all work out.'

'Like Jane Eyre and Mr. Rochester.'

He smiled. 'I'm glad you finished it.'

'It's a good ending.'

'One of the best.'

And he wrapped his arms around her as they both looked back towards the island and their future.

PRAYING

Eliza sat in the dappled light beneath the willow tree. She had been there all night, waiting for Isaac to return. From inside the house, she could smell toast and coffee and hear tender laughter. Happiness. That was all she had wanted to gift, and she had succeeded, but at what cost. Yes, she had meddled, but she had also had a little luck in finding Mark's business card on the spare bedroom carpet. Luck was much under-rated, she thought. There was only so much you could do on your own without good fortune in your corner. Of course, she knew the Major would jump to the wrong conclusions when he found the card in the potting shed just as she knew that Irene would do her best to put things right, provided she could find her car keys. Guy had hidden them well, but Irene was nothing if not tenacious. And of course, she had hoped that Guy would pursue Carrie, not known for sure, because even people in love could deny themselves the chance of happiness, especially if they were afraid of being hurt again.

She may not be able to remember portions of her own life, but Eliza had learned about people over the years and the patterns of their behaviour, the predictability of their reactions.

Was it not her beloved Isaac who had said to her, 'That's your gift, Eliza, knowing what others need in advance of their own awareness.' Except for Isaac. For the first time that she could recall, she had misjudged what he needed. Perhaps she didn't know as much about love as she thought. Perhaps there was still more to learn. If he had gone without her, what should she do? It would be so hard to leave this place even though she knew that it was in safe hands with Guy. She and Isaac were bound together just as she believed that Carrie and Guy were. Perhaps Isaac was right, perhaps she had achieved what was needed and it was time to leave. But what if she passed over and Isaac wasn't there? What then?

As the breeze parted the fronds of the willow tree she gazed out towards the Solent. She sensed a golden-haired woman who spent her life helping others. But there was a crisis brewing. This woman was about to need a sanctuary. She might need guidance, too. Eliza felt that Hideaway Cottage wasn't yet ready to let her go. She resolved to wait just a little longer and pray that Isaac would return.

A LETTER FROM THE AUTHOR

Dear reader,

Huge thanks for reading *The Sanctuary Keepers*. I hope you were hooked on Carrie and Guy and Isaac and Eliza's journeys. If you would like to join other readers in hearing all about my new releases and bonus content, you can sign up here:

www.stormpublishing.co/alexandra-barber

If you have enjoyed this book and could spare a few moments to leave a review that would be hugely appreciated. Even a short review can make all the difference in encouraging a reader to discover my books for the first time. Thank you so much!

Inspiration is capricious. When we are looking for it, it can elude us. Conversely, it can spring upon us when least expected. It was early evening and I was idling through a small churchyard in springtime when the seeds of this story were sown. We were on a family holiday on the Isle of Wight, and I had escaped the hurly-burly of a busy household for a few minutes of quiet while someone else was getting supper. Although it was only March, the sun had shone all day. Primroses glowed brightly amongst the unmown grass, birds sang, and the sky was still blue. For some reason I stepped away from the path and headed towards a pair of moss-covered, weathered gravestones. In retrospect it almost feels as if I was led there by an invisible force. To my astonishment I discovered that these headstones were for people who had our family name which is not particularly common. By the end of our week on the island I had the beginnings of a story.

I have discovered many things about the Isle of Wight since then. Apparently, it is the most haunted island on the planet! There are more sightings and hauntings on this small patch of land than anywhere else in the world which is just amazing for an island which is only twenty-three miles across and thirteen miles long. In literary terms, the word 'wight' actually means ghost, phantom or supernatural being. I've always been interested in 'thin places' where heaven comes close to earth, where we can find a sense of connection with something greater than ourselves. For me, the Isle of Wight feels like a soul home. As soon as I step on that ferry to cross the Solent, I feel my shoulders drop and my mood lift. It is a place where I can truly be myself.

Writing this book about a place which I love and characters I care deeply about has been a real joy and a privilege. My hope is that, even if you have never been there, you are able to absorb a little of the special quality of this fascinating place just off the south coast of England. I also hope that this story whisks you away from the cares of daily life for a short while and gives you the opportunity to take some relaxing time for yourself. My heartfelt wish is that reading about the cottage and the community connected to it brings you a small degree of happiness.

Almost finished now! If you would like to connect with me on social media, I'd love to hear from you.

Alexandra Barber

 instagram.com/alexandrabarberauthor

ACKNOWLEDGEMENTS

Finally, I can't go without thanking a few people who have worked so hard to make this book possible. Firstly, my family and friends, without whose support the ups and downs of a writing life would be so much harder to navigate. Secondly, the wonderful team at Storm, who have welcomed me into their fold with such enthusiasm and generosity, especially my editor, Kathryn, whose advice and guidance has been invaluable. I cannot thank her enough. And as a writer, I also have to honour the mysterious force of inspiration which is present all around us if only we take the time to look, listen and sometimes deviate from our normal path. That day in the churchyard I stepped to one side. I send thanks to whatever or whoever prompted me to do so. Without that small detour this book may never have been written.

www.ingramcontent.com/pod-product-compliance
Lightning Source LLC
Chambersburg PA
CBHW010431170726
48283CB00011B/3161

9 781837 002214